I0670472

Lucifer Laughed

Matthew Stramoski

No deities were harmed in the writing of this book. Any resemblance to people or entities who may serve as your spiritual guide(s) is unintended and/or accidental. If you do recognize your personal savior or prophet in this work of fiction, then the author recommends that you consider finding a new religion.

CONTENTS

Part I	**In the Beginning**	**9**
1	The Loss of Lucifer	10
2	Beelzebub Awakens	21
3	Paradise Prepared	26
4	Paradise Improved	35
5	Lucifer Lessened	45
6	Man, Before Woman	52
7	Paradise Perfected	58
8	Lucifer's Lessons	68
9	Paradise Passed Over	76
Part II	**The Beatification of Beelzebub**	**83**
10	The Rebel from the Fiery Pit	84
11	The Exodus from the Fiery Pit	92
12	The Disposition of Demons	95
13	Job Search	100
14	On the Job Training	108
15	Hitches in Stardom	113

| 16 | What to my Wondering Eyes | 121 |
| 17 | The White Crane Ascends | 125 |

Part III | **Mystic Maneuvers** | **131**

18	Battle of the Besties	132
19	A Star is Berthed	141
20	Religion in the Rough	145
21	The Star Goes Nova	152
22	The Starless Sequel	161
23	Ba'al Rocks	166
24	Road Trip	173
25	Pastoral Call	179
26	The Apostles Strike Back	183
27	Tracking the Truant	190
28	Basking on the Beach with Ba'al	201
29	The Return of the King	211

Part IV | **Sin and Punishment** | **223**

30	Roman Fever	224
31	Clothes Make the Angel	239
32	The Trials of My Tribulations	253

33	High Tea in the Himalayas	264
34	Breakfasts with Beelzebub	273
Part V	**Trying to Try Again**	**285**
35	The Invitation	286
36	The Case of the Vanishing Tablets	295
Part VI	**After Math**	**309**
37	Lunch with Lucifer	310
38	The Epistle to the Recorders	328
39	Dining with the Devils	343
	About the Author	358

Matthew Stramoski

Part I
In the Beginning

CHAPTER 1

THE LOSS OF LUCIFER

I was there almost from the beginning, milliseconds after time began. Heaven was already brimming with angels, shoulder to shoulder, wing to chest. It was a marvel of packing, as dense as a black hole but without the pressure. Facing away from the center, all I could see, besides the halos of other angels and the apexes of their wings, was a void, formless and dark, beyond the edge of heaven. Some think it's impossible to see a void, but that disbelief simply proves that they haven't seen nothing yet. Indeed, nothing looked as natural as heaven.

Seconds later, while I was still astonished that I existed at all, from behind me an explosion like a sneeze sent a shock wave over the angels' heads, knocking the halos of the taller ones askew. Suddenly, they were surrounded by a vast, deep, substantial darkness, a subtle yet significant change. Then a gentle sigh swept from the center of heaven and undulated the darkness as if it were water. In unison, the angels all turned to see whose breath it was. Heaven was shaped like an amphitheater but sloping from the lowest and outermost semicircle of angels to a central pinnacle where, on a throne at the summit, sat a figure resembling yet different than themselves. We didn't know what he was, but we knew he was no angel. A power flowed from him, brighter than light, and swept into my chest, causing me to lean a degree off plumb. Behind him and extending over his gleaming white throne towered a radiant arch within whose recess stood a portal. He seemed to pay no attention to us angels but went on muttering to himself, as if talking in his sleep, barely audible.

At that moment, he looked young; the timeless eternity before creation had not aged him.

The angel on my right cried out, "What's he saying?"

"We can't hear a single word back here." This time the faint call came from behind.

The whispered reply was transferred, angel to angel, from inner to outer arc. I heard, "Something about light--day--night...." But when it was repeated to the angels in the back row, the message had become "Licht--Tag--Nacht...." This process seemed unending.

I glanced over my shoulder to see what was happening where nothing had been. Now that something existed, nothing seemed unnatural.

The mystery enthroned at the center muttered, and

water whooshed overhead and splashed beyond heaven. He then appeared to concentrate his attention on a space at the edge of the clouds. A storage shed appeared. Another incomprehensible phrase, and vegetation flew across heaven's vault. I almost broke ranks when I saw a carrot on a stick. The Mystery spoke again, and stars sailed over our heads, so close we felt we could touch them. Fish jumped from nowhere, land animals followed as if in pursuit. I caught a glimpse of a creature as upright as an angel. I was convinced this extraordinary specimen was destined to rule the universe, but it was just a kangaroo. From time to time, the mystery at the center of it all would declare, "Oh! That was a good one!" With every mumble, he aged prodigiously.

Finally, he stopped murmuring and seemed to doze off.

During the lull in the action, we angels spontaneously began to get acquainted. Immediately, it became too noisy to hear anything clearly. The angel to my right asked my name.

"Samuel." Shouting was the only way to be heard.

"Hi, Some-Mule. I'm Ba'al."

"Sa-mu-el."

"Yes, I'm well, and you?"

I wondered what I could have done in the short time I'd

existed to deserve a spot beside an idiot. I hoped our places had been assigned randomly and temporarily. I groaned at the thought that our positions might be based on merit. In the back of my mind, a vague sense of eternity formed and gave me the heebie-jeebies.

This moment of dread was interrupted when the angel nearest the center turned and faced outward. His clear voice sounded a low note with a tight vibrato, a rich, lucid note whose pitch began to rise in a smooth glissando and strengthen in a controlled crescendo; a compelling, enticing, inviting note which he effortlessly sustained until the last angel in the farthest row nearest the undulating waters grew quiet with astonished admiration. In the moment that followed, we swayed and undulated as the reverberation tuned our hearts.

The angel nearest the center scanned, swiftly yet intensely, the ranks of the heavenly host, his glance a caress that filled us with a sense of being unconditionally respected and accepted. A brilliant softness, sweet and loving, swept through and embraced us. I glowed with love for everyone, even the idiot on my right. (The angels still cherish the experience, their first moment of kinship, which they discretely refer to as "the Event before the Incident.")

The angel nearest the center spoke. "I am Lucifer." He was resplendent, brightly clad in stunning white, light merrily dancing in his eyes, not the glaring light that causes the eyes to turn away and close in fear and pain, but the glow that mesmerizes the predator's prey. His halo radiated purest gold, a stunning complement to the brilliance of his immaculate garments. He was by far the tallest of the angels, arguably only a smidgeon shorter than the Mystery behind him at the center. Lucifer stood comfortably with the confident posture of an angel of destiny. For that moment, I trusted him completely. He slightly elongated sibilants when he spoke, but his voice was melodious and resonant, projecting without strain to the farthest ear. It was obvious he was here to lead.

"I was the first angel to pop into existence. I had only a microsecond to get my bearings and then a millisecond to chat with the one who's napping right now, but it was enough time to learn that we all have a role to play, although I don't yet know what role in what play. He said it would take an eternity to explain the whole plan. I have faith, though. As you can see, he is the epitome of glorious light and love. As soon as I became, I sensed him embracing me. I felt first a bubbling, a tingling throughout from toes to wingtips to halo, then a pulsing energy."

I felt the joy radiate from Lucifer, and in unison our essences effervesced, as if filled with sparkling wine.

Lucifer continued, "The moment I heard him let light be, I could feel it in my heart and see it in my mind, more brilliant even then the light here, all around us. It pierced and overwhelmed me, permeated me, overflowed and reflected through me." Lucifer paused. Choked with emotion, he whispered, "I will devote my existence to concentrating, reflecting and transmitting light."

For a moment he was quiet, as if focusing his energy into this vow. This may have been the first prayer and the first vocation; it was certainly the first moment of adoration. I was not the only angel who felt privileged and blessed to have witnessed it.

Suddenly bursting with exuberance, Lucifer sang out, "Let's all enlighten each other, one at a time, about our names and, if you have realized it, what you would like to choose to do. It seems like that would take an eternity, but we can't all talk at once until we learn to chant, so be succinct."

"Hi and pleased to meet you, Lucifer," said the angel to his right. He turned away from the center and faced the other angels. "And hello to all of you. My name is Beelzebub. I don't know how I know that, but it's without a doubt my name. I haven't prepared anything to say, but I'll try to come up with something on the fly. By the way, Lucifer, did you happen to catch Sleepy's name?"

"He told me, but I couldn't pronounce it. It was all consonants."

"If you couldn't say it, I doubt if anyone else can. Maybe we should ask him to simplify it. He would be more approachable if we could say his name."

Lucifer asked, "What makes you think he's unapproachable? He was quite willing to chat with me."

"When he was changing nothing into something, only a few of us in the front loop could hear him. But now here we are, the two of us, chatting quietly a wingspan and a half from him, yet every angel can hear us clearly. That difference alone makes him seem a little exclusive, a little unapproachable. Could you wake him up and ask him for a simpler version of his name?"

Lucifer looked perplexed. "Ask him for a nickname? It sounds a little presumptuous."

Beelzebub pressed his point. "It wouldn't hurt to ask, would it? Otherwise, we'll have to call him 'Unpronounceable.' That doesn't sound proper to me, not at all. And while you're chatting, you might want to find out if there's a protocol for requesting a face-to-face meeting with him. After all, that current nudging us away from him is off-putting. Oh, and what's behind the door?"

Lucifer answered, "I don't think we should wake him, much less ask him to dumb his name down for us. As for--"

They had been so involved in their conversation that they did not notice the figure with the unpronounceable name had opened his eyes. "I'm not asleep; I'm resting." He looked in all directions simultaneously, which amazed the angels. It also made me dizzy. "I just created an entire universe--my first one, too, and in just six days--so you can hardly fault me for wanting a little private time to catch my breath."

We angels had not yet developed a sense of time, so we didn't know how impressive the accomplishment was.

Lucifer said, "We were just trying to figure out what to call you since we can't pronounce your name. How about if we call you The One?"

"I can't be The One because I am before all."

"Ah," said Lucifer with a wink at Beelzebub, "then that would make me the one, and you would be the zero."

There was hell to pay for that remark. With a wave of Unpronounceable's little finger, the half of the heavenly host who laughed went down in flames.

You could have heard a feather fall on fleece.

Half an epoch passed before an angel, the one to my left, found enough courage to whisper, "Well, what do we call him?"

"Maybe," I said, "it would be best to drop the question."

"I'm going to go with Almighty," the courageous one said.

To my right, an angel said, "I'm going to call him Unpronounceable. It seems to be the safest choice."

When I turned to face this angel, my mouth dropped open. The place where Ba'al had stood was vacant. A ring of singed cloud was slowly scabbing over the hole where he had stood. I was disappointed. I felt we could've been good friends, if we'd had half an eternity to get used to each other.

When I looked up again, I saw the one with the troublesome name glaring at the angel to my right.

"It's not unpronounceable. I can say it easily." And he said it as if to illustrate his point.

The entire congregation of angels in unison said, "Huh?"

"Let me try," said the angel who stood beside Beelzebub's vacant spot.

"And who are you?" said the angel next to him.

"Call me Michael." Michael splayed his wings proudly. He almost tipped over.

The other angel turned away and smirked. When he turned back, he extended his hand and said, "Gabriel."

"No, I just told you I'm Michael. Are you senile, or just dense?"

Along with most other angels, I gasped, appalled that

anyone would question another angel's subtlety. A feminine voice from the edge of heaven stage whispered, "Did he just call him opaque?"

Gabriel pretended to brush a bit of dust off his left shoulder with the three middle fingers of his right hand. "Were you born yesterday? Gabriel's _my_ name."

Michael's cheeks tinged with pink. He drew his sword, lofted it over his head and cleared his throat. Trying to pronounce the unpronounceable, he screeched a series of scratchy sounds that trailed off and ended randomly. In unison, the rest of the angels covered their ears, wailed in pain, and shook their heads.

Gabriel blared, "My turn! I can do this!" In spite of his confidence, he mangled his attempt so badly that he stopped and covered his face before he finished.

The angel to my right said, "It's too hard. If he doesn't like Unpronounceable, maybe we could call him Unsayable or Unnameable or Whozit?"

"He's treading on thin cloud," I thought and started to warn him off.

The angel on the opposite side intervened before I could get a word out. "When we say Unpronounceable, it's with total respect."

"I'll keep an ear tuned to make certain," Unpronounceable said.

The angel toward the edge asked very quietly, "Why are none of the angels at the top female?" She was instantaneously transported to the spot between Michael and Gabriel, who was forced to step back with an oof into the vacant spot below him. "Call me Angelica," she announced.

Since that beginning, those millions of angels left in heaven have been assigned to care for trillions of worlds. They are all overworked due to the flame out. Although they do their best, none of them have reported unconditional success. My home base was Earth, and my initial assignment was to manage Eden. At first, I was disappointed that I hadn't been assigned the one thousand worlds that most angels were given, but I soon learned that I'd been burdened with one of the most difficult tasks.

CHAPTER 2

BEELZEBUB AWAKENS

I did not witness much of what I reveal in this Testament. However, unlike most scriptures, this narration has been reconstructed from the personal accounts of those directly involved and cross referenced as often as possible with eyewitnesses. It is the product of my efforts to reestablish, maintain, and nourish the trust and friendship felt among all the angels--including those who have not yet returned home--before the Incident.

At the time of the apocalyptic fall, not one of the angels left in heaven knew what had happened to the Fallen Angels or where they had gone, but we felt they were somewhere. We also believed that they would soon be back with us. In fact, most of the angels left in heaven thought Lucifer, first to be created and closest to Unpronounceable, would be the first to apologize for disrespectfully making Unpronounceable the butt of a joke. We hoped for his quick return, leading the rest of the gigglers, but his path home has proven longer than any of us imagined. He has chosen to explore a seemingly infinite number of detours and dead ends.

Beelzebub, choking on the noxious fumes from burning tar, was the first of the Fallen Angels to regain consciousness. He had no idea how long he had been comatose. His thoughts were hazy, his vision blurry, his tongue coated with brimstone. He heard only the flickering of the enveloping flames and the sputtering of burning sulfur. "Where am I?" he asked as he wrenched his face from the viscous floor.

As his head began to clear, he tried to recall what had happened. He had a vague impression that it was something to do with nothing. At last, he remembered the joke and the joker, Lucifer, winking at the start of the punch line. And Beelzebub recalled vividly how the butt of the joke inflicted without warning a flaming punishment with a miniscule movement of a single finger. No hint had been given that such a place as this fiery pit existed, that such incomprehensible retribution could be possible, that such torment could be inflicted. He was incredulous, despite the overwhelming evidence engulfing him. He dropped his head in despair. Ooze squished into his nostrils.

Beelzebub yanked his head out of the tar and pushed with his hands until his torso was freed. He rose to his knees and then managed to stand and look around. He could see no farther than a few miles. The light of the flames tinted the fumes a sickening yellowish brown. Above him, he could see the ceiling, as black as the soot coating his own body. The cavern's gelatinous floor oozed between his toes. He concentrated his strength; frantically, desperately he flailed his wings. He grabbed and yanked on his ankles until he managed to extricate his feet from the tar.

Black sludge dripped from his feet as he hovered a dozen feet off the floor. Around him, the bodies of millions of unconscious angels littered the ground. A few were struggling to get to their feet, some were on their knees, others barely managed to lift their heads, most lay stunned and immobile. The only positive feature was the expanse of unoccupied space between bodies. He could not help but notice that there was room for at least another trillion. He felt an urge to regurgitate.

"What," he asked himself, "gave me the bright idea that The Zero with the unpronounceable name was the manifestation of love, justice, and mercy?" He lowered himself onto a boulder of sulfur. "I remember now. Lucifer told me. He might have been mistaken."

He felt his jaw drop to his belly. He sat motionless while he tried to make sense of what had happened.

He had thought the Creator, perched imperiously on a luminous white throne, enshrined within a glorious grotto of polished alabaster, was beyond reproach, even perfect. He could deny either the perfection of the one who created him or the existence of this burning pit. He reasoned, "If my maker is perfect, he couldn't make a mistake. I'd be perfect, too. If I'm perfect, then I couldn't have made a mistake. If I didn't make a mistake, then I couldn't have been punished. But if the punishment happened, then I made a mistake and I am not perfect, and neither is my maker.

"On the other hand, if I'm not perfect, then I can't be expected to act like I am. And if I'm allowed to make mistakes, because I'm not perfect, then I can't be punished for them; it wouldn't be just.

"Therefore, this cannot possibly be just and therefore cannot be real."

Without warning, he felt a surge of anger explode within him. He asked (rhetorically because no one could hear his thoughts), "What kind of creator devises a visible void, a secret Fiery Pit, punishment without a trial by a panel of peers? This must be a joke. It does not tickle me in the least."

Recognizing that his befuddlement was overwhelming his rationality, he decided to seek Lucifer. Beelzebub knew he needed explanations and advice, and Lucifer, by his very name, was certainly the most qualified to shed light on this mystery of unrelenting dark fire. He rose from his sulfur seat, flew systematically in ever widening spirals, and eventually found the twisted, charred body of Lucifer sinking sideways into the tar and chanting incessantly, "I'm number one!" Without disturbing Lucifer's reverie, Beelzebub left the smoldering, oblivious lump who obviously could not help. Lucifer had apparently shed his light.

As he flew toward his sulfur perch, Beelzebub swerved left and cursed Lucifer then veered right and cursed Unpronounceable, as if nastiness could free him from his punishment and ruin. The maledictions ricocheted off the starless vault. Through the darkening fumes, he heard bodies in the distance jerk and whimper as if struck by spikes.

When he landed on his bolder, the Fallen Angels around him stirred. He felt his despair reverberate through the pit and resonate with the anguish in the hearts of his neighbors. It grew in intensity, creating swells that swept as far as he could sense. Beelzebub screeched from the depths of his tormented soul, "I declare myself to be forever the enemy of The Zero. Never will I repent. I will carry my struggle for justice to victory or the end of my own existence. May victory come first."

The circle of Fallen Angels that surrounded him shrunk back, cowering before his audacity, fearing the inevitable retribution.

CHAPTER 3

PARADISE PREPARED

Those who have never been to Eden praise it mightily. More realistic appraisers have rated it as problematic at best. When paradise is promised, perfection is expected, and every detail becomes a potential catastrophe.

I was less impressed than later historians have reported me. I struggled with the nearly impossible task of converting a barren, ugly plot of hard brown clay into a verdant Paradise. Together, my meager, inexperienced, untrained crew and I toiled tirelessly, bravely to perfect the dump that was to be the cradle of terrestrial life.

Eden's location at the center of the most desolate desert on Earth made it almost impossible to reach on foot. Even my angelic crew had difficulty navigating the unpredictable crosswinds and downdrafts.

Surrounded by a drab baked-brick wall, Eden's exterior had neither charm nor personality. In fact, if either Adam or Eve, the original residents, had started life outside its gate, they would have turned their back and walked away without the slightest temptation to peek over the wall.

When I discussed the problem with my crew, only Raphael volunteered a solution. "Might a mural make the exterior more appealing?"

"Paint and plaster," I said, "are not in the budget. We're stuck with what's in the storage shed." Among those angels who had paid attention, none could recall seeing building supplies.

"Let's concentrate on the interior," I said with a shrug. "I've been told there are big plans for the space."

Sofiel suggested timidly, "Some greenery might make it more inviting. Perhaps a lotus? I remember seeing one sail into the shed."

The rest of the crew agreed. She flew away to retrieve a seedling from the shed. When she returned holding it gently between her thumb and forefinger, a crosswind almost ripped it away. As she carefully planted the bent stem in the brown dust and caressed its leaves with her delicate fingers, the crew admired its fragile beauty and her sensitive touch. Two minutes later, it had wilted so badly that she uprooted it and rushed it back to the safety of the shed.

I said, "It looked thirsty. Water, evidently, will be another obstacle."

One of the crew optimistically suggested, "Heaven will provide." The entire crew looked up at the cloudless sky in hopeful anticipation.

Reluctant to disturb Unpronounceable over what seemed a minor problem and unwilling to risk the appearance of criticism, we waited for rain. Some of the angels, grown bored, invented the game of kick-the-dust.

Three months later, I decided to seek divine guidance, but when I arrived in heaven, the throne was vacant.

I asked Michael, who was twiddling his thumbs and humming a ditty, "Where's Unpronounceable?"

Michael answered, "About a month ago, he went through the Portal and he hasn't been seen since, although I've heard an occasional rumble."

Carefully avoiding contact with the throne, I skirted it and approached the Portal. As he lifted his hand to knock, the door swung open. I was yanked into the chamber, as if by a vacuum, and then released so abruptly that I lost my balance and fell face down.

I lay still until Unpronounceable spoke. "Water, eh? I'd hoped you'd be able to find it on your own. Here's a clue. A spring will flow from the dry ground."

"Forgive my obtuseness, but I don't see how."

"Of course not." Unpronounceable described a

nondescript rock, gave vague instructions, and shooed me away with orders to make it happen.

When I thought I'd found the right rock, I tapped it as instructed and waited. I was unversed in universal law, and response time was slow. Anticipation became uncertainty. Still, I clung to faith like a lifeline while nothing happened. Then suddenly, the waters spewed more copiously than I'd imagined possible, jetting from the rock like a geyser.

Sighing with relief, I tapped the rock a second time, more lightly, hoping to throttle the flow to the volume of an abundant spring. Instead, it doubled. Soon, the water was ankle deep within the walls. All my helper-angels fled, except Raphael. I tapped the rock a third time, but instead of lessening, the volume redoubled.

We panicked. Raphael pointed his staff at the brick wall and blasted a tunnel at its base. The water gushed through the hole into the desert. Hoping to divert the flood away from Eden, we channeled it into a dry riverbed.

Raphael pointed at where the river divided into four wadis at a seemingly safe distance. "I'm certain," he said, "the water will follow the channels and find its way somewhere else."

"And where would that be?" I asked.

"I'm not sure where, but I'm certain it won't be here."

Unfortunately, Eden was at the lowest point in a basin. The river backed up, filling the enclosure and submerging the baked brick walls. I flew around the periphery in a panic, trying to blow the water away from Eden by frantically fluttering my wings. I was about to call out for divine intervention when Raphael, the showoff, stopped the springs with a simple incantation.

We waited for the water to recede. It was deep, and the ground was saturated; the level dropped by infinitesimal increments.

A week passed. I asked, "Are you sure your incantation shut the spring off completely?" My impatient tone startled me.

"Huh? Sorry, but I was drifting in a daydream about floating on an ocean wave."

I repeated my question.

"It's mesmerizing, watching the water, its waves slipping slowly lower every day by the thickness of a wing feather." Raphael shook his head as if to clear it. "Of course, I'm sure the incantation worked. Well, now that I think about it, no, I can't be sure. It's my first time to cast a spell. I think it did. I wonder, did I shut my mouth tight enough at the end?"

"I can barely discern a difference in the depth. Magic is new to me, too. Is there such a thing as a spell to stop a stopper from seeping?"

"Do you want to dive in and check my work?"

"It's yours, so you should be the one."

"Patience would be a soothing supplement to your lack of faith." Raphael stared again at the wavelets.

"There must be something we can do while we wait."

"We could practice being nonjudgmental."

"Will that lower the water level?"

We chose instead to return to heaven and seek an audience with Unpronounceable.

At the edge of the Portal to the Presence, Raphael asked, "Would you mind terribly if I waited here? I get nervous enough in the Presence when everything is going well, and I'm sure I'll freak out from fright when we have to face the consequences of our failure." He lowered his voice and shuddered. "I remember the flames."

"You do know his wrath can slap you down just as easily out here?"

"Yeah, maybe he'll mistake my timidity for innocence."

"Good luck with that." I sighed, resigned to my fate. "I'm the one in charge, so I'll face the judgement alone. But don't believe for a second that you're any safer out here."

I entered the Portal with trepidation and stood quietly and patiently at the edge of the aura. Unpronounceable was poring over some plans sketched on the surface of the clouds, paying particular attention to a strange shape that resembled a tailless kangaroo with inordinately long arms. I learned later that this was a monkey mockup.

Unpronounceable looked away from the drawing and the plans vanished. "Ah, Samuel. No need to explain why you're here. I heard about the flood. Sooner than scheduled." He chuckled.

"Forgive me, but I don't get the joke."

"Never mind. You'll understand it later."

I pressed ahead. "This water thing is a problem. It's going to take forever to dry out, and I know we're on a tight schedule. I think it would be better to relocate to the higher ground east of Eden where an impressive escarpment has a great panorama."

"I have other plans for that area."

"But surely the flood changes everything. If we restart the springs, Eden will be inundated again. After all, if we can't get past step one, we'll never reach step-- whatever it is."

"Watch me fix it without lifting a finger. You'll be

impressed. Go back, and while you're waiting for the ground to dry, imagine a lush, colorful garden in place of the brown water. Sketch a few ideas on your own. To help you get started, I've thrown together a few hints about what I want. Take these watercolors with you and look them over. I don't mean for you to replicate what I've done. I'm asking you to develop an artistic sense, not an echo, but your own voice." I heard a whoosh coming from behind me, and Raphael landed on his butt beside me. "Raphael will help you."

Raphael and I were each handed several folders. I wanted to ask for more information, but Unpronounceable waved us off. I glanced over my shoulder and saw the stick drawing re-emerged on the clouds at his feet.

When Raphael and I splashed down in Eden, the watercolors washed away before we could open the folders.

A stiff, relentless, arid wind blew from the south. We waited while the waters receded over the course of two months. The ground, finally bone dry again, was uplifted in an earthquake that left the baked brick walls severely cracked and uneven. Eden's charm dropped to a new low, but drainage improved.

Much later, empirical evidence led some angels to formulate a theory that water, left to itself, invariably flows downhill. It may seem self-evident, but millennia were to pass before the advent of science. Even at this late date, Free Water Fundamentalists assert that the existence of waterspouts, fog, and steam is evidence enough to refute the theory.

CHAPTER 4

PARADISE IMPROVED

Despite the minor defect of hard, barren ground, Raphael and I thought that Eden was ready to accept its first resident, but word came by Messenger Angel that Unpronounceable had not yet finished detailing the two trees which were to adorn his shrine at the center of the garden. She turned to leave, but I stopped her to complain about the delay. She advised patience and explained that a committee had been formed. I felt an urgent need to cover my ears. The word sounded like a curse.

Unpronounceable had appointed an advisory council to give the angels an opportunity to discuss issues before agreeing with him. The qualities of one tree were still undecided because of a circular debate in the inner council about the niceties of culpability. It wasn't until he threatened to hurl all lawyers, philosophers, and grammarians into the Fiery Pit that they precipitously and unanimously agreed on the principle of arbitrary flexibility. Unpronounceable knew all along that he could create new rules from moment to moment and was well pleased that the council had finally understood.

As for the second tree, the head of the committee asked for a unanimous voice vote. However, one dissenting angel dared point out that overpopulation would be the probable, almost inevitable, result of eternal life.

Unpronounceable answered curtly, "It's not about them; it's about me. It's life; it's eternal. Get over it." The question died on the vine.

After Unpronounceable returned to his inner sanctum, the dissenting angel asked, "Can we at least prevent the Tree of Eternal Life from bearing fruit?"

The other council members hushed her.

She pressed her point; "It just doesn't seem wise to plant them right next to each other. Shouldn't we at least--"

The other angels drowned out her voice with loud litanies of unsubstantiated praise for the divine while running for cover.

All alone, the dissenter mumbled, "Why on Earth plant them on Earth?" She shrugged her shoulders and turned her attention to a picturesque crater on an uninhabited planet in the Andromeda Galaxy. "Enough work! It's time for a vacation."

In the meantime, mostly from boredom, we two worker-angels in Eden installed myriad plants in the garden. We made frequent raids on the storage shed and had profound discussions about flower arrangements. Raphael connected with his innate talent and endowed the garden with an artistic touch that transformed it into a masterpiece of composition and color. But when the leaves began to turn yellow and wilt, he recalled Sofiel's lotus and realized that plants need water. As a precaution, he replaced the stopper on the spring with a control valve while I constructed a rudimentary irrigation system of open ditches.

With trepidation, Raphael reopened the spring. The valve metered the flow precisely. I believed there was no danger of another flood and complimented my coworker on his mechanical virtuosity. Then Raphael pointed out that the water was flowing downhill only. I tried to hide my chagrin as we reworked potential trouble spots.

The moment we finished the final touches, another Messenger arrived. One of her arms was three times thicker than the other. I thought it would be impolite to mention the deformity and tried not to stare at it.

She announced, "The Trees will arrive at noon tomorrow."

I asked, "They're being delivered? Who's delivering them?"

"Angels from the Department of Transportation."

"We'd expected to pick up and install them ourselves, so pardon my surprise that it's being handled by others."

Raphael asked, "A new department? Why?"

She explained that angels, left to decide for themselves how, when, and where they would travel, had caused a traffic jam at the bottleneck of Heaven's Gate. Guardian Angels, still awaiting permanent assignments, had been given temporary duty to regulate the flow. All other choirs of angels were required to apply for and obtain a permit before traveling beyond the gate, except in cases of emergency.

"What's considered an emergency?" asked Raphael.

"I brought part one of the list." She pulled from her thicker sleeve a hefty scroll that was covered in a miniscule scrawl. "There are forty-seven more sections."

Raphael turned his eyes away and faced his palm toward her. "Thank you, but never mind."

The next morning, Raphael and I spent less than an hour digging the holes for the root balls. Once finished, we were unable to contain our excitement. Our hearts and minds quivered so rapidly the very air vibrated around us. We played with modulating our exhilaration so that the pitches emitted formed consonant intervals, as clear and harmonious as two flutes in love. Raphael suddenly bleated like a bassoon with a broken reed. I blatted like an ovine trombonist. We giggled like two boys eating stolen pies in a treehouse. Settling down beside the holes in the ground, we sang and plucked, double checked the holes against the specs, and plucked and sang.

Noon approached. Noon arrived. Noon passed. Noon became a faint memory. Finally, we heard someone gently tapping at Eden's Gate. I didn't want to miss the delivery which I was certain would be directly to the center of Eden, but I went, grudgingly, to see who was knocking. When I swung the gate open, I recognized two angels from among the Choir of Guardians. Behind them, two trees lay flat on the ground.

"Your trees. Sign here." The right guard pointed to a line at the bottom of a page.

"Bring them in. I'll show you where they go."

The right guard skimmed the paper. "There's nothing here about installing them."

"Well, you're going to stay to guard them, so you may as well help us move them inside."

The right guard pored over the paper, brows knit, eyelids narrowed. "Nothing about that on the manifest either."

I sighed and signed. The left guard sheepishly muttered, "We're just on temporary assignment. We're not fully trained, so we can't risk the dangerous stuff like lifting."

"How did you get them here without lifting?"

"We lowered them," the left guard explained, pointing toward the sky.

"A few assistants have been sent to cheer you on," said the right guard. A flurry of tiny angels descended over us and fluttered around our heads like flies.

Raphael helped me haul the cumbersome trees to the center of the garden, one at a time, while the chubby-cheeked cherubs sang our praises without lifting a finger to help. Many leaves and twigs were scraped off along the way. Raphael and I hoisted the nearly naked trunks into the air and dropped the root balls into the holes. At first, the trees leaned off plumb. Raphael pushed each one upright and steadied them while I kicked and tamped dirt around the root balls. The cherubs finally chipped in by cheerfully gathering and reattaching the lost leaves and twigs with precision. The trees were shaped in perfect proportion and color coordinated with the surrounding plants, as if they had been custom designed.

The cherubs then congratulated each other and fluttered back to heaven where they took credit for the installation, wrote innumerable pages about countless leaves, and received bountiful rewards for their meticulous and exhausting work.

At long last, Unpronounceable declared that all was ready to create The Man. Those angels who had glimpsed the drawing board speculated how this was going to be accomplished. Some believed a lightning bolt would shock a bit of water and dirt into standing upright; others thought an incantation and ritual dance would materialize him out of thin air; a third group asserted he would spurt from a nut. Having seen more mockups than most of his colleagues, I guessed that a prototype monkey would be renovated with softer skin, less fur, and a more prominent forehead. I was baffled when I learned that primates were to be created after The Man. I hadn't yet realized that logic and design were neither divine traits nor divine aspirations. No one predicted that The Man would be nothing more than dust and a bit of breath, just moist enough to clump together. Like the vowels in his name, Unpronounceable often omitted what he considered to be unessential details.

When The Man was fashioned in Eden, he lay face up in the dust. In fact, it was hard to distinguish him from dirt until Unpronounceable leaned over the mound and breathed on it. The Man coalesced and then spasmed as if he had been stung by a thousand wasps. He opened his eyes. His first sight was of the formidable figure hovering over and breathing on him. His eyebrows rose and his lips formed a fatuous smile.

Before the Man could say a word, the figure spoke. I caught only part of it. "Call me" and then something I couldn't understand, much less pronounce.

The Man said, "I beg your pardon?"

"That was my name. But don't worry about it. No one gets it right when they first hear it. Take me at my word: I'll know when you're talking to me even if you get the name wrong. By the way, I will call you Adam."

"Are there other options?"

Unpronounceable smiled indulgently. "No. I don't give options."

"Well, then. I'll be a dam."

"Not 'a dam'. AA--dum. It's a pun. Would you like me to explain it to you?"

"If it's insulting, I'd rather not know."

Unpronounceable withheld the explanation, as is his habit. He unbent to his full height. "Stand up, Adam." Adam tried, but he moved as if he had dust for legs. "Samuel, help him to his feet."

Once Adam was able to stand and had learned to walk forward, I handed him a pouch made from banana leaves and bid him drink from it. Adam hesitantly sipped the water. His eyebrows rose as if he were surprised and pleased with the taste. I had to take it away and caution him not to drink too much. Thinking that Adam might be hungry, I reached to pick an apple from the nearest tree, but Unpronounceable stopped me.

"Give him an orange instead."

Confused by a name that sounded more like a color than a fruit, I hesitated and looked around.

Unpronounceable pointed at a tree near the edge of the clearing. "You can recognize the fruit by its color."

I blushed and sheepishly fetched it.

Unpronounceable said, "You turned out better than I expected." He was always the first to compliment his own work. "Don't you agree, Samuel?"

"I don't know what your expectations were," I answered diplomatically. I secretly thought Unpronounceable must have incredibly low expectations.

Unpronounceable smiled indulgently at me, as if he had read my mind, and turned his attention back to Adam. Twirling a finger in a tight circle over his head, he asked, "Are you ready for a tour of your home? Of course, you are."

He led Adam in a promenade around Eden's perimeter, all the while chattering about the goodness and perfection of all that he had done. When they came to where the river flowed through the tunnel in the garden wall, he invited Adam to sit on a flat rock. "There are a few rules to be aware of. First, ..." And he proceeded to list six hundred thirty-one rules for daily life. Adam became completely confused. He tried to pay attention. Soon his eyes drifted shut, and his jaw slacked open. I thought even ten rules would have been a stretch for him.

Mixed among the many tidbits was an admonition to refrain from eating the fruit of the special trees at the center of the garden, the Tree of the Knowledge of Good and Evil and the Tree of Life. Samuel noted that Unpronounceable omitted the word 'eternal' from the second title, but he did say the first tree's fruit resembled an apple and the other's a jackfruit.

CHAPTER 5

LUCIFER LESSENED

L ucifer struggled to his feet, wiped the steaming tar from his face and, after a gasp of acrid air, screamed. At his feet, he saw the sulfur rock his head had shattered.

He pressed his fingertips against his forehead. It stung and the sulfur shards seemed to burrow into his skull. His flesh felt like the incarnation of flame. A rash covered his torso. He pawed frantically at his chest; his pointed fingernails cut into his skin; a black gel oozed from the fissures. He backed into a nearby boulder to scratch between his wings. He exploded in a second hellacious screech.

"Where? Why?"

His mind whirled through images of flame, a precipitous chute, chaos, darkness, concussion. "I remember--. What? A moment of love, a giddy trance, a unity of angels, a harmless witticism." A grimace twisted his upper lip. "The Zero! That was clever!" He surveyed his neighborhood and noticed other burnt bodies struggling to be free of the tar. "Who knew he would be so sensitive?"

Lucifer grabbed a thought: The fall-in-flames did not really happen. The punishment was disproportionate to the crime. "No, not a crime; at worst, a deed; no, even less than that; a mere word. I did nothing wrong! How can this be? An impossibility! That he could take a happy remark and twist it into sin? Who's the real perpetrator? The one who pretends to be perfect?" Lucifer curled his lips like a horse taking an apple.

"This can only be his joke in answer to my joke. At worst, perhaps there's a lesson to learn."

Lucifer assured himself, "We'll all soon be back in heaven having a good laugh with the rest of the angels." He imagined the host of angels clinking and hoisting half-full glasses of fermented holy water in an optimistic toast to the Primal Comic's eternal good cheer.

The heat intensified, and a profound sense of abandonment swept over Lucifer and drowned his fantastical dream. Within, he felt a ravenous abyss and recoiled from its brink. He sought a feather's heft of hope to balance against his despair but found only the weight of emptiness.

"Obviously," he said, "the eviction from heaven was undeserved, but I will give him, for now, the benefit of doubt. After all, this was his first attempt at creating; he lacked experience working with underlings; his hypersensitivity must have been due to self-doubt. Therefore, he should apologize to all the Fried Angels for overreacting."

Lucifer remembered his first sensation, the surge of love that flooded him; but now he wondered if his own inexperience had led him astray. Perhaps he had mistaken The Zero's pride of accomplishment for love of the created. Lucifer could only say with certainty that a dimension existed within the Creator that he was too naïve to comprehend. Lucifer felt confounded and muddled. Life had seemed in those first moments simple and clear, but now existence dripped danger. It was a convoluted, duplicitous, tortuous complexity.

Lucifer wept for his lost innocence.

He dragged his fingers through his hair and gasped. His halo was missing. He dropped to his knees and searched in the tar as deep as his arm's length but found nothing, not even a solid bottom. He pulled his arm from the muck and stood erect. All around, as far as he could see, were smoke and dull flames. Here and there, a body tried and failed to pull free of the tar.

He knew then that there would be no restoration. Without his own apology, his contrite abasement, he would be trapped, hopeless, for eternity. His anger rose into his mouth and stuck to his tongue. He tried to spit out the bile but failed.

"I will never apologize. I am the one who has been wronged. It's so obvious, the least among the angels could see it."

In his heart, he knew that even if restored to his rightful place, he could never again know trust, confidence, security. This pit of flames and fumes was now and forever his home. The creator had ruined his eternity.

Lucifer soared to the apex of the cavern. "I am sovereign over all I see. Here I am almighty. From here I will strike at my enemy. I consecrate my power and passion to work persistently to foil all his plans. When he has finally apologized, I will banish him from the universe. I will lead my fallen brethren to glory and victory."

Convinced of his righteousness and power, he speculated aloud what the universe would be like with the Creator in exile, but no other angel near him was conscious enough to hear or comprehend.

With a great flapping of wings, Lucifer burst through the ceiling of the Fiery Pit and circled through the chaotic abyss until he came to a place on the outskirts of heaven which he later learned was called Purgatory. There he eavesdropped on three angels discussing the latest plan of Unpronounceable. Divine "likenesses" had taken up residence, rent free, in an alleged paradise. This pair of humans, Adam and Eve, had apparently supplanted the angels as the centerpiece of this creation. Lucifer put the exile of Adam and Eve as the first item on his list of things to do. No other deed imaginable could prick the potentate's pride more profoundly.

When he returned from his reconnaissance, Lucifer heard Beelzebub's oath against the Almighty still echoing through the Fiery Pit. He was well pleased. Flying in an ever-widening spiral, he began a systematic search for the beloved blasphemer.

Beelzebub had continued to stew. Soon after his vow, while he gnashed his teeth counterclockwise, into his head popped an unexpected fact. Although created second, at the side of Lucifer, he had not been privy to the whims of Unpronounceable. His jaw dropped to his belly when he realized that Lucifer was to blame for everything. It was Lucifer who had known the Creator nanoseconds longer. It was Lucifer who must have known how touchy Almighty was. And it was Lucifer who had shirked his duty as elder brother by failing to warn and protect Beelzebub. Lucifer's wink, given so freely before the punch line, was the seal of Beelzebub's doom. How could the Creator think he, Beelzebub, a mere neonatal-angel, not yet a celestial week old, had been aware of such subtleties? Deeper and hotter burned Beelzebub's resentment, searing into his soul. He thought, "Lucifer's the one at fault! Why am I being punished? Lucifer should have warned me.

Lucifer should have seen what was coming. Lucifer needs to take full responsibility."

Lucifer arrived above him at that very moment. Beelzebub shot up from the sulfur boulder. They hovered face to face. Lucifer saw the hatred in his brother's eyes but was unaware that Beelzebub had recast him as the Adversary, so he dismissed the blazing glare as one would brush off an ambling fly. "I've been investigating this flawed creation while others have been lying around suffering from inertia and self-pity. I've even infiltrated the outskirts of heaven. They call it Purgatory. I heard that Unpronounceable (that's what the Leftover Angels are calling The Zero)—"

Beelzebub tried to interrupt. "That's what I was afraid of!"

But Lucifer forged ahead as if he had not heard, "--has focused on a miniscule part of a worthless area on a pointless planet." Lucifer, thinking he was talking to his right-hand angel, his dedicated comrade-in-arms, revealed to Beelzebub his plan to spoil Eden.

Beelzebub bowed in fawning agreement. "Yes, Master," and "As you wish, Master," fell unctuously from his lips.

Lucifer was certain he could secure the souls of Adam and Eve with ease. "I will give you Eve for your very own to torment as you please. And I will keep Adam eternally close, in a teensy corner, his very own fiery pittance."

"I live only to serve you, Master."

Lucifer rose a few feet above him. "By the way, there's a band of Chaos separating this pit from heaven and Earth. It ruffled my feathers something fierce. We'll have to find a way to smooth the journey." As he flew away, he squealed gleefully, "Prepare the rotisserie!"

In his heart, Beelzebub wanted nothing more than to defeat Lucifer and restore himself to his rightful place in heaven, which would then be second to none but Unpronounceable. He especially liked the sound of "second to none." He resolved to forge an alliance with Almighty. Together they would save Eden from their common adversary.

CHAPTER 6

MAN, BEFORE WOMAN

Having completed the tour of the garden and finished his lecture, Unpronounceable excused himself, saying he had a parallel universe to redesign. In his absence, Adam wandered from wall to wall and tried to engage the trees and bushes in conversation. I plucked my harp to entertain him, but he was too restive to pay attention. Again and again, he asked the cacti and thorn bushes, "What's the point of this noise?" Over and over he interrupted to complain of boredom.

I said, "Boring? How can it be boring? This is celestial music, composed by Gabriel himself in one of his quieter moods. It's one of the most popular tunes among the angels."

"These harmonies are too predictable. How about something less organized? Maybe a little dissonance would perk it up."

"There is no dissonance in the heavenly choirs. Well, I

admit Uriel is off-key sometimes, but he's getting better."

"But it's just cloying--"

"Perhaps you would like a visit from the Fallen Angels? A little weeping and gnashing of teeth to soothe the soul?"

He straightened from hips to neck, and his eyes perked up. "Fallen Angels? What happened?"

"Never mind." I thought about turning him over to Lucifer, who is much better at inventing entertaining diversions, but I had an unnerving vision of Adam slowly roasting on a rotisserie, an experience I felt he was not yet ready for. Instead, I reported the malcontent to Unpronounceable.

"Can't he climb a tree, make a raft, invent the wheel? I knew he'd be high maintenance, but this is ridiculous. I've only been away a few days."

I said, "He seems to prefer talking to material things over harmonizing with angelic emanations."

"Ah, well, I knew that, of course. I'll indulge him, but only because he's in paradise."

"I was thinking about escorting him on a visit with Lucifer so that he can learn to appreciate what he's got."

"No, it's best that Lucifer does not know about Adam for now. I'll create some entertainment for the man on my next visit to Eden."

It was almost a month before Unpronounceable fulfilled his promise. When he finally appeared in the garden, he created an amazing array of creatures to entertain Adam. The animals were glad to be in paradise. They willingly paraded in front of the man, whom they considered one of their own. When Unpronounceable asked Adam to give them all names, they looked surprised.

The naming process did not go without a hitch. For example, a pair of small, hairy rodents scampered before him, reared up on their tiny hind legs and sniffed the air. With a broad smile Adam said confidently, "Daffodils."

Unpronounceable asked, "Doesn't that sound more like a plant name to you?"

"Oh, rats!" said Adam petulantly.

"That's right!" said Unpronounceable patiently.

After a full day of watching the parade, identifying the animals and reviewing the correct names, Unpronounceable announced with that proclaiming tone that is his hallmark, "The Man will be in charge during my absence. I want all of you to do whatever he says when he calls you. Remember, he knows your names."

"Great," mumbled Adam under his breath. "Now I'm a tattletale."

Before Unpronounceable returned to heaven to finish perfecting the parallel universe, he instructed me to watch over his pet project. "Keep an eye out, especially for unexpected visitors. And try to teach the man focus and self-discipline."

Unpronounceable seemed to think that Adam would remember the ten thousand names he'd learned that day. Having spent more time with Adam, I had less faith. I wondered as well how knowing their names would give Adam some mysterious power over them. I noticed that most of the animals sulked as if harboring resentment.

I asked a nearby, scowling gorilla, "Is something bothering you?"

"No one asked me what I'd like to be called."

"I'm sure it was an oversight. What name would you like?"

"Koko. It's gentle yet intimidating." I couldn't be certain, but I thought she might have blushed.

Only the dogs (and much later the parrots) readily accepted the names Adam gave them. The cats, after all these millennia, are still pouting.

A few times when walking with Adam, I noticed behavior that I thought was inexplicable. He would tell me he had to urinate, a non-angelic action I did not yet understand (but later learned to appreciate). Usually, he'd only be gone a half minute or so, but sometimes when he was alone behind the bushes, he would linger much longer, and I could hear inexplicable heavy panting. One time, with a far-off, dreamy stare, he told me that he thought Koko, the gorilla, was somewhat attractive although her chest was too flat to be ideal and too hairy for his taste. I couldn't begin to fathom what he was talking about. He often slipped away when I was distracted by anything interesting. I had no idea what he was up to until the rumors about the sheep surfaced. He had discovered an effective way to tell them apart and memorize their names.

Reluctantly, I reported the allegations to Almighty, fearing that I might be blamed and become the victim of another display of fireworks. I wasn't addicted to my job, but I had grown accustomed to Adam's company. He was not an engrossing conversationalist, but his stupidity was occasionally entertaining. He could hardly carry a tune, but he was a pioneer in the field of quartertone harmonies. He complained far too often, but finding solutions sometimes challenged my ingenuity. All things considered, watching his antics was better than sitting alone under an apple tree waiting for eternity's end.

When I marshalled sufficient courage, I tried to look

casual and described Adams's activities as if they were amusing anecdotes. Unpronounceable, instead of lashing out with his little finger, muttered something. I caught only the one word, "propensities". Returning to his sketch on a cloud bank, he said, "I'll take care of it on my next visit."

"I hope it's not too late. The rats tell me that habits are easy to form and hard to break."

"That's what I've heard, too."

CHAPTER 7

PARADISE PERFECTED

The distraction of fashioning a parallel universe delayed Unpronounceable much longer than I felt was wise. It seemed like months before he finally put aside his trips to alternate realities and returned to visit Eden. Adam and I were arguing about whether a bird he had spied in a tree was a macaw or a budgie. Because we disagreed, he thought I wasn't looking at the same bird. He stood in front of me so that I could sight along his right arm. I had just assured him that we were looking at the same bird--in fact, the only bird on the limb--when up popped Unpronounceable a foot in front of him. Adam jumped, screamed, and fainted away into my arms. I lowered him to the ground.

"You scared us both."

"Fearing me is wise, so don't complain about it. By the way, that's a lory."

"Are you sure?" Immediately, I repented my doubt. "Sorry. A lory."

Adam regained consciousness and sat up. He shook his head and rubbed his eyes. "Could you send an omen next time?"

Unpronounceable ignored the request. "It would be better if you slept through this." Adam immediately slumped over. Almighty pushed him flat on the ground, yanked out one rib and reached toward the ground as if to scoop up some dirt. "Oh, right. It's a meadow now. Good job, Samuel. Tell Raphael I completely approve."

He pulled dust out of thin air. When he sculpted it around the rib, it transformed into something that resembled Adam's flesh, but softer and more supple. I thought he must have been impatient or distracted because he left a few lumps here and there and, in place of a set of protruding items, there was an orifice. I had never known him to be sloppy, even in a rush, so I practiced faith, hoping it would atone for my fleeting flight of doubt.

As he bent over the figure, his form blurred into a pillar of fog. He exhaled gently on the mound.

The new figure's eyes opened immediately and smiled at the glowing fog floating over her.

Unpronounceable said, "Welcome to Eden. I will call you--"

"Eve. I like the name Eve," the new arrival said.

"What a coincidence," said Unpronounceable. He straightened up and coalesced into the familiar quasi-angelic shape I recognized.

She rose with a graceful assurance and a balance foreign to Adam. I concluded that her dust must be wetter on the inside. That thought momentarily titillated me.

She pointed at the lump of flesh asleep on the ground. "Is that for me?"

"All yours," he answered, "although he'll think you're for him."

She looked him over carefully from his toes to his head, walked around to the opposite side and reexamined him meticulously. "He'll do, but I would have preferred a hairy chest and more muscular arms."

"You'll find he's already too much like an ape."

"Can we do something about the hair in his ears?"

"I'll let you handle that." He turned to me. "Samuel, tell Adam to teach the rules to--uh--Eve. Tell him to be sure to mention the trees." I thought he might have winked.

As Unpronounceable turned to leave, I asked, "How long before Adam stops bleeding?"

Unpronounceable healed the wound with an offhanded wave and rose rapidly in the direction of heaven, making quite a show of wind, cloud and lightning.

Eve muttered, "Quite a showman--or maybe just a showoff."

I cringed and looked over my shoulder toward the sky. "I'd be careful what I say, if I were you."

Eve wrinkled her brow and looked askance at me. "Is he really that sensitive?"

I cringed again and protected my head with my wings, but there was no fireball.

"You are a jumpy one, aren't you?" She looked at the body snoring on the ground and drew her foot back as if preparing to kick him. "Should we wake him?"

"Not yet. He's had a rough morning."

Eve ambled around the meadow, keeping close to the edge of the forest. Occasionally she paused and gazed into the shadows beneath its canopy. Twice I saw her lean forward as if intrigued by the darkness. Each time, though, she breathed deeply, smiled as if sensing a sweet aroma, and then continued around the meadow. When she spied a yellow tubular bloom on a squat bush, she oohed. She bent over, sniffed it and sneezed. She pinched the flower from its lifeline and displayed its carcass in her hair.

I refrained from commenting on what seemed like arrogant retaliation, but I couldn't help gasping. I looked away and awaited Adam's awakening, wondering if he would be at all pleased with this knockoff, this thing I thought of as "The Malformed," who apparently had a quick and vicious temper.

She asked me, "Is he going to sleep forever?"

"I doubt it. Are you in a rush? We have eternity."

She picked a blade of grass with her toes and lifted it to her hand. "He's going to sleep half of it away."

She waited. She yawned. She softly hummed random notes. Her arrhythmic, tuneless attempt at music I attributed to her youth and resolved to teach her a few celestial melodies once she got comfortably settled.

Adam began to moan. He grasped his side at the wound and rolled to his opposite side. "Owie. Owie."

Rolling her lower lip out, Eve said, "Aw, poor baby."

His eyes popped open. He murmured, "That sound-- what?" He looked at me. "Not you, not the harp; it sounded like--a voice more mellifluous than anything I've ever heard." He sat up, saw Eve and floated to his feet.

Although I had always thought Adam was rather thickheaded and slow to appreciate, he reacted immediately and acted straight away.

Eve pushed him away. "Introduce yourself." She turned to me, "Tell him to mind his manners."

Adam could not keep his eyes off her chest. "What are those?" His voice was almost a growl.

"They're not for you," she said.

"That's not what I asked."

"We can talk about them later. For now, try to look into my eyes."

He raised his gaze to her face. "Has anyone ever told you that you have incredibly beautiful eyes? I've never seen that shade of brown before. They're so deep, so glossy, so--uh, deep. And glossy." He had a tone in his voice that I had never heard before, as if he were both amazed and enthralled. He clasped her hand and tried to pull her close.

She jerked her hand out of his and moved to his side. She slid her left arm into the crook of his right arm and applied gentle pressure to urge him forward.

"What do you call this green thing?" she asked pointing at the bush she had mutilated.

Adam, eager to show off the immense vocabulary that he himself had invented (with divine guidance), told her they were plants and began identifying each of the trees and bushes surrounding the clearing as either a tree or a bush.

Soon, Eve interrupted. "You can't call everything shorter than yourself a bush and all the taller plants trees. You're missing the complexity."

"This is a short bush, and that's a tall--"

"I don't think you understood my point."

"If you're so creative and discerning," he said, "why don't you tell me what they're called?"

"As an example, we could call this one with the pretty little flower a rose."

"That pretty little flower over there is another rose," Adam said, pushing his shoulders back as if proud that he had learned the lesson so quickly.

"Notice how it has fewer petals and a different color. Let's say it's a buttercup."

"What a silly name. I think it's a primrose."

"It doesn't look prim to me. After all, its petals are spread wide open."

Together they wandered off toward the center of Eden, stopping every few yards to identify a plant or an animal. Twice I heard The Woman say, "No, they're not oranges; and no, they're not for you; and no, you cannot touch them. Pay attention to the plants."

I was debating whether I should follow them when I

heard the call of Almighty. He was ready to create a paradise in a parallel universe and wanted to discuss a few ideas with me. This time, I thought, he must be aiming at intelligent design. Not one of my ideas was accepted. Later I figured out that he was distracting me to allow the new couple some private time.

Several weeks later I returned to Eden to visit with the happy couple. I found Eve, under a lean-to, sitting alone, with a parakeet on her shoulder. She told me in an exasperated tone, "I hope you're not looking for Adam. He's off betting on the races."

"Races? What races?"

"I really don't see the point," she said, ignoring my question. "Every race, Adam bets against no one that the horses will all win, and every time, the horses all tie for first place. He races rats in a maze, and they all finish first. What else could happen in Paradise? When he started talking about cockfights, I drew the line. He's always looking for a reason to get away."

"But you seemed inseparable. What happened?"

"Oh, he's passionate of course for up to a half hour at a time, if I pretend for twenty minutes that I'm not interested, and right after, he asks what's for dinner."

"You make dinner for him? But there's food all around. All he has to do--"

Too wrapped up in her ruminations to pay attention me, she petted her parakeet (which continually babbled, "Got to go! Got to go!") and barged ahead. "He mutters about feeling tied down and having a job to do. He talks about not wanting to commit to the first woman he meets and about looking for fresh fish in the sea. When I point out that I'm the only woman on Earth and that he doesn't even know where the sea is, much less how to fish, he says I'm missing the point. Then he leads the sheep out to pasture, claiming that he's got to be a good shepherd, if only as an example for someone who might follow. He rarely makes it home on time for dinner no matter how hard I slave over a hot pit."

"You cook for him?"

Without pausing, she continued, "There's no appreciation in the man. Washoe--"

"Who?"

"The chimpanzee. She told me that a good meal would be the quickest way to his heart. That backfired. Adam is convinced I cook for him because I enjoy doing things for him. He acts as if all he has to do is eat it without complaint, as if that's the quickest way to my heart. Well! He's a bit confused. He doesn't seem to understand about needing to repay my generosity."

"If I could suggest--"

"Koko tells me he's always been selfish. She says it

comes from being coddled from the moment of his creation. Her cousin Nim says he feels entitlement because he's the only man in the neighborhood. But the lioness Leona tells me that all males act that way when they're alone with a female."

I promised to inform the All-knowing and hurried away to report the impossible: There was trouble in Paradise.

As I left her lean-to, I caught a glimpse of a snake coiled just to the left of the entrance. Softly hissing, he slithered in as soon as I was clear.

Creatures of every sort inhabited Eden. I hadn't met all of them, but I knew that even the ones who looked dangerous were innocuous. I had often seen a lion laying down with a lamb. They both appeared to be happily enjoying the tenderness.

I didn't recognize Lucifer in his disguise, so I thought nothing of another reptile apparently nestling peacefully in the shade. I hurried back to heaven and ignored my microscopic twinge of doubt. As I found out later, this was a mistake.

CHAPTER 8

LUCIFER'S LESSONS

Eve saw the silver and white snake sliding slowly and serenely across the lean-to's packed earth floor. She didn't recognize it, but she welcomed it with a smile, completely unaware that peril might exist in the garden.

The snake softly coiled around her leg, smoothly spiraled up her thigh, her waist, her ribcage, her shoulders. It gazed into her eyes, tickled her cheek with its tongue and introduced itself.

"I am Lucifer."

She tried but could not remember the last time Adam had gazed, as if mesmerized, into her eyes.

Lucifer's satiny scales titillated and caressed her skin. The soft, rhythmic, sensuous contraction of its body around her torso swept from hips to shoulders, sweeter and more fluid than Adam's rushed and rough embrace. The serpent's head slowly swirled before her, leaving her breathless, lightheaded, enthralled. She felt totally desired, appreciated, possessed. Adam had always been the center of her life, but this serpent seemed to offer-- she didn't know what to call it. But, focused on it, intrigued by it, yearning for it, she craved it. Tingling warmth surged in waves through her spine into her head. She swayed like a kelp in a gentle neap tide.

"I sense a disturbance in your thoughts, an emptiness in your heart, a longing for fulfillment."

The dissonance within her amplified, as if sharpened and intensified by the serpent's sweet voice. The pulsing effervescence now spread into her limbs and overflowed into the air around her. Confused, she searched for some thought to hold her steady, but could not find even one word to speak with conviction.

An image of Adam's frustrated face began to take shape in her mind. Lucifer whispered, "Adam wants to please you, but he doesn't know how. You want to possess his love, but you don't know what to do."

She nodded, still unable to name what she desired from this serpent.

Lucifer squeezed softly and slithered another loop of its tail around her, never moving its gaze from hers. "He doesn't know how to change, so the change must come from you. First, you must learn right and wrong."

"That sounds dangerous," she said hesitantly. "Is it?"

The snake's head drew back the width of a rose petal. "The right way to act to keep the man at home with you; the wrong things he does when he's away; what keeps you apart; what can bring you together: Why would--how could such knowledge be dangerous?"

She hesitated, confused even about why she was concerned.

The smoothness of the serpent's scales slipped across her bare skin, but its unblinking gaze never wandered from hers. Its tongue emerged, flickered tantalizingly between them and then swept lightly across her lips. She shivered.

Lucifer promised, "You will both learn to love in ways you have never imagined."

"Will I be able to make this magic?"

Its coils pulsated lightly; her body throbbed. "You will. Yes. You will know the wrong things Adam does, and then you will be able to lure him to be the man you know he can be. He needs work, struggle, achievement. Without challenges to test his strength, without obstacles to break through, without failures to learn from and reverse, he will drift through eternity, lost in the pointlessness of Paradise. You will give him the chance to be his complete self. He will love you forever for this gift."

Coupled with the smooth scales stroking her skin and

the unwavering, unblinking eyes mesmerizing her, the promise of requited, fulfilling love she could not resist. "How do I learn this mystery?"

"Come, follow me to the center of the garden."

There the serpent showed her the Tree of the Knowledge of Good and Evil. It wrapped itself around the trunk from the base to the first branch. It stretched out its neck and nudged an apple toward Eve.

"But Adam told me Unpronounceable has forbidden us to eat the apples from this tree."

"He prohibits things because it makes him feel powerful. What could happen?"

"Adam said he's forbidden us to disobey him."

The snake sneered. "The one giving the orders has ordered you to obey the order, a convenient circle. I could do the same trick by swallowing my own tail. Unpronounceable is addicted to power. He told Adam hundreds of rules, to intimidate him, to keep him enslaved."

"Adam said he's in charge."

"A little disobedience, what harm could it do?"

Eve didn't understand these unfathomable mysteries; the prohibition was followed from mere rote obedience without roots in wisdom. Still she hesitated, remembering another caution Adam had shared with her. "He said we would die."

"And what does that mean?"

"I don't know. I've never seen it happen."

"Death is just another empty word, as meaningless as life."

She reached for the apple, felt its smooth skin. It reminded her of Lucifer's sleek scales. And she tugged. A twig came off the tree with the apple.

The serpent said, "See how simple it was to pluck the fruit? This harvest must have been your destiny."

She bit.

Her first thought was how sweet disobedience tasted. Then she had an idea about how to style her hair. Next, she pictured herself in a grass skirt. She was not surprised that such superficialities would impress Adam; in fact, she was absolutely convinced they would enthrall him.

"Wasn't I right?" asked the snake.

She smiled distractedly. "Adam too will need to know right and wrong so that he can treat me the right way and leave behind his wrong habits."

"Exactly," said Lucifer. "You have a lot to do, so I will

leave you for a while."

She harvested more fruit before returning to the lean-to.

As soon as Adam came home, he was hypnotized by the skirt. 'How,' he wondered, 'could covering so little make so much so irresistible?' He began to drool.

Eve asked, "Do you like my hair like this?" She handed him the fruit.

He looked up at her hair and said, "Did you do something different with it?"

She scowled at him.

"Oh, yes, of course. It's beautiful." He looked down and away, hoping that she would not ask him for a detailed list of the changes. He saw the remains of a fruit on the ground. Then he noticed that what she had handed him was an apple. He drew a quick, astonished breath. "Is this from--"

"Yes, it is. I got it for you. It's your dinner."

At first, he hesitated. Unpronounceable had been generous and patient with him; Eden had been paradisiacal, and the animals were fun and game for anything, especially racing. He was inordinately fond of the sheep.

She broke into his thoughts with a deep sensuous purr.

"Knowing that sex is sinful will make it twice as intense. Once you're done with that apple, I have these oranges for you."

That assurance alone might have been enough to persuade him, but he wondered what would happen if he did not join her. They had been threatened with death if they ate the fruit. He did not know what this death could be, but he had looked over the baked brick wall and seen the desert beyond. He thought that death might be something like being on the other side. He knew that he could remain here, in nondeath, because he had not bitten the apple. He recalled about how stale paradise had been before she arrived, how enchanted he was by the first experience of her eyes and voice, how they had walked arm in arm while renaming the plants and animals, how being with her was fundamentally more real than everything else he had experienced.

Their relationship had not been perfect. They had disagreed on priorities. He had neglected her to play frivolous games. She had insisted they spend time together on meaningless activities. He still did not understand why they should watch an unnecessary fire burn evenly and safely on air alone. It seemed frivolous to till the soil so that she could plant a row of vegetables in the midst of an abundantly fruitful garden. He thought building a shelter was a waste of time; the mild, comfortable weather changed but imperceptibly through the day. He yawned watching a moon that changed more slowly than the weather.

But, when he pictured her struggling alone, suffering in the desolation that he had glimpsed over and beyond the baked brick walls, he knew that he, isolated in Eden for eternity, would be plagued with longing for her. Still he hesitated. Perhaps he could put off the decision and later--. Then he saw that the flower in her hair was wilting.

He took two enormous bites: the first for her, the second for both of them.

CHAPTER 9

PARADISE PASSED OVER

I was halfway to heaven when the realization struck me: The hissing serpent beside the lean-to exuded a faint aroma of sulfurous smoke. "It's a Fallen Angel! It's Lucifer!"

Immediately I doubled back and tripled my speed. I arrived just as Adam was eating his second apple. They were oblivious to my presence. I knew there was nothing I could do now to save the future or reverse history. Divine intervention was needed. I hurried back to heaven.

When I arrived in the presence of the Almighty, he was in an audience with Beelzebub. The Fallen Angel was prostrate before Unpronounceable, muttering into the cloud where his face was buried.

I was too agitated to hear what they were talking about and too alarmed to wait my turn. I interrupted, screaming as soon as I passed through the Portal to the Presence, "There's trouble in Paradise!"

"Slow down those wings," Unpronounceable said. "You're causing an unholy draft."

"They're mixing apples with oranges!"

The audience was immediately aborted. He said something to Beelzebub, but I was too bound up in my own consternation to pay attention.

As Unpronounceable and I sailed to Eden, I heard him muttering to himself. "Now that they know good from evil, if they live forever, we'll never hear the end of it. Constant criticism and second guessing! I should never have let the lawyers talk me into arbitrary flexibility. Damn them all!" Suddenly, heaven had more space.

I wondered at the time if Lucifer had sent Beelzebub to distract Unpronounceable while he seduced Eve. I reminded myself that Almighty had the capacity to look in all directions at once and discarded the theory.

We burst into the lean-to without knocking and found the entwined couple simultaneously biting into an apple. Half a dozen cores surrounded them.

Unpronounceable launched into one of his infamous, long-winded, open-ended curses, exiling Adam, Eve, and the snake. He didn't seem to notice that the serpent had already left. Lucifer, I believe, did not want his special day spoiled by a temper tantrum. The curse accidently fell on a passing garter snake. I heard its last thought as its head was crushed: "What did I do?"

Without excuses or objections, the couple packed their few possessions into the bundle of their blanket. Adam whispered, "Eve, don't forget the skirt." She slipped it into the bundle along with the water sack made from banana leaves, a few apples and the flower she had picked the first day, pressed between two fig leaves. Adam hoisted the light bundle over his shoulder.

Eve said to her parakeet, "You'd better stay here."

The parakeet flew to his perch on her shoulder and sang, "Got to go! Got to go!"

And they left.

I was dumbfounded. "Where will they go? What will they do?"

Unpronounceable said, "Frankly, my dear Samuel, I don't . . .. I'll think about it tomorrow."

"Well, tomorrow is another day. I'll remind you."

"Stay out of it, Samuel."

I stared at the point in the trees where they had disappeared. "Would it be okay--"

"Yes, yes, go ahead." Unpronounceable shook his head. "That heart of yours, it will get you into trouble if you're not careful."

It is almost impossible to appear nonchalant while

rushing to catch up. I was within earshot of the couple when they arrived at the edge of Eden.

As Adam was passing with Eve through the gate in the wall, he said, "I gave names to all the animals and plants, with your help, but we never named Unpronounceable. I think we should call him--"

"Don't!" interrupted Eve. "We're in enough trouble as it is."

"But he--"

"No, Adam. Just drop it."

"But--"

"A name is not worth fighting over."

As the gate swung closed behind them, I flew to the top of the wall. Eve looked back and caught a last glimpse of Paradise before the gates clanked. A twinge of sadness surfaced on her face but then was swept away by a great peacefulness. She drew her shoulders back, held her head high, and turned to face the desert.

"Let's go to the other side of that ridge," she said. "And maybe the next one, too. I don't want to have to look at this ugly wall. Hard to believe they never thought to use a little plaster and paint." As they reached the slope of the ridge, she took Adam's hand in hers. The couple crossed to the other side, out of sight.

An angel in a robe with singed cuffs, wielding a blazing sword, but keeping it at arm's length from his body, landed on the top of the gate, wobbled a smidgeon, then found his balance. He asked me, "When's my replacement coming? Rubiel's got a game going, and I was about to break even."

A week later, I noticed that the sheep had left Eden. Within two months all the animals had gone, except for a lone salmon gamely swimming upstream.

The debate in heaven after the eviction centered on justice. Of course, the arguments were hypothetical and academic because we all knew that Unpronounceable would never do anything unjust. We rarely understood his justice, but we had faith in it, just to be on the safe side.

Adam and Eve could not know good and evil, not even theoretically, until they ate the fruit. They could not possibly have understood that disobedience was bad until they disobeyed, yet they were severely and implacably punished for it. Angel Gabriel blasts all the arguments into smithereens by asserting, "You can't say it isn't just, just because it isn't. The obvious isn't always credible, and mysterious ends can justify mysterious ways. Who are we to judge? We only know some of the facts." Some angels remained unconvinced.

On certain celebratory days, especially the summer and

winter solstices, the Fallen Angels entertain themselves with pointless debate about whether Adam had been shown specifically which tree was forbidden. Adam never denied that he knew exactly which it was. I know that he was seated near the tunnel in the wall when Unpronounceable told him not to eat the fruit from "the tree at the center of the garden." Adam might have remembered the fruit I had reached for when Unpronounceable suggested I offer an orange instead. Undoubtedly Adam recognized the forbidden fruit when he saw it in Eve's hand.

Another problematic point perplexes me still. Adam was threatened with instantaneous death if he ate the fruit. At that moment, he was completely ignorant of what death meant, having never witnessed it, so the admonition meant absolutely nothing to him. And when the fruit touched his lips, death didn't happen after all. He was nine hundred thirty years old when he died, and less than a year old when he bit the banned fruit. This is the earliest verified example of inconsistent parenting.

Matthew Stramoski

Part II
The Beatification
of Beelzebub

CHAPTER 10

THE REBEL FROM THE FIERY PIT

While Lucifer was slithering into Eden, Beelzebub begged his way up the ladder of angels and pleaded his way through the archangels, until he was prostrate in the presence of Almighty.

His voice muffled by the cloud, Beelzebub revealed to Unpronounceable Lucifer's plan to disrupt Eden. Trying to sound humble, he suggested, "I believe, in all honesty, that I could prevent Adam and Eve from succumbing to Lucifer's efforts."

"What do you know about disobedience? Your sin was disrespect."

Beelzebub simmered, but he refrained from arguing. Focusing on his mission, he said, "I think that Adam and Eve might find it difficult to talk freely with you. You are omnipotent; even among the angels, that can stifle open and honest communication. I'm less intimidating than you. In fact, with my appearance, they'd probably want to learn my history, if only to avoid repeating my mistake. While I'm explaining my charcoal robe, I could slip in a fable--perhaps linking disrespect with disobedience--and then reason with them."

"You haven't met him yet, but I can tell you Adam's less rational, so far, than I'd hoped."

"It's probably just confusion. I heard from a couple angels on my way up the ladder that you listed somewhere near six hundred rules for him. That's a lot to assimilate all at once, especially on the first day of his life. I'm not second guessing you—"

"Go on."

"My plan is to start with Eve. I'm sure I can talk sense to her. Once she's on track, I think we can count on Adam following along. I hear he's completely enraptured by her."

Beelzebub, still face down, hazarded a sidelong glance at Unpronounceable who seemed to be thinking over the proposition.

A few moments passed before Unpronounceable said, "She likes pretty things, like flowers and gems. You could start there. She thinks Adam's one of those pretty things. I had to tell her not to pick his head off like she did the flower."

"And what would you suggest for keeping Adam in line?"

"He likes sex, but don't start there. Let Eve take care of it."

"Do we have an agreement then?"

"I know the answer to this, but we have to go through the formality of verbalizing the question and response. What are you asking in exchange?"

"For restoration to my place in the hierarchy."

"Without penalty? I believe a demotion is appropriate."

"But it was--"

This was the exact moment when I flew in, without fanfare or patience, and screamed, without apology or courtesy, what sounded to Beelzebub like an announcement that someone had invented a fruit salad. "They're mixing apples and oranges."

Unpronounceable stepped over Beelzebub. "Already? Time flies when you're contemplating eternity." Over his shoulder, he said to Beelzebub, "It looks like I'll have to handle this myself. Hang in there. It will all turn out fine." And we hurried off to deter disaster, leaving him face down in the clouds.

Beelzebub drew an exasperated breath. The inhaled cloud tickled his nose hairs and caused him to sneeze.

He struggled to his feet, his singed sinews still achy and stiff. "'It will all turn out fine?' What about he now? He could've at least given me a new robe. My burnt skin is sensitive, and this charcoal is scratchy. This is the second time I've been chucked aside because someone else has screwed up."

He scratched his face and felt tiny bumps covering his cheeks. "Great. Don't tell me I've become allergic to cloud."

He moped on his way back to the Fiery Pit, all the time muttering to himself. "Demotion? I've already been penalized. I don't think he's ever been to the Pit, or he wouldn't say things like that. Who has ever heard of a demon getting a demotion!"

Focusing his thoughts through the lens of resentment onto the options that would spark and flare into the result he desired, he decided to do something so ostentatious, so dramatically unexpected that even Unpronounceable, as obsessed as he was with his own creativity and power, could not ignore it.

Beelzebub first thought he could fashion substitutes for the disobedient couple by possessing and shaving the bodies of chimpanzees. Without free will, they would remain forever the docile pets of the All Powerful. But he knew that he himself would be controlled indirectly; he would have to continuously monitor the chimpanzees' behavior.

Then, he considered recreating the humans by molding new ones from the desert dust. However, his breath would undoubtedly bake them into figurines. Unpronounceable didn't seem the type to be swayed by cuteness alone. He realized that he hadn't the wherewithal to create anything except, perhaps, chaos, which would accomplish nothing.

He considered seeking out the humans and teaching them the secret of gratitude. But had he mastered it himself? What had he to be grateful for?

At last, the magnificent solution came to him. Beelzebub would rally the Fallen Angels and overthrow Lucifer. He would triumphantly lead the march of the repentant to heaven's gate. A conquering hero's welcome would be bestowed on him. All the angels, both the restored and the Leftovers, joined by Unpronounceable himself, would shower him with gratitude. His robe would be cleansed, his allergy healed.

This coup would require most of the fallen to rebel against Lucifer and align with the one who had punished them. An overwhelmingly difficult task it seemed, but he bolstered his courage, telling himself that he could not call it impossible until he had failed. His mind made up, he set himself to the task with no more hesitation. He knew he had barely enough time to organize the rebellion while Lucifer was still occupied in Eden. Unfortunately, he had miscalculated how quickly the woman would be persuaded. In fact, she was already succumbing to the serpent's temptation, and Adam was soon to take his first bite.

Beelzebub ascended from his perch on the sulfur boulder until his head touched the ceiling. He formed a trumpet with his lips. "Attention! Your attention! Gather around and hear the way of salvation! I know how to escape from this den of suffering!"

The Fallen Angels struggled to turn toward the voice. The burning, oozing goo sucked at their feet, but most managed to pivot and face Beelzebub. The rest bent over backwards to see him.

"We have been tricked, seduced by the Joker's humor. There is no place in heaven for humor; there is barely enough room for joy and serenity. We must admit to Unpronounceable--"

"Who?" asked the closest angel.

"Unpronounceable. That's what the leftover angels call the one at the center. We must admit to Unpronounceable that we were wrong to laugh at anything concerning him. Now that we know that the sacred is not laughable, we must beg for forgiveness. We must even be willing to accept the possibility of a temporary demotion, maybe as low as Guardians, in exchange for returning to heaven. It will only be for a short time, I'm absolutely sure. Satan has gone--"

"Who?" interrupted the closest angel.

"Satan. It means Adversary. That's my new name for Lucifer."

"Does he know that?"

"No. Not yet. He doesn't know about any of this yet. So far, it's our little secret. Anyway, back to topic. We've got to be quick. He's in Eden (don't ask;" he said to the closest angel, "I'll explain later) corrupting Eve (don't ask) in order to avenge our punishment. Satan will want all of us to join him in a war against our brothers, the host of angels left in heaven. Satan has already directed me to gather an army of Fallen Angels. Revenge is not the way! Revenge can only exacerbate and prolong the strife. Instead, we must renounce Satan--"

"And who is this Satan?" The expansive voice of Lucifer, freshly returned triumphant from Eden, echoed in the fiery pit.

Nonchalantly, the angel closest to Beelzebub said, "You are."

Lucifer said, "Apostasy? So soon? I _am_ disappointed." Without waiting for an explanation or a trial, he flew at Beelzebub faster than light and blasted him through the ceiling.

The fallen stood silent. The crumbs from the ceiling sploshed in the molten tar. Within the whisper of flames, they could hear the crisping of flesh.

Lucifer, with a self-satisfied smirk, turned his attention from the hole above him to the remaining demons surrounding him. "Would anyone else like to be in charge?" There being no volunteer, Lucifer began to regale the fallen with the epic of his facile victory in Eden.

CHAPTER 11

THE EXODUS FROM THE FIERY PIT

Lucifer, shivering in the Fiery Pit with his icy, sadistic joy, bragged about his triumph over Eve. His eyes focused on the ceiling as if a shadow play were reenacted on that stage. He did not notice the scene unfolding around him.

Slowly, the fallen brethren began to breathe again. They stood frozen, openmouthed and wide-eyed, appalled by what they had witnessed. They had all been ejected only a few cosmic moments before from heaven, without warning or trial, dropped like trash through a chute. Beelzebub's ejection seemed equally unjust, intolerant, and impulsive. The fallen expected better from one of their own, especially from Lucifer. Not just any random angel, he was The One, The Harmonizer of the Angels, The Founder of Angelic Brotherhood.

Ba'al, gaping and aghast like the rest of the multitude, recognized astonished despair on the faces around him. The thick, stifling air vibrated with disbelief, undulated with repulsion, and rippled with fear. Each smoke-filled inhalation amplified the burning in their lungs and the gloom in their thoughts.

Lucifer remained oblivious, trembling with his own power, pulsating with cold-blooded pride, and cocooned in his own purposes. The fumes before him became viscous. The vision of his conquest, shapes in the smog, played out his triumph. Repeatedly Eve stretched out her hand, plucked the fruit and brought it to her lips.

The angel in front of Ba'al slipped like quicksilver across the floor, up the wall and out the pit through Beelzebub's hole. Then another and another followed stealthily. Although many stood enthralled by Lucifer's silvery rhetoric, most disappeared into the smog. Ba'al wrapped a veil around himself and slunk away, being careful never to turn his back on Satan.

He vowed as he emerged from the fire into the chaos, "I will bring hope to the lost, even if it's a lie." He struggled against the torque of chaos to keep his body intact. He broke at last into the relative serenity of the universe, having lost only three blackened feathers to the shearing forces. He sat on a jagged chunk of rock near the edge of Earth's solar system and untwisted his body. Even millennia later, while basking on a beach, Ba'al shuddered as he recalled for me the angst he suffered at that moment.

When Lucifer reached the end of his repetitious epic, he looked down toward the floor of the Fiery Pit, expecting a vision of adoring, uplifted angelic faces thronged around him, their eager hands stretching to caress the hem of his robe. Instead, he saw a vast emptiness. The few who remained were spaced randomly, and most of them seemed to be focused on extracting their feet from the tar.

CHAPTER 12

THE DISPOSITION OF DEMONS

Adam and Eve had three sons. They also had four daughters, but they are rarely mentioned. In addition, due to a defective gene that has since been rectified, the close contact between Adam and the ewes populated the Earth with hundreds of step-daughters. Eve refrained from acknowledging them, and Adam, at a loss for girls' names, eventually fell to referring to them as random pretty objects, such as flowers and cute animals.

Supplementing the population were many of the Fallen Angels who fled Lucifer. The majority stopped on Earth to rest and plan their future, but most decided to stay. The planet was close and comfortable and could, with a little effort, be made to resemble a home. The more restless spread across the galaxy, as thick as dark matter.

I didn't realize how densely infested with demons the planet under my care had become until I saw, too late, that the descendants of Eve and Adam had become enamored with them.

I have never been able to substantiate the claim, but some Fallen Angels are said to have started families with the daughters of men. The rumor, as far as I have been able to ascertain, originated from a few garbled lines scrawled by a scribe on an old scroll. Perhaps he was trying his hand at pornography, but he evidently suffered from either a fear of censure or a lack of hands-on experience. In an apparent attempt to ennoble his crassness, he left out the penetrating details that he obviously knew nothing about and ended with an unsubstantiated claim that the "sons of god" and the "daughters of men" were begetting the heroes of yesteryear "of whom many tales have been told." But it seems the author fell into a crapulous stupor before he could recount a single lascivious or heroic detail.

Later, a few influential scholars who did not understand the passage concluded that it must be the unimpeachable word of some divinity. I tried to intervene, arguing that the entire passage was a vain boast by a Fallen Angel too ugly and too poor to have had a chance with any daughters of men. The scholars countered that they could not doubt what was written.

As I said, I have seen no evidence to support this rumor, but it has been frequently and variously reproduced in human folklore.

I admit, in retrospect, that I should have been worried from the start, but it was hard to see the threat. Most of the Fallen who stayed on Earth found diversion in harmless hobbies, such as possessing pigs or haunting mansions, manipulating 77Ouija boards or hosting book clubs, masquerading as vampires or teaching spelling. Some became immersed in the care of lakes, springs, and rivers. A popular choice was managing sacred groves, grottos, and graveyards. Many learned a specialized trade: guiding the potter's wheel, the smithy's hammer, the gardener's rake. The more enterprising started cottage industries, some of which are still profitable. In exchange for a temple and a few sacrifices, they managed the weather, stimulated fertility, or gave political guidance.

My friend Circe, one of the more reclusive entrepreneurs among the fallen, sequestered herself on an island which she named Aeaea. When I asked her how she decided on that name, she said she didn't want to risk angering Unpronounceable a second time by trespassing on his consonants. She harvested lotus pods and marketed the refined products throughout the Mediterranean. She has since diversified her portfolio with peyote and tobacco.

Shankara, whom I met during an extended stay in India, had the slogan, "Easy to please, slow to anger." I must admit, that's a tempting promise. Unfortunately, he had trouble keeping it. I believe the lice and fleas in his hair made him grumpy. Obsessed with cockroaches and rats, he established himself as the preeminent cultivator of Earthly vermin. His garden contained the world's most extensive collection of millipedes and venomous spiders, unsurpassed until the middle of the twentieth century.

Ba'al wandered Earth for several centuries in search of meaningful work, but he was unable to find any he was qualified for. His first attempts at being a local deity were unsuccessful due to his inexperience. Unschooled in the mechanics of the physical universe, he proved ineffective as a provider of fertility or victory. His being almost deaf did not help. He finally convinced a Nubian tribe near the Nile's first cataract that he was a seasonal divinity specializing in spring floods. It was a cushy job, but the pay was sporadic. He persuaded another tribe in the mountains of Anatolia that they needed a divinity to manage winter snows. He proved to be exceptionally talented at accomplishing easy, self-regulating tasks. However, he discovered later that travel between his engagements was fraught with danger.

Naturally, I thought that Unpronounceable would personally manage the Reconciliation of the Fallen. Instead, he seemed to be completely uninterested in the project. While he retained the right of final approval, responsibility for vetting candidates for reinstatement was delegated to committees who then created subcommittees who hired bureaucracies. A low-level official decided to create an Application for Readmittance to the Sacred Environs (ARSE). Under the question, "What is your current state of being?" he provided a single box to check: "Evil." He authored an official informational pamphlet promulgating that all the fallen were equally wicked, through and through, without hope of redemption. His head clerk kicked the form upstairs, attached the pamphlet as supporting documentation, and asked the supervisor for a position paper on degrees of culpability. The manager sent the proposed application to the Department of Canon Law where it was referred to the newly instituted Committee on the Readmittance of Original Snickering Sinners (CROSS).

I came to believe that the Committee wanted to avoid the laborious and seemingly unending drudgery of individual reevaluation. They did not want to admit that a continuum of redemptability existed, from those who are raging through those who are merely obstinate, from those still giggling to those ignorant of their options. Among the most adamant was the Archangel Michael who insisted that long lines of charcoal figures awaiting assessment for readmittance would discourage immigration from Earth. I suspected that Michael, who had been created third among the angels, was motivated more by a desire to keep his new spot as arch-archangel than by a desire for justice.

While I waited for decisive action from above, the Fallen Angels became entrenched on Earth. Lucifer's influence took root and flourished.

CHAPTER 13

JOB SEARCH

Because of the spin Lucifer put on his strike, Beelzebub, breathless and unconscious, took a thousand years to spiral through the abyss before breaking through the shell of the universe. He sailed past Neptune and drilled through Uranus, awoke in time to grab at and miss the rings of Saturn, and laughed giddily as he just barely evaded the long gravitational reach of Jupiter. Ricocheting among the asteroids delayed him another thousand years. At last, he careened free and shot past Mars. When he impacted Earth, the low angle created a long south-north gash that later was called the Jordan River Valley.

Already stripped featherless by his rough travels, he was nearly skinned alive scraping though the rock and gravel. Immediately, flies, thinking him dead, descended to drill into his raw flesh and lay their eggs in his open, bleeding wounds. He awoke long enough to try to crawl out of the crater, but he had hardly begun to move when he rolled back to the nadir where he lay stunned and incredulous until he passed out again.

When he recovered consciousness and tried once more to crawl out of the crater, he failed again. Remaining still seemed to be the best choice. After two days and nights of striving to recover the ability to breathe easily, he felt strong enough to sit up. Rather than risk another failure at trying to crawl out of the crater, he contented himself with staring at the landscape. To the south, the narrow vista, undulating in the summer heat, was of barren and broken rock devoid of shade and nuance. His jaw dropped to his belly. "It's a fate worse than the Fiery Pit." He lay back with a resigned sigh. "I hope the neighbors are quiet."

The Philistine priests in Ekron witnessed the meteoric descent in the east and commissioned the stonemason to record it on the wall of the central well. They proclaimed to the citizens that an omen had been sighted, not confined to the sky as was usually the case, but evidently falling all the way to Earth.

Rather than listen to the sacred interpretation, the laity immediately argued among themselves. Had it had been a comet, falling star, mass hallucination, or archetypal dream? Work ceased in the fields, markets devolved into forums, rituals were neglected, friendships were deferred until the debates over the mystery could be resolved. A noisy mass of farmers waving their planting sticks came to the West Gate of the city and insisted that the government resolve the question. A similarly armed mob besieged the East Gate.

Within the week, the King called an assembly in the town square and decreed the Philistine priests go unearth the truth.

The Chief Priest suggested the military would be the logical choice of envoy in case the Messenger from the Sky Gods proved petulant.

The King, as leader of the Municipal Army, thought the Messenger might require rituals, speak a mystic language, or expect special obeisance that only the arcane knowledge and fabled purity of the priests could plumb and satisfy. The soldiers rattled their swords against their shields to show their agreement with the royal opinion, although they didn't understand it.

The Chief Priest agreed with the King and declared him magnificently insightful.

A sergeant proposed to grant the King through acclamation the new royal title Ever Wise.

"It is so obvious, it hardly needs to be announced," the Chief Priest said.

"Hear! Hear!" the sergeant shouted.

And the obvious remained unacclaimed. The King was none the wiser.

Ever optimistic, the Assistant High Priest suggested the name of the central well be changed from *Sweat of the Earth* to *Star Juice*.

The King proclaimed, "Be it so! Now pack your bags."

The quasi-mathematical among the priests calculated the trajectory of the star fallen in the east and estimated the time it would take them to arrive in the presence of--they did not know what but they assumed it would be a heavenly being, perhaps even a divinity, a benevolent one if luck was with them.

They were in sore need of a new god. The graven image that had been their hope was proving unresponsive. Tweaking the rituals, reciting intuited magic words, offering sacrifices, withholding sacrifices, following their dreams, doubling tribute, offering virgins: Nothing succeeded in persuading the entity to break his stony silence.

As a precaution, the priests performed ablutions before the idol that they planned to supplant, and then with hope, the townspeople and soldiers, waving planting sticks and swords, escorted them as far as the east gate.

They rode on their asses (the camel had not yet been domesticated) and drove along with them the beasts they had commandeered, packed with food and water. The second day, they passed from Philistine lands into the unfriendly domain of the Canaanites. A few well-placed jewels bought them safe passage.

A week passed before they found Beelzebub, sitting in a heart-shaped depression that was to become the Sea of Galilee. The priests were unsure how to approach the mystery.

The Assistant Chief Priest thought the safest way was to prostrate themselves and slide down the slope on their bellies.

"Crawling will take another day or two. We should use the quickest approach: walk down."

"But strutting brazenly towards a divinity might appear disrespectful and merit a quick rebuke. We don't know what we're dealing with, so let's maximize caution."

After much debate and some regrettable epithets, they decided to combine walking and prostration. The Chief Priest volunteered to watch their asses. The others insisted they stake the animals so that all the clergy could go together, and no one of them would be saddled with the onerous task of tending to their asses.

When Beelzebub saw them descending from the crest of the crater, he expected the worst. He remembered that humans had at one time been seduced by Lucifer. How could they possibly be friendly to him? He noted that the strangers alternated between walking stealthily toward him and hiding flat on the ground. He resigned himself to his fate. "I'm immortal, so I won't be killed. That's the downside. Perhaps stabbing and drubbing me will scare away these flies. In any case, showing friendliness is probably my best option."

A half day passed in the descent to Beelzebub. When they were twenty cubits away, the group prodded the Chief Priest to the fore and insisted in hushed voices that he approach alone. Beelzebub, impatient at the long delay, waved them closer and called out to them. The priests fell quaking to the ground. Finally, the Chief Priest accepted his destiny and strode forward with only his shaky legs to support him. When he was five cubits in front of the visitor from the skies, his legs gave out, and he fell flat on his face.

Beelzebub winced in empathy. "I am Beelzebub, and I'm new around here. Do you have any recommendations on where to live?"

The Chief Priest sighed with relief. He thought that anyone who could endure the flies so calmly and create such a crater without bragging must be powerful on a divine level. It was time to recruit him.

"I know a town about a week away that needs a new resident for the temple. It's hardly been used; it's practically new. I could arrange for immediate occupation."

"I was hoping for something completely new, with the latest amenities."

"In exchange for what? Pardon my bluntness, but I don't want to risk disappointing you if we find out later that the town can't afford you."

"Don't worry about it. I'm here to help. Food, water, a little tribute, maybe some sacrifices."

"Animal or human?"

"How about something durable, like minerals?"

"The usual?"

Beelzebub had no idea what that meant. "For a start, but I may want some variety from time to time; nothing you can't afford. Wouldn't want to bankrupt my own company."

"How about we donate the equivalent of one percent in gems and animals?"

"Why do you persist in offering animals?"

"It's the latest trend. The neighbors would ridicule us if we didn't keep current."

"If you're going to feed me carcasses, I'll need something to calm my stomach. Twenty percent of the village's gross ought to buy me enough milk of magnesia."

The Chief Priest was hesitant. "Can we agree on ten? Mind you, now, we might not be able to spare that much in hard times. Here's a modest proposal: If we're short of resources, can we substitute a baby now and then? That's a premium product. I hear they're tender and juicy when slow roasted."

"Here's a reasonable proposal: a fatted calf, euthanized, with a foot-long loaf of well-buttered rye bread every other week plus a mug of mead on major holidays."

The Chief Priest smiled and prayed that Beelzebub was telling the truth.

Beelzebub smiled back and hoped that the villagers would be easily pleased.

CHAPTER 14

ON THE JOB TRAINING

It was a sweltering day when Beelzebub entered the city's east gate riding on an ass. Many of the townspeople stood along the street fanning themselves with palm fronds while saying, "Hoh! Sun's hot today."

A rumor had sprung to life and spread among the Philistines like a vine: A secret pact between the priests of Ekron and the military of Jericho had been formed to frighten the farmers into ceding their crops to the Egyptians in exchange for a multicolored robe for the king of Petra. The rumor was weakened, but not disproved, by the return of the expedition with an actual candidate for the position of deity.

When the Chief Priest learned about the conspiracy theory, he declared it heresy. It persisted until he suggested that those caught repeating it would make ideal sacrifices to the new deity. The townspeople immediately diverted their attention from speculation to erection.

Beelzebub perched and patiently waited on the pinnacle of the royal palace. His apparent supervision seemed to spur the assiduous craftsmen to work faster. With the detritus of the idol's temple, supplemented with the idol itself repurposed as part of the foundation, as well as some nicely polished stone and a few slabs of granite purchased from the quarries of the neighboring tribe, they built a taller, broader and more luxurious sanctum.

The Canaanites who sold the slabs were later chastised by their own deity for helping a rival god. The repentant tribe claimed the infidelity meant nothing to them. They were only in it for the money, and they promised it would never happen again. The deity pouted for a decade, accepted half a thousand sacrifices on the anniversary of the sale and claimed he had forgotten all about it. (However, he did refer to the event the next seven times they erred.)

No requests were made of Beelzebub at first. The Ekronites had heard frightening tales of the neighboring deity's wrath. He was said to be quick in anger and slow in forgiveness, deaf to suffering and oblivious to need, rigid in rules and unsparing in penalties. Secretly the Canaanites joked, "He says, 'Ask me for anything, so I can slap you down.'" The devotees of Beelzebub mitigated their personal risk by waiting for some sign of benevolence.

A fortnight after Beelzebub took up residence in the rebuilt temple, he asked the Chief Priest, "Doesn't it rain around here? I haven't seen a drop since I landed."

"It's been four months since the last rain."

"No wonder the crops are--what color would you say that is? Yellow? Brown? sallow?"

"It's a judgement call. I'd say between a light tan and blond. Of course, you could say--"

"Never mind. I'll see what I can do."

Beelzebub flew southwest. After three days, the Chief Priest informed the King of the absence. On the sixth day, the King consulted his counsellors who, having already weak faith in the new deity, advised that the old idol be dug up and reinstated in the temple. They suggested that sacrificing the Chief Priest would cheaply atone for their infidelity. They hired a stonemason to begin the excavation, an architect to design the repairs, and a carpenter to erect a pyre. They promised to begin in the morning.

In the nick of time, at sunrise, Beelzebub returned pushing a raincloud before him. Thus, he watered the crops and cultivated the people's gratitude and devotion simultaneously. For this, they called him Lord of the Skies and declared they were satisfied with his performance.

When three women pleaded for him to help them become pregnant, he levied a tribute on the townspeople to finance the acquisition of a fertility herb from Mesopotamia. The people grumbled about the added expense but decided it was easier to pay than to listen to the wives complain about unfulfilled maternal desires and the fruitlessness of their husbands' best efforts.

Having obtained the blend of herbs at a discount from a Babylonian merchant, Beelzebub surreptitiously added it at midnight to the Star Juice Well. All the women between twelve and fifty-five became pregnant. All the babies were males. Undoubtedly the discount herb was old stock. For what the Ekronites saw as simultaneously granting the wish and playing a joke, the disgruntled but resigned townspeople called him Lord of the Flies.

The people continued eagerly seeking favors, but the priests acted as mediators, cautiously analyzing and editing the requests before submitting them.

Overall, the Ekronites considered Beelzebub a fair to middling deity. His miracles ingratiated them, and his mistakes endeared them. They grew to love him the way one loves a bothersome brother or a clumsy uncle. He found the favor of the people satisfying and refreshing, despite their being fickle, whining, and insatiable. He soon grew rich and popular enough to have vacation and weekend cottages in Ashkelon and Ashdod.

Although Beelzebub slowly grew weary of their constant requests, he continued to feast on the sacrifices and accept tribute.

CHAPTER 15

HITCHES IN STARDOM

Beelzebub learned soon after his arrival that the tribes neighboring the Philistines were mercenaries and proselytizers for Unpronounceable. He often heard them crying out in the wilderness, "There is only one god, therefore we must destroy all other gods." Of course, these exhortations made him anxious for his own future. Fearing that he might be forced into an early retirement, Beelzebub stockpiled as much treasure as he could in the basements of his three temples. He dreamed of a serene life in a far land: a cottage, a vegetable garden, and an attached solarium conducive to painting.

It was clear to Beelzebub that Unpronounceable assumed his opponent was a carved idol, an unconscious stone stele, and felt no need to exercise his prodigious power. Rather than arouse suspicion, Beelzebub confined his military activities to aiding and abetting the Philistines within their own territory. But the ever more frequent encroachments by the belligerent neighbors became intolerable. The

Philistines begged for more decisive actions, for more intimidating victories. They had treated him well, most of the time, and he wished he could be of better service. Winning the few minor scrapes and skirmishes that he thought would be beneath Almighty's notice left everyone dissatisfied. Then a goon, who had been captured through the wiles of a beautiful woman, destroyed his cottage by the sea. Beelzebub worried about his status, but he still refrained from any ostentatious retaliation that might reveal his identity.

The Chief Priest confided to Beelzebub that he might be getting too old for warfare and suggested that the blood of newborns might restore his youth. Sacrifices could start as early as the following week.

Beelzebub declined the offer. He decided the time had come to move his hoard of treasure to a cache in the Caucasus Mountains and started to pack. He had yet to realize that danger approached sooner than expected and from another direction.

Lucifer, taking a break from fomenting internecine warfare among the Edomites, checked his ledgers and noticed that the tribute from Ashdod had stopped centuries ago.

He dispatched Ishtar, his assistant assigned to Mesopotamia, to investigate. She ascertained that the beautiful, yet unresponsive, block of stone had been replaced by Hell's rebel rouser. She had personally trained and coached the sculptor whose skillful creation had surpassed the meager efforts of the most talented of the Assyrian artists. Rather than submit the region to her fury and risk the obliteration of an asset, Lucifer elected to handle the situation in person.

Beelzebub was surreptitiously packing a few small trinkets when the Chief Priest interrupted him. "I hate to bother you again, but--. Oh. Are you going somewhere?"

"Uh, yes. Headed off to Ashkelon to help stack the bricks for the new city wall. What's up?"

"It's the same old story, the jawless jackass in the barley field. It's been rotting for, oh, I don't know, maybe a half a decade, judging by the stench. The farmer's acting out. Seems the carcass is interfering with his planting. He claims it's spooking his donkeys."

"Why doesn't he move it out of the way?"

"He's afraid it's a sacred animal; looks to him like a sacrifice. He wants a deity's dispensation to touch it."

"That's asinine."

"He's mulish about it. He needs assurance that he won't get assassinated when the blame's assigned. He's been blindsided before."

"Does he expect me to move it for him?"

"I think he can haul the ass himself."

"Tell him that I assent to reassigning the carcass and--"

Lucifer strolled into the temple and casually extinguished the candles with a fetid exhalation.

"You!" Beelzebub gasped.

"Me!" Lucifer said with a sneer. He spread his wings from wall to wall like a hawk menacing a snake. His scalp brushed the ceiling, his feet seared the stone floor.

To the Chief Priest, Beelzebub said, "Go now. We can finish later. I forgot a dear friend was dropping by."

The man crept along the wall, head bowed, eyes covered, more frightened than he had ever felt before. As he passed beneath the tip of Lucifer's wing, he fell to the ground as if knocked down. He crawled out of the temple, tried and failed to stand, crawled to the wall of the Star Juice Well, pulled himself to his feet, wobbled out the West Gate, and then ran without stopping to the next town where he hid in a stable and ate hay for the remainder of his short life.

"You," snarled Lucifer, "you have been stealing my tribute."

"I had no idea. I thought I'd replaced a statue. It didn't look anything like you. It was rather cute in a perver--"

Lucifer hissed. His breath singed the sparse feathers of Beelzebub's wings. "Earth is mine. I won it in Eden. Why didn't you beg for my permission?"

"I never even considered that you'd be interested in a dilapidated, ugly town like this one."

"Dilapidated and ugly are pleasing to me."

"Would you like me to leave it in ruins for you? I'd be happy to help."

Lucifer spit a wad of fire at Beelzebub's feet. The molten stone between his toes jolted his memory. "I don't need help." Lucifer pointed his clawed middle finger at Beelzebub's chest.

"Of course, not, but I can lighten the load. And I love what you've done with your nails. Have you considered crimson paint? It would bring out the red of your eyes."

"Surrender the tribute you've stolen."

"Absolutely! You can have it all. I had to spend some of it on renovations. And buying off the Egyptians hasn't been cheap. I've had to purchase rain from central Africa forty-eigh--no, it's forty-nine times now. And fertility herbs from Mesopotamia don't come cheap. I've got a complete list of expenses, all legitimate. But you can have the rest."

"You'll owe me the difference."

"Of course. I'll start restitution as soon as I have another paying position. I swear, I had no idea you had a financial interest here. I would have cut a deal with you and taken just a little off the top."

"If--?"

"If you had agreed. Ha-ha! Heh? I'm sure you would have. I'm a good administrator, and I don't need much. Ten--no, make it one percent?"

Lucifer snapped his fingers. Fifty-five and a half dozen hobgoblins clamored in and carted away the trove.

"Are those your children?" asked Beelzebub. "So cute, look just like you."

"Are you fomenting another rebellion, here on Earth, like you failed to do in the Fiery Pit?"

"No, no! I wouldn't dream of opposing you again. I remember excruciatingly well what happened last time. Very ill-advis--."

"Torture, terror and torment are yours, Beelzebub, unless you swear eternal and unwavering allegiance to me."

"Yes, of course, Master," said Beelzebub with his head bowed and his chin on his belly. "I will do whatever it takes to atone, whatever pleases you."

"I'll leave you here temporarily as my agent until I can

find a worthier deputy. You have not even begun to earn my forgiveness. It may not be possible."

"I'm certain that there is nothing I can do to make it up to you. I can only rely on the--." Beelzebub hesitated, searching for the right word, then gave up. "--the goodness in your heart. In the meantime, whatever you say is my sincerest desire."

Lucifer then instructed him at length in the use of dark propaganda to foment unrest in the neighboring tribes. "Eventually, the followers of Unpronounceable will recognize the emptiness of his love and rebel against him. In the meantime, I will send Ishtar to help you. You will find her both useful and observant." He turned to leave and said over his shoulder, "Remember: 'failed creation' and 'failed paradise' and 'failed compassion.' Repeat 'failed' until they stop questioning. If they argue, remind them that all their facts are fake."

"As simple as that?" Beelzebub asked.

"Strange as it seems, it can't fail." Lucifer paused on the threshold of the temple. "I will decide your punishment later."

As soon as Beelzebub was alone, he abandoned his temples, without saying goodbye to his people, and fled into the desert. When the flies, his last and most faithful devotees, could no longer endure the relentless heat, they deserted him. For forty years, give or take a few decades, across the desolation between the Jordan and the Tigris, he trekked, too fearful of drawing attention to himself to risk flying. His grateful feet finally waded through the reeds and sedges of the Euphrates, trying not to disturb the cranes and blackbirds. He scrambled through a range of precipitous mountains and hid in the land where Cain, alone and rejected by his children, had ended his second exile.

CHAPTER 16

WHAT TO MY WONDERING EYES

I applied for a long overdue and much deserved vacation. The Committee Offering Vacation Escapes and Negotiations (COVEN) summarily refused my request to revisit Chaos. My first visit involved multiple wild rides balancing on a meson while avoiding collisions with photons. I was rendered so discombobulated that twenty years passed before my head cleared enough to refocus on my terrestrial duties. Angelica, the new Chief of the COVEN, allocated me a week atop the third tallest Himalayan mountain and scheduled it in the third fortnight of Winter. The nearest cave was already booked. I was issued a jacket and promised a cord of pine. To be effective the former was too flimsy and the latter too green. Luckily, the Travel Department mistakenly made the reservations for midsummer.

I reported a week before my scheduled departure date. The angel Angela informed me that I had almost missed my shuttle. I showed her my documents, but she brushed them aside, calling them irrelevant. I apologized for being a slow learner and hopped aboard the empty express.

When it jolted to a stop, I climbed out of the half-sunken car and swam to the left bank. Atop a boulder, I stretched my wings and shook the feathers until they were dry, a trick I had learned from observing wild chickens in the jungles of southeast Asia.

I turned to head upstream, wondering where I could possibly have landed. My jaw dropped open: There, not more than thirty cubits away, stood a featherless angel, his jaw hanging to his belly. He resembled a frightened fawn, frozen in terror.

"Beelzebub!"

He dropped to his knees on the bare rocks. "Don't, don't, don't--."

I let a minute pass before I asked, "Don't what?"

He pointed up. "Whatever he sent you to do to me!"

I scanned the sky and the slopes of the canyon. "Who? There's no one there."

He fell flat. His forehead cracked a piece of driftwood. He whimpered, "Don't let him hear you deny him."

I hopped near him and sat on a boulder. "It's good to

see you again. What brings you to this--canyon? And where is this canyon?"

Beelzebub eyed me through narrow slits. "You're not acting as Angel of Retribution?"

"Fiddle-dee-dee. I wouldn't be any good in the role. At best, I'm a character actor, but even when I play myself the rest of the cast roll their eyes. Once they assigned me the part of a sea captain, but I sounded more like a sea lion."

He struggled to his feet and pulled a few splinters from above his brow, "We're east of Eden, but I don't know exactly where. I'm hiding, I mean, hanging out in a cave, keeping my head down, waiting--. I just thought it was a good idea to relocate. New environment, new growth; you get the picture."

"Yes. Your feather is growing back nicely. Let's hope it's progress encourages the others."

He smiled, inhaled deeply, exhaled slowly, and his shoulders dropped. "I've got a little place nearby. Nothing fancy, but we could have some tea if you're up to it." He picked up the broken branch and lead the way.

As soon as we entered the cave, I said, "Do I detect the scent of Cain?"

"I thought so too."

"I'd often wondered what'd happened to him."

He warmed a crude stone goblet between his hands and offered it to me. "I'm afraid all I have is hemlock."

"My favorite!"

CHAPTER 17

THE WHITE CRANE ASCENDS

When Beelzebub emerged from his cave several decades later, and crossed the Indus River, as quietly as the evening star, he thought it would be wise to continue to hide from Lucifer and Unpronounceable, although he was far enough away from their lands to feel safe, at least for a while. He knew they were both actively seeking to widen and maintain their influence and dominion on Earth.

He disguised himself as a servant, then a soldier, a lover of ten thousand maiden cowherders (although forty-seven of them misrepresented their profession and fifty-four were no longer qualified), as well as twenty-three other personae. At last, having risen in the world to the rank of prince, he felt exhausted by the constant conflict between striving to achieve and preserving anonymity. He knew for certain that someday, somewhere, he was destined to meet Lucifer or Unpronounceable again.

He sat beneath a Bodhi tree and wept for seven years. Then he spent twenty-two years trying to clear his mind and heart of the regret, sorrow, and disappointment of having lost heaven. After another thirty-three years he asked himself, "What is the point of it all?" For forty years he considered ways to end his existence, all the while regretting his immortality. Then, with the heaviness of certitude that there could be no escape, he sighed, so deeply that he felt the Earth quiver underneath him. He whispered with a sob and a sigh, "All is suffering."

Beelzebub spent the next fifty years contemplating the truth of his depression, feeling sorry for and pitying all the angels who had been unable to control their sense of humor. Toward the end of this "mood-itation," he realized that he suffered because he had been in heaven and craved to reexperience those moments. He was surprised that it was not Unpronounceable that he missed most. Unpronounceable was great, he was good, he was unsurpassed, he was beyond all others in everything. Beelzebub could only imagine him as a not-an-angel, some not-a-thing that was so different that Beelzebub could never feel truly close.

Those few moments alone with Lucifer and the other angels while Almighty rested had indelibly marked his soul. If he had never known them, he would probably be content. It was the desire for the pleasure of Lucifer's company and the comradery of the angels under the care of the Almighty that was the root of his suffering. That depressed him to a nadir lower than he had felt in the Fiery Pit. One hundred eight years later he thought that if he could release himself from the memory of heaven, he might be able to stop suffering. But the memory, fundamental to his identity, could not be expunged. Sixteen hundred years later, he set his mind and heart on the path to accepting both his suffering and his echo of elation.

Centuries passed. His breathing slowed. His mind stilled. His heart calmed.

When next he opened his eyes, he saw a gathering stretching in all directions around the tree. There were thousands of people from all levels and occupations. There were even some he recognized as Fallen Angels. A few he thought looked like refurbished monkeys. I had been sitting in the crowd, shifting to the back row every decade or so, for almost five hundred years, curious about where he was in his mind and where he was going in his life. When he looked in my direction, a trace of a smile crossed his lips. He nodded, and I felt the same brotherly caress that had come with Lucifer's gaze.

Someone close to his right hand said, "We await your words of wisdom."

"I'm not sure I have anything worth saying. Why do you think I am wise?"

"Some of us have been sitting here for hundreds of

years, life after life, ever since word went out that a new meditation record had been set. We thought you would certainly have something to share."

"Have you really spent lifetimes waiting for me to become wise?"

Many in the crowd nodded. The man on his right said, "We've tried out a few ideas on our own. Like, 'Know Yourself' and 'Self-Reliance' and 'Be Nice.' They all seem to lead nowhere. No matter how deep you dig into yourself, there's always another mystery deeper down; it just keeps getting scarier. Rely on yourself alone and you cut off all the benefits of society. Some mornings, it's impossible to be nice, especially before breakfast."

"Have you tried, 'Do unto others as you would have them do unto you?'"

"I'm into getting flogged."

"Okay, maybe that won't work." Beelzebub asked, "By the way, just to satisfy my own curiosity, do you know who I am or anything else about me?" He believed that the crowd would flee when they discovered he was the Fallen Angel who had been exiled from both Heaven and Hell.

"Of course, we have heard rumors, some qualify as legends, many of them uncomplimentary, but we prefer to think about who we believe you are now rather than what some say you may have been in the mythic past. We call you the Bud of the Bodhi, as if you materialized right here as fresh as a blossom from this very tree. Is that okay with you?"

Beelzebub nodded. "I prefer Bub, but Bud will do nicely." And the word went out in widening circles until in the outermost ring I heard, "We can call him Bubbha."

The person on his right asked again for some wise word of guidance.

"Let me think it over."

The newly named Bud sat in silence for another month.

Finally, he said, "There's danger everywhere. Good and Evil are equally intent on trapping us. Both sides are locked in dubious battle and both sides want you to join the war. Everything here on Earth is designed to entice you to enlist in the service of Good or Evil. Neither Master is worth the strife and struggle. It would appear that there's no escaping it, but if we work together to dissolve our ties to these ideals, to gain and remain in equanimity, to live and die without clinging to life or death, to ignore the snares of Good and Evil, then we can all leave safely at the same instant, like birds in a flock rising from a tranquil lake."

Matthew Stramoski

Part III
Mystic
Maneuvers

CHAPTER 18

BATTLE OF THE BESTIES

Most Fallen Angels chose to remain free agents in the foul times when Satan's goal to retake heaven was first hatched, opting to duck like chickens while keeping out an eagle eye for the hawks. When either of the Big Two crowed, the Fallen would turn and flee as fast as flycatchers.

Lucifer's plan to conquer heaven required myriad millions of humans for paramilitary service. To recruit the necessary numbers, Lucifer devised promises that appealed to visceral desires, disguised them as necessities, and recycled them from one generation to the next until they seemed instinctive. Lucifer looked for help to manage the mobs, but the Fallen Angels remaining in the Fiery Pit hesitated. Despite the limited support of his allies, Satan made great strides recruiting people to train at his "time share." The pace at which his influence spread convinced many of the more secular-minded angels that demons had become overrepresented in the human gene pool.

Lucifer attributed his success to superior insight about people's hearts. He recognized that offering hope was more persuasive than threatening damnation, even though the hope was unrealistic and undeliverable while damnation was a certainty. He saw that hope, for most human hearts, grew from greed, lust, gluttony, envy, gall, and pride. The promise of heaven was readily traded for empty words, worthless trinkets, and fleeting sensations.

The Guardian Angels fretted about losing their jobs and frequently dismayed over their plummeting performance ratings, but Unpronounceable seemed unperturbed. In fact, he gave us the impression that skimming ten percent off the top of Lucifer's take was satisfactory.

Two of the most exalted of the archangels, Michael and Gabriel, feared that Lucifer's plan to amass an army large enough to storm Heaven and eject them from their rightful places would succeed. They discussed counterplots to send a rival power to Earth. Neither wanted to assume the risk himself, but both wanted credit. Michael preferred commissioning a zealot who, while castrating the Adversary's armies with his flaming sword, would grow increasingly berserk until the final victorious battle at the gates of Hell. Gabriel favored dispatching a magician whose irresistible power over water would quench the fire in the pit of each demon's heart and leave him an oozing pile of sludge. Neither entertained the possibility of reconciliation with the

Fallen. The discussions grew so heated, they scorched the clouds. The other archangels forced them to delegate the negotiations to their agents, who immediately attacked the question of their commissions and, much later, who would get top billing for the final script.

I questioned the sincerity of both archangels. Michael, for example, had become the subject of rumors among the few people who made it past Purgatory. They had gotten the idea that Michael had been responsible for casting out the Fallen Angels. According to the legend, he'd raised an army of loyal angels, led them to victory, and quietly, meekly restored heaven to Unpronounceable. Although Michael must have been aware that these falsehoods were circulating, he did nothing to discourage, much less repudiate, them. Instead, he seemed to wallow in the unmerited prestige. On the other hand, Gabriel openly presented himself as one trusted with inside information, often sent alone on secret missions confided directly from the divine lips to his eager ears. He frequently blew his own horn but rarely gave credit to any other Messenger. I cannot say with certitude if he is aware of my own prominent role on Earth. I have never heard him mention it.

The archangel's agents, who had played out their own personal drama and narrowly avoided making a scene in front of the newest arrivals in heaven, were about to ink the agreement ("Play by Gabriel & Michael based on a story by Michael & Gabriel from an idea by Michael after a word by Gabriel") when Unpronounceable called for a meeting.

Wondering why I had been asked to join the ruckus and hoping to avoid uncomfortable entanglements, I stood a discreet distance behind Michael and Gabriel. Without hesitation, Unpronounceable struck at the heart of the matter. "We need to send a representative to Earth to stem the surge of Satan's allies. We can't send just any angel; he needs impeccable credentials."

Gabriel and Michael simultaneously burst into sales pitches promoting their favorite underlings.

Unpronounceable interrupted. "I already have someone in mind."

Gabriel and Michael simultaneously burst into sales pitches promoting their own scripts.

"Yes, yes, I know all about your plots," Unpronounceable said. "I thought about incorporating your ideas into a single script, and I even went so far as to write a few scenes. Then I decided that merely making a few changes to the script wouldn't solve the fundamental problems. Suspension of disbelief is the basis of religion, but it still has to be at least superficially realistic. Neither of you have hit on a believable premise. No one will buy into the invincible warrior who destroys all but never gets a scratch. And no one will take a flood seriously if you pretend it will wash away culpability and extinguish the passions. You may as well call it baptism and get laughed out of the theater. I've kept a few elements from your weak efforts, but really everything in my morality play, from high concept down to devilish details, is my own creation. I'll leave the execution to you two. Samuel will take charge of continuity and be the arbitrator-director."

He handed each of us a script whose by-line was nothing but consonants. Dismissed from the meeting, we adjourned to a private corner of heaven. Michael and Gabriel immediately began to argue over whose name would appear as principal producer. I slipped away unnoticed to read the script undisturbed in a small, out of the way tavern in Bethany. They served an excellent honey bread whose aroma helped me relax.

I hesitated over the lead role, a combination son-of-man and son-of-god. I wondered if the titles were intended to be literal. I wrote a question mark in the margin adjacent to the son's first appearance, but it vanished as quickly as ink from a lemon. "Of course," I thought, "there are as many sons of men as there are alleged sons of deities scattered across Earth."

Knowing Unpronounceable's obsession with center stage, I assumed he would play the roles of both father and son, make cameo appearances as needed, upstage everyone, and float back to heaven whenever the parallel universes called him.

In our first pre-production meeting, Michael wondered, "Who could this mother be? Where is she? The script implies she's human and already living on Earth. A mob will answer the casting call. We'll need to hire someone to screen them."

I answered, "Unpronounceable may have someone already picked out. We should start by asking him."

Michael was skeptical. "Wouldn't he have told us? Where's she hiding? I've been nosing into every fold in the clouds and haven't seen anything."

Gabriel shushed him. "We do not want to know if heaven has an attic or a secret chamber."

I whispered, "I hope the son-of-god role will be either an actor or an honorary title."

Michael answered me shaking his head. "There's going to be an immense herd of wannabes for that role. I bet there's a mystery here that we aren't in on yet."

Gabriel, in the quietest voice I had ever heard him use, said, "We are all aware that some of the fallen have fathered and mothered children. Maybe--."

Michael whispered more softly still, "But such a deed would be out of character for You Know Who."

I said, most softly of all, "We know he is capable of anything."

Although working covertly, we inadvertently started a cascade of speculative theories culminating in one by a fringe group of conspiracy-minded angels. They asserted that Gabriel had been instructed by the highest authority to collude with Lucifer to produce a hybrid spawn. These demonic, zombie-like offspring would rise from a deep state of sleep, overthrow human governments, and establish kangaroo courts. The future of koalas was in peril, but very few worried for them. The consensus was that koalas have more cuteness than usefulness.

We decided to schedule the audition for the mother's role and leave the problem of the son until later. That it could work itself out without our assistance, we hoped fervently.

On my recommendation, Michael and Gabriel agreed to hire Raphael to head the casting department. We suggested he begin with the role of Mother. Immediately, the heavenly host were rife with rumors: An unacknowledged lovechild, a non-disclosure agreement, a clandestine chamber wrapped in clouds.

Instead of squelching the falsehoods by announcing the truth, Unpronounceable ignored the chatter. He called me to come see the one who was to be Jess but swore me to secrecy. "There's enough noise in heaven as it is." He waved his hand over a clump of cloud. "Of course, he hasn't been born yet, this is the model. I'm well pleased with him. There's only one--maybe two--tweaks to be done, like the nose. I'm not satisfied with that nose."

"It looks fine to me," I said, thinking that it looked a lot like mine.

"As soon as you have the mother picked out, I'll animate Jess and send him in."

"Without rehearsals? Can't we have a dozen run-throughs?"

"We're on a tight schedule."

I decided to ask the son later, when we were alone, for the truth of his origins, but I changed my mind when I remembered that no humans are ever observers of their own conception. After all, no one can swear to know exactly how it had happened. I opted to give Unpronounceable the benefit of faith and doubt by calling it a joyful mystery. I resolved to treat Jess as he was portrayed in the script. I noted that the father never appears on stage, although he has a voice-over at the end of the first act.

Michael complained endlessly about the episodic structure of the second act. Gabriel admitted that it was "preachy," but he thought the tension with the Pharisees would keep the plot moving. I distracted Michael by asking him to take charge as location manager of the manifestation.

When I told them there would be no rehearsals, Gabriel appealed to Unpronounceable. Jess could not possibly be skilled enough as an actor to pull off a performance in Jerusalem, known to be a tough and unforgiving crowd: If you fail, they write it down and call it scripture. Unpronounceable relented after Gabriel orchestrated an unabridged performance of the Book of Psalms. An out-of-town tryout was arranged with the Olmecs and a select group of Jews who had gotten lost when they wandered out of Egypt; they turned west instead of east and eventually beached on the far side of the Atlantic. Our tight schedule demanded that we keep rehearsals to a minimum, but we managed to hold a cold reading before we left. It was not convincing. Michael, Gabriel, and I carefully reviewed the itinerary and then notified the Transportation Department that we were ready.

The next thing we knew, Jess had landed in Bethlehem.

CHAPTER 19

A STAR IS BERTHED

The birthplace reservations weren't for another 30 years, so we had to put him up in a manger for a couple nights then rush him off to a slum in Nazareth. Miriam, the woman who had been cast as Mother, was appalled to find out that she was not just playing the role during the rehearsals and performances but was actually expected to care for the child every day from infancy to manhood. And she was expected to provide him with room and board, as well as enough criticism to make him feel part of the family.

Before the end of the first night, she had become exhausted by his constant hungry crying. Having never been pregnant, she had no milk to satisfy his appetite. A visit from Gabriel convinced her that child support would eventually be paid in the heavenly currency, a coin called "grace" which was said to be more valuable than gold although you couldn't buy half a loaf of bread with it at the corner bakery. As an immediate incentive, he doubled the size of her breasts and enabled them to produce milk. When baby Jess smiled at her from the crib, she said, "How could I stay cross at such an adorable baby?"

In the original script, no one got killed; everyone found happiness, true love, riches; kids looked like their fathers; and their people first rulers put. I saw immediately that under current circumstances a happy ending was improbable at best.

Michael whined that he couldn't work under such conditions and haughtily headed heavenward. Gabriel blasted a few fanfares and made one announcement to some wandering rustlers posing as shepherds, then he wished us luck and soared after Michael. Four years passed before anyone thought to reset the calendar to year one.

It was do or die, for certain. Immediately I found another extra named Joe to play Jess's stepfather, now rewritten as a mute. He proved to be less necessary than I had thought. The only essential family member was Mother. As a breadwinner in a crossroads town, she was an exceptional provider. She was also admired locally for her baking skills.

I concentrated on preparing Jess for his mission. Every night we rehearsed his lines. Every day we practiced acting in an effort to build his confidence. "Imagine," I coached him, "you're sawing a board, building a cabinet, preaching to the multitudes." At first, he wasn't getting the hang of pretending to saw while preaching. I gave him a dozen boards that I found in a pit and had him experience carpentry firsthand. By coincidence, a Roman Centurion saw him at work and thought he had talent. He gave Jess a steady stream of commissions, mostly making crosses. His mother was glad for the money but thought collaborating with the enemy could come to no good. She had found that Gabriel's gift had tripled her personal income, but the increasing size of her family ate up the gain.

Jess seemed confused, and his priorities conflicted with our mission. Instead of attending rehearsals or studying his lines, he showed an inadvisable interest in the company and "redemption" of adulteresses and "women of the well." We frequently had to claim certain events were intended to be rehearsals of scenes. I can't remember how many times I had to yell "Cut!" to halt his inappropriate actions before they became crimes. But it was often enough that the villagers nicknamed me "Mohel."

Later, when we were on the road, we were forced to cover his actions with "alternate interpretations." If they involved random strangers encountered at common, unidentifiable locations like a community well or a public stoning, we preferred to explain them as acts of righteous mercy that had been misread. We often obliterated the real names, not to protect the innocent, but to shield the scandalous from scurrilous scrutiny. The rumors, though, persisted and multiplied. The company he kept made it difficult, almost impossible, to maintain his reputation as a holy representative.

One day, Miriam scolded him for neglecting his duties. "If you don't learn your part, you'll never move out, and I'll be stuck with you the rest of my life, eating up my wages like they grew on trees. Well, let me tell you, life hasn't grown on trees since Eden was plowed under. All I suffer and sacrifice--I wouldn't wish it on another soul."

That evening, Jess complained to me that the script was too difficult to memorize. He found the stories he was to tell too mysterious and disjointed. I had to agree that the text lacked continuity and was rife with obscurity; the plot wandered aimlessly, worse than a directionally challenged nomad under a jungle canopy. I urged him to continue trying and assured him his best efforts would be rewarded.

"Not many people are born knowing their purpose. How lucky you are to have been blessed with a divine mission!"

Jess sighed deeply and slowly, staring at the ground. He kicked a pebble. "I wish someone else could do this."

He disappeared the next day.

CHAPTER 20

RELIGION IN THE ROUGH

We searched for Jess in all the usual places: around the taverns where people gathered in hope of finding a dog's hair, at the wells where the women waited to draw water, in the neighborhood near the Roman garrison guarding the crossroads. I called on Michael and Gabriel to help in the search, but they had moved on to other projects. Miriam was too exhausted by caring for and feeding her family to be of any use. The actor playing the role of Earthly Stepfather finally earned his keep by checking the town tavern every day, sometimes twice. I saw no evidence that Jess had brought along food, water, money or a map. My worry grew stronger each day. It took us over a month of canvassing the countryside to locate him.

Jess had isolated himself in the wilderness, doggedly trying to learn his lines by rote. He fed on sparse wild figs and dates, neither abundant enough to satisfy his appetite. After a couple weeks, even those resources were exhausted. He yearned to munch on grasshoppers, but they were out of season, or honey, but he was allergic to bees.

His hungry stomach, crying out in the wilderness, was heard by Lucifer. Satan flew unnoticed into the ravine behind Jess, folded his wings behind his back, and climbed to the crest where Jess sat inaccurately repeating the first of the Beatitudes.

"You look famished, my friend." Lucifer interrupted without apology.

Jess jumped, but quickly recovered his composure. "I haven't eaten for I don't know how long."

"That lean and hungry look does not become you. Why don't you take a moment to grab a bite?"

"I can't stop until I finish. I've got to learn my lines. It's a huge part, and I haven't even gotten my first big speech memorized."

"I could hear your stomach growling down in the ravine. Hunger is a poor tutor. I know a nice tavern near here, just a hop away. The bread is as hard as stone, but it becomes edible if you dunk it. Care to join me? My treat!"

"It's kind of you to offer, but I've got to memorize every word of this speech today, and it's got to be verbatim."

"Why? Surely a paraphrase will suffice. It's not as if they came from the mouth of some god."

"I was told they did."

Lucifer chuckled. "You believed them? Did they offer any proof?"

"Samuel gave me his word on it. He's an honorable man."

"Has he told you about whose will he's following?"

"No. But right now, I don't have the time to debate the issue. I'm way behind schedule. I keep tripping over these mind-boggling blessings. Which comes first, the meek or the poor?"

"Who cares? What do either have to offer?"

Jess consulted the script he was holding. "According to this, Earth and the Kingdom of Heaven, eventually."

"Power gets you Earth, and Heaven already has a monarch. But if it's important to you, I am willing help. To keep you from stumbling over the words, I have a way to carve them into your mind as if in stone. You'll never be able to forget them. It will be like a miracle."

"Don't tempt me. If it doesn't work, I'll be in grave trouble, even further behind from wasting time. It's not like I can pretend to stub my toe and read from a cheat sheet with my back to the audience. The speech has to give the impression that I mean it, that it comes from my heart."

"Then don't think it through. If you understand the meaning, you'll never give a convincing performance. Just repeat the words by rote and try to look inspired. Keeping your eyes on a distant cloud usually gives bystanders the impression that you're channeling the divine."

Jess sat silent, contemplating the words of the stranger, vacillating between believing the seemingly wise visitor and keeping his faith in his old friend.

Lucifer saw the doubt and conflict in his eyes. "I'll be honest with you, Jess."

"You know my name. How?"

"Back home, I heard that a wannabe star named Jess was struggling in the wilderness, so I came to see for myself. When I saw you, I recognized immediately that you were undeniably a man of destiny, with untold theatrical potential. You've got a terrible agent, a clumsy director, and an author who thinks only of his precious phrases, as if they were poetry. There's nothing worse than an author who's obsessed with his own career. He'll cast the gig aside with a flick of his wrist if he gets whiff of a better deal. I know the type from personal experience. Just try to ad lib, and he'll burn you. I can help you break free and realize your true potential."

"But I can't turn my back on my friends. They've been with me from before my birth. I have to stick with them."

"Have you signed a contract?"

"Contract? Among friends?"

"Believe me. It's the only way to go." Lucifer smiled, half shut his eyes and nodded his head with a knowing look on his face. He had mastered the appearance of confiding sincerity.

"Still--"

"Are you absolutely certain that you don't want my help? You're settling for less than your potential, hampered by a misfit inept cast and a limited budget. Your agent is working for someone else, your director hasn't a clue about the purpose of the plot, and the producer has moved on to other projects. I have not only the money to back a full production but also the friends to make it happen. Greek chorus? Got it. Special effects? Easy! Lead roles? Before you know it, you'll be turning down heavenly roles that others pray for! You can be the master of all this. All you have to do is sign me as your agent, and I will give you the world."

"You'll get behind me, completely?"

From my flight overhead, I spied the two of them on the rocks, facing and leaning toward each other as if they were in a close conversation. My meticulous search, spiraling out from Nazareth, had at last paid off. I dropped down lightly beside Jess. "Lucifer! What a surprise! I haven't seen you since that day in the garden. How have you been?"

Lucifer was startled. He had been too focused on his prey to notice my approach. His jaw dropped, but only a millimeter, too little for Jess to be able to notice. Quickly, seamlessly Lucifer regained his composure. "Oh, just fine, thank you," he muttered. Then in a clearer voice, he said, "I intended to come see you, but I've been busy as hell. You understand: one thing or another always seems to manage to burn a hole in your schedule."

Jess asked, "You two know each other? What a coincidence!"

To me, Lucifer said, "I was just leaving." To Jess, he said, "I'll catch you later." Lucifer flew away east in a whirlwind. In spite of the commotion, I could hear him mutter, "This is the Anti-Satan? Really? What a joke! I can't wait to tell the gang back home."

With an open mouth, Jess watched him leave. "Wow! What a sound effect! And the visual was awe inspiring! Can we work it into some scene?"

"Maybe at the end. I'll have to check the budget."

Jess sighed, as if he regretted not making the decision he almost made.

I touched his shoulder gently. "It's easy to make people say wow. And making big promises is easier still. But creating a profound experience, one that will be remembered and talked about for generations, that's real magic. Change people at their core, from selfish to generous. Lead them from fearful hate to confident love. What a miracle that would be! It's within your grasp if you believe in the script." I could see in his downcast eyes a lack of confidence. It would take time for him to discover the truth. I knew I could not rush him. "Would you like me to go over the lines with you?"

I stayed with him, consoled, and coddled him with as much care as I could muster, until he was ready to return home. I often wondered if he would ever recover from the temptations in the wilderness. The shadows of doubted aspirations and regretted choices darkened his eyes.

CHAPTER 21

THE STAR GOES NOVA

Finally, bolstered with hefty doses of encouragement from me and the rest of the cast, Jess felt ready to go in front of a live audience. He wanted to "get it over with" by opening in Jerusalem, but I convinced him to start off-off-Jerusalem, in the unsophisticated provinces to the north. He pleaded to go for the gold with a resurrection from the dead, but I convinced him to start with a simple substitution, wine for water. It was more complicated than it seemed on the surface, I told him, because the Law of Object Permanence had been in effect since Moses escaped from Egypt.

Jess played the scene as written, except for an adlib directed at his mother about not wanting to be pressured "before his time."

Miriam angrily rebuffed him. "What? Now you're a fine wine?"

I suggested he was trying to be profound, without

success, which brought her ire down on my halo.

"You got the coin to buy enough wine to souse a wedding party, but you ain't got enough to pay me for the last thirty years. This production don't got much of an angel."

She went out in a huff and acted like she was slamming a door, but the curtain just flapped back into place. She didn't return to the set until the final scene, three years later.

Jess was devastated.

I tried to bring his attention back to the scene. "Let's stay in character. The show must go on."

He pasted a halfhearted smile on his face and began to strut confidently toward the raucous festivities in the next room.

The Steward blustered in and grabbed him by the tunic. "Are you in charge of the wine? Can't you tell good from mediocre! Sherry at a wedding? Even if they're all drunk, they still have taste. You're making me look stupid."

The least criticism always deflated Jess, but this disparagement was particularly devastating; the insult stuck in his craw like a thistle. His chest caved and a tear rolled down his cheek.

The steward grabbed a jug of wine and a loaf of bread

and headed back to the party.

I placed my hand gently on Jess's right shoulder. "Don't take it to heart. He's just a shepherd who doubles as a sommelier in a tiny town down the road from Nowhere. What does he know?"

Jess wiped his nose on the hem of his sleeve. "Yet he still knows more than me."

"Hey," I said, trying to cajole a smile to his lips by lifting his chin with my forefinger; "he can't tell wine from blood."

"I could forgive him more easily if it <u>had</u> been my blood."

This sensitivity persisted throughout his life. Years later, at our last meal together, he was still harping about it.

We returned to Nazareth. To rebuild his confidence, we worked on a few other scenes, alternating long speeches with pithy aphorisms. We almost busted our budget practicing a few simple special effects. We even tried them out in front of small, personally selected audiences from among those tavern regulars chosen by Jess's stepfather. Soon the locals were spreading the word that one of their own was proving to be someone special.

I thought we were too far away from the elite, self-appointed culture guardians in Jerusalem to draw their attention, but word got back to the critics. We were attracting crowds from the unsophisticated villages, but it was obvious to me we weren't prepared for the big-time. The few professional critics who came to see us wrote that we had a few passable tricks, but they looked fishy. When we told them how much bread we made, they accused us of cooking the books. The snootiest one said, if we were remembered at all, it would be as the worst act in history. It would take divine intervention, he claimed, to bring about a second showing. Although I thought the general public would find this scathing review intriguing, that it would generate enough interest to bring in the curious, very few bought it. No one seemed to care enough to cross the road. A well-meaning neighbor claimed we had the biggest crowds ever, but an impartial assessor counted fewer followers than John the Baptist had. Jess lost his confidence and begged to go back to Nazareth. I did everything I could to steady his nerves. Then our time ran out.

We were way over budget. Unpronounceable, either unaware or unmoved by Jess's crisis, commanded us to open in Jerusalem the following week. Jess, feeling the pressure of potentially disappointing the sponsor, opted for a well scripted, impeccably directed, and well-rehearsed scene concerning the denunciation of sinful masses. Our Publicity Department coughed up enough money for a small reception line with a couple dozen palm fronds at the city gate, a donkey ride for the star, and a grossly underfunded promotional event in the temple courtyard.

We couldn't afford extras, so we had to improvise with audience-participation. Unfortunately, the audience hadn't understood the symbolism, the methodology, or the message, and even objected to being flogged without prior consent. The result? A flop! Dead in the water!

For the cast dinner that night, we assembled at a tavern near the Serpent's Pool, which was within sight of Herod's Pillar and close to the Palace of the High Priest. Jess ordered a simple meal of bread and lamb. He chose a light white wine and asked for a couple of casks. The server mentioned that the legume salad would perfectly round out the meal and suggested that a hearty red would be a better complement. Jess acquiesced, but he was in a sulky mood the rest of the evening.

Jess picked at his food. He drank at least one glass too many and let slip that the company didn't have the funds to cover salaries. Judas left in a snit. Jess then implied some creepy things about eating flesh and drinking blood. I was afraid that he would lose the last of his cast, but they were too inebriated to realize the import or to remember accurately what he said. When the bill arrived, they told the server that Judas had gone out to retrieve the money and would pay the bill when he returned. The server left the room, and they all slipped out the window. I went with them, even though everyone was far off script.

Jess led us to a favorite secluded spot in an olive grove overlooking the city. He asked the eleven to try to stay awake despite their crapulous condition. Then he wandered away by himself, softly humming a psalm off key. I flew into a tree and waited for the sunrise.

We did not know it, but charges had been brought against Jess for destruction of private property, assault and battery, unlicensed theatrical use of the temple set, and assuming a false identity. An official of the court recognized Judas pouting beside the Serpent's Pool. To avoid being imprisoned, he turned state's evidence. A posse was raised, and Judas led them to the tavern, where he settled the bill, and then to the garden spot where Jess had collapsed.

They found Jess hallucinating and mumbling to himself. "No, no more, pass this cup to the blonde at the end of the bar. Tell her it's on me."

He was arrested. The eleven remaining cast members would have been detained as well if it were not for Simon Peter's improvised sword play. The loss of one ear seemed to intimidate the entire posse. Jess was escorted back to Jerusalem.

We thought that nothing would happen until the next day, but the authorities were ahead of us by a league and a half. Before we could even think how to arrange bail, the local authorities ran him through the night court, denied his plea of "innocent by divine decree", declared him guilty and sentenced him to death. It was not in the original script, but there was nothing we could do to regain control. Immediately, the lawyers in heaven, in a futile attempt to prevent future audience participation, began drafting approval clauses for unauthorized script changes, but it was too late for this production.

As soon as the climactic earthquake scene started, Jess declared himself "done with this" and invoked his escape clause. Unpronounceable pointed out that the clause had not been included in the final contract, but he agreed to cancel the engagement, declaring that he was "well pleased" with Jess's performance. Only fifty-six angels thought it worthy of anything more than polite applause.

Unpronounceable insisted that we try again, from the top. Still under contract, Jess was sent back to Earth to restart the franchise, this time with the Jews lost in the Caribbean. At immigration, Jess told them that he came from the land of milk and honey; the customs agent told him to get real. When he gave his name, he was offered the option to change it to either Winged Serpent or Feathered Boa. They were even more incredulous when I listed my occupation as "Superintendent of Earth." When the laughter subsided, I tried to namedrop who had sent me, but my facial contortions as I tried to pronounce it sent them rolling on the floor. The agents waved me through after Jess agreed to be responsible for my behavior.

When we arrived at our lodgings, more than thirty-three years late for our reservation, we found that we owed an astronomical sum for a room we had not yet used. The proprietors insisted that we had failed to cancel before the deadline, that there was no expiration date on the stay, and that we pay either with cacao or gold. To raise the money, Jess put a bowl on the ground in the city plaza and mimed generosity. The spectators reacted as if they were staring at a wall. Jess then tried reciting his best parable, but the authorities closed the performance and threatened to arrest him for preaching without a permit.

Unpronounceable decided to start fresh. He called Jess home, but it was too late to avoid paying the innkeeper. After seven years of indentured servitude, the bill was finally settled.

In lieu of severance pay and in compensation for the end of his previous engagement, Unpronounceable granted Jess a glorious ascension, complete with a chorus of cherubs lifting him on glowing clouds, custom designed lightning by Baraqiel, and thunderous applause orchestrated by Ramiel. While he postured triumph, I was unceremoniously hauled up in a hopper car atop a heap of unrefined gold ore.

Nine days later, I was sent to retrieve Jess from the

stratosphere.

My subsequent petition to retrain the Transportation Department was lost in transit.

In the circles of Mediterranean pundits, Jess's reputation had transmogrified from bad actor to legend to superhero. The posthumous explanations of his ancestry, much to Unpronounceable's dismay, had taken root in the fertile soil of human imagination. The debate had turned from "How bad an actor was he?" to "How much of his performance was divine?"

Jess had prayed for retirement, but he was destined to make yet another appearance.

CHAPTER 22

THE STARLESS SEQUEL

Thomas, who played a minor role in the original drama, predicted a second appearance for Jess in a major remake of the original. Many doubted Thomas. Because the return engagement was delayed again and again, each delay explained away with mumbled excuses about the complexities of the lunar calendar and the whimsicality of the divine will, "doubting Thomas" became synonymous with "being realistic."

The cast decided to revive the Calvary drama without divine intervention, hoping it would become a cult hit that would generate enough revenue to support them. They formed a company, The Apostles. They found a few backers, The Disciples. They recruited a director, me.

Although Michael had abandoned his position as director of the earlier production, I knew crossing into his territory without asking would irritate him. We did not need to add his resentment to the list of impediments. He had been created the third highest in heaven, and his power was rumored to be the equal of Lucifer's and his ambition a close second. On each return from a mission, he alighted a nanometer closer to Beelzebub's vacant spot. I decided not to risk walking on vapor with a flaming sword at my back. I begged for his permission to pitch the new plot to Jess. Michael withheld consent until I promised him first option on directing.

I offered Jess a stunning, cloud-wrapped, brilliantly backlit descent from heaven. A host of bare-bottomed cherubic babes would scatter buttercup petals before his golden, ruby-studded sandals. A legion of avenging angels would flank him on each side, every other one wielding a flaming sword, the others blasting bolts of lightning from their bare palms.

"Vengeance?" he said. "It's so not me."

I offered to let him keep the slippers. He objected that they would distract attention from his brown eyes. He complained the script was too long. He expressed hesitation over risking a second crucifixion. Amazingly, he passed over this opportunity to give fresh life to his flagging career.

When I delivered the news to Peter, he remained stone-faced and maintained an optimistic mien. Even without the star, Peter was certain the sequel would draw the necessary crowds to generate a decent return on investment. As proof, he cited the enormous crowd the crucifixion had drawn. He suggested taking advantage of Jess's notoriety by crediting him as "Creator of the Role."

I reminded him, "'Creator' is a jealously guarded trademark."

He then suggested, "We can promote it as based on the life of Jess."

Most of The Apostles opined that Jess's role was essential and insisted he appear in some form. We discussed at ecclesiastical length recasting the part, but no one knew how Unpronounceable would react, and no one dared to ask him.

In the end, The Apostles reimagined his part as a hallowed ghost, an unseen presence guiding the action through voiceovers and visions. The onstage lead went to Simon Peter.

Michael, without having read the script, accepted the challenge of directing. Then he complained the action was burdened with ponderous, yet quaint, parables that seemed pointless. He demanded miracles, extravagantly beyond our budget. He insisted on dozens of rewrites and revised six acts himself. And at every ad lib, he flew off his cloud waving his flaming blade in our faces.

After two dozen rehearsals, the cast, weary yet optimistic, felt ready for the public. Steven, one of The

Disciples, went to the town square to announce that the next performance was at hand.

The Apostles were astonished when word came back that Steven had died at the hands of fundamentalists. Every member of the original cast and crew had been indicted as accomplices in the Temple Attack, and Steven had exacerbated their ire by delivering an excruciatingly long and tedious history lesson. That Steven was a Greek lecturing Hebrews on their own history irked the crowd. That he knew the facts less well than they did irritated them. That he skewed the tale to imply they were the favorites only until something better came along enraged them. That he tried to whip up enthusiasm for the very criminal whom they had condemned for flogging them inspired them to devout violence.

As soon as the stones began to fly, an innocent bystander named Saul panicked. He tried to flee the scene but was captured by the fundamentalists before he reached the edge of the square. They accused him of refusing to honor the law by declining to participate in the stoning. He explained meekly that he was merely trying to avoid being accidentally hit by a stray rock. Deciding that no innocent person would be afraid of stones thrown in the name of justice, the authorities condemned him for slander and stoned him for his fear of dying at the hands of the righteous for a crime he did not commit.

Ba'al witnessed both deaths.

CHAPTER 23

BA'AL ROCKS

S ummering in the mountains of Anatolia and wintering along the banks of the upper Nile, Ba'al carefully avoided the territories under the control of Lucifer and Unpronounceable. However, signs of the inevitable expansion by Lucifer's minions could no longer be denied. Romans had reached the second cataract; a fetish had been spotted floating down the Blue Nile from the Ethiopian highlands. They were projected to meet in Kush before the end of the century. Knowing he was no match for Lucifer, he abandoned the entirety of Africa. In his early retirement, he most missed cat-sitting and fashioning goblin-faced goblets from the steam generated when he dipped his toes in the spring floods. Now he had half a year to wander leisurely through the Crescent. Visiting the traders and temples, brothels and barracks from the Gulf of Akaba to the delta of the Tigris, he often met other Fallen Angels who caught him up on the news and doings of the Celestial Leftovers.

However, this spring, following a whim, he vacationed

in Jerusalem. In an unanticipated turn, an alert sentry at the Dung Gate noticed the scent of burnt feathers. Completely addled by the sudden appearance of soldiers bearing shields emblazoned with a six-pointed star, Ba'al was apprehended without a struggle.

The Sanhedrin and Pharisees prosecuted him for being himself, a Fallen Angel, and sentenced him to one hundred hours of community service. Each day, he was required to stone blasphemers, idolaters, and random women in case they were prostitutes. He would have preferred to blast the accusers with spiked fireballs, but he resisted the urge from fear the razzle-dazzle would attract the attention of Lucifer or, worse yet, Unpronounceable. He decided to finish his sentence and move along as quickly as possible.

Still, the task did not engage his heart. He agreed with the blasphemers, felt grateful to the idolaters, and knew there were more appropriate and satisfying ways to treat random women. His reluctance shortened his wind-up, ratcheted his delivery, and aborted his follow-through. Every stone that missed the mark added another hour to his sentence. After throwing three hundred thirty-five stones, he owed four hundred thirty-two hours of service. Ba'al became convinced he would spend more time in Jerusalem than he had in the Fiery Pit.

When Saul dropped dead from a stone to his forehead, Ba'al fell ravenously on the opportunity to escape. He dragged Saul's body, as he explained to the Pharisee overseer, "out of the way so no stoner will have a bad trip because of it." Out of sight in an alley, he covered himself with Saul's bloody cloak and strolled down narrow, twisting lanes toward freedom.

As he approached the city gate, he found a pair of gems in the inner pocket of the cloak. He was still fingering them when he gave his new name to the guard.

"How was your stay, Saul? Did you find everything you were looking for?"

"Oh, just fine, I had a wonderful visit. Managed to pick up a couple of gems for the wife. She's going to laugh heartily."

"She likes a good joke, does she?"

"She prefers the egg whites."

The answer didn't register with the guard. He was distracted by the stains on the traveler's garment. "May I ask how you got blood on your cloak?"

"There's mud on my throat? I didn't know."

The guard enunciated loudly. "I said, 'blood on your cloak.'"

"Oh, that. I got in on a little action while I was here. One of the accomplices of the Temple Twelve was stoned. Can you believe they actually announced a second attack?"

"There's no explaining zealots. But it was certainly good fortune for you. We don't get as many stonings as we used to. It's killed tourism."

"It's the fault of the Romans, I'm sure."

"True," said the guard. "Crucifixions just don't get a crowd involved the way a good stoning does. You weren't hurt, were you? I know of a great faith healer on Gentile Alley."

"No. I'm fine. I was standing too close when a stone went astray and struck a by-stander." Ba'al added casually, "Unfortunately, it was that Fallen Angel, the one doing community service. I can't recall his name. It'll probably come to me in the middle of the night."

"Ba'al."

"That's it! Another accidental victim during a stoning."

"Bystander damage is inevitable, and sometimes seems regrettable, but at least this time it was someone who obviously deserved it. Too many people second guess nowadays. If only Faith was as blind as it was in the good old days."

The traveler nodded. "True, all too true. It was fortunate he was the one. But they really ought to consider hiring a team of professional stoners. These amateurs are dangerous--righteous but dangerous. I wish the Lord would take a more proactive role and guide their stones, like he did with David and that tall guy."

"It's dangerous to question the ways of the Lord, my friend. When the reason's hidden, it's hard to understand divine justice. You just have to believe."

"Oh, I didn't mean to imply doubt, much less criticism. Heaven, forbid!"

The guard said, "The Lord is perfect, that's why he wraps himself in mystery."

"I never could understand the Almighty, much less follow his ways. I doubt if I ever will. It's my greatest shortcoming."

"I admire your honesty."

"Very few people do."

"Such is the way of the world. Still, we must give the stoners an Aleph for amateur effort." The Guard gestured

"Don't you mean a branch? One olive isn't much of a reward. Still, I love a minced olive spread on a slab of bread."

The guard shouted, "Aleph, the letter."

"That's right. I couldn't do any better than the other

tossers either, that's for sure. Nothing but wild pitches from this arm ever since I got hit by a speeding chariot on Pharisee Lane."

"That happens way too often. They ought to put up a sign, but I don't think the Romans would slow down. What's doubly amazing to me, Saul, is that the Fallen Angel was killed. I didn't know that was possible."

"I would never have guessed it, either. Maybe he was just stunned. In any case, as you can see, he lost a lot of blood."

"Pardon me if I'm out of line, but you also smell like smoke."

"I offered a burnt sacrifice at the temple. The south wind blew the smoke back in my face. I teared up. That's how I managed to stumble into the square when the stoning started."

"Lucky you. If you don't mind my asking, what was the purpose of the offering?"

"For a safe journey home."

"Always a wise investment. Have a good trip. May the Lord find you alive in your home!"

Ba'al stepped back frowning, then he realized the guard's wish was meant as a blessing. "From your lips, my friend."

And the new Saul strolled into the desert nonchalantly, quietly singing "The Shadow of the Valley of Death."

CHAPTER 24

ROAD TRIP

U nsure if he had pulled off his escape, Ba'al continually glanced over his shoulder. He was certain that the mostly naked body of the real Saul must have been found by now in the alley, certain that Ba'al's failure to return to the scene must have already been noticed, certain that the gate guard would connect reports of these circumstances with the departure of a man in a bloody cloak who had a faint odor of charcoal about him. The imposter Saul grew increasingly obsessed with the idea that a posse was in hot pursuit.

Within a few miles of the border of Galilee, paranoia seized him. He thought he could hear someone overtaking him. His body trembled, his shoulders rose halfway to his ears, sweat dripped from his armpits and bathed his torso. He whirled around and walked backward, searching the road which had been behind but was now before him. As he put it later, a stone in the road seized him by the heel and flung him to the ground. Still later, he claimed he fell off a horse.

Whatever the truth, he hit his head on a rock and passed out.

When he came to, he saw a lean face with a dark, trimmed beard leaning over him. His brown eyes looked both concerned and hesitant. "How many fingers am I holding up?" asked the hooded stranger.

The first arithmetic problem Ba'al had encountered made him wary. "I can't see," he said. "Let's hope the blindness is only temporary. I hit my head you know."

"You've lost a lot of blood."

"Have I? How can you tell? Is my hair drenched in it?"

"No, your hair's messy but fine. There's dried blood all over your cloak."

"That's from an accident in Jericho. I was splattered during a stoning."

"That happens if you stand too close. You've got to be more careful. Those amateurs are dangerous, even if they have good intentions. Their aim can go wild in a stoning frenzy."

"I've learned my lesson. I've said for years that we ought to have professional death squads."

"What is your name, my friend?"

"B--Saul."

"Bsaul? What an odd name. What language is that from?"

"It's Psaul, and it's a Roman name."

"You're telling me you're small?"

"It's just a family name and has nothing to do with my personal attributes."

"Well, friend Psaul, I am going to help you stand up. Lying in the middle of the road is not a good choice. I've got a cart, and I can take you as far as Damascus. You can lie there just as effectively."

"Just roll me into the gutter and I'll find my own way home once my sight returns. God must be punishing me for my sins. You would be wise to avoid getting into the line of fire."

"I could never show my face in Samaria again if I left you injured and in need. Do you have family I can take you to?"

"Oh, no, they're all in another world now."

"My condolences. You can stay for a while at my home in Damascus."

"Thank you, friend. What is your name?"

"Judas."

"I heard you were dead."

"Apparently not."

"Why would someone repeat a wrong rumor?"

"It happens."

"What was it I heard? Fell off a cliff? Hanged yourself?"

"Must've been someone else. I'm not the only Judas on Earth. Let's not get lost in rumors. I'm a respected intercity merchant trading in slaves and chicory. And I own a house in Damascus. It was a steal at thirty pieces of silver." Judas averted his gaze and pointed across the road. "Look! There's a possessed pig!"

Ba'al reminded him of his blindness.

Judas carted Ba'al home. He waited three days for Ba'al's sight to be restored. Ba'al stayed seated on a stool in the corner, whimpering about how much his head hurt and complaining first that he could not see and second that there would be nothing to see if he could see. Judas noticed a subtle aroma of charcoal that grew stronger the longer Ba'al lingered.

Worried and suspicious, he sent for his friend Ananias, who was reputed to have gained healing powers when he auditioned for a bit part with an acting troop in Jerusalem. Allegedly, the chief of The Apostles had encouraged him to practice the role of healer until it became "his" and promised to get in touch. Because the Apostles advocated dramatic realism on paper, Ananias believed the promise to send for him meant his power to heal was real.

When Judas sent the invitation, Ananias was unsure if this was another audition or a rehearsal. He decided it did not matter; he would give a stellar performance. Focused on his role and determined to impress, he ran out of his house and down the street without his sandals. As he scudded around a corner, he accidentally knocked over an old woman struggling home with a cumbersome basket of wheat. Oblivious, he ran on without pausing and had already turned the corner when she cursed him. "May you welcome the unwelcomed into your home!"

Ba'al was still sitting in the corner looking like a whipped puppy when Ananias, eager to prove himself, entered in character. He didn't need to ask about his motivation or his patient. Improvisation was his forte. All he needed to do was follow his intuition. He towered over Ba'al, placed his hands forcefully on the man's head and screamed, "Heal!" He then struck Ba'al's right cheek with the back of his right hand. He swung the back of his left hand toward Ba'al's left cheek, but Ba'al blocked the slap with his left arm.

"Healed!" cried Judas, and he patted Ananias on the back. "Another great performance by the master healer." Then he whispered, "Can you take him with you?"

Ananias willingly invited Ba'al to come live with him and in his enthusiasm unintentionally exaggerated the benefits of sharing his home. Ba'al, aware that Judas had undergone a change in heart toward him, cheerfully agreed. On the way, they came across an old woman on her knees scraping up wheat mixed with the dust of dried dung.

Ananias said to Ba'al, "Such is the remarkable piety of those who approach death: they pray openly in the street!"

She smiled smugly after they passed. They had not thought to pause and pray with her.

CHAPTER 25

PASTORAL CALL

B a'al had seized what he thought was a great opportunity. He would no longer need to pretend to be blind; Ananias had promised riches greater than money and food from heaven.

The house had a pleasant, cozy walled garden where Ba'al could bask the day away. The sunshine reminded him faintly of his time in the Fiery Pit. A part of him missed his old comrades, although their time together had been short, but the memory of Beelzebub's expulsion and Lucifer's cavalier attitude nibbled at his nostalgia. Still, he had found the unrestrained warmth comforting.

The first few days with Ananias, Ba'al dozed away the afternoons while his host prattled about the thespian life. A few days later, Ba'al realized that Ananias, now beginning the thirty-seventh repetition of the same tale with only wispy variations, was never going to stop blathering about his stay in Jerusalem and his apprenticeship with the master actor Simon Peter.

'Peter said' and 'Peter did' were his unending refrains. Ananias varied his monologue but rarely, and when he did, it was only to include some numbingly inane notes on the life of someone he had never met. Jess had failed as an actor despite his best efforts, diligence, discipline, persistence and divinely bestowed talents. The script, peppered with obscure parables that appeared profound to the superficial, was doomed to failure, at least as it was retold by Ananias, who hadn't witnessed even fragments of the original performances. Ba'al wondered if it had been as awful as it sounded twice removed. He decided to reserve his doubt and store the gist of the tale in case he ever needed it.

Ba'al was resting in the garden when Ananias sat beside him. Near the middle of the thirty-eighth fond recounting of the saga of Peter, Ba'al leapt to his feet. "I feel the spirit moving me to preach to the flocks. I must escape! I mean, I must answer their call!"

"What call?"

"From the sheep, bleeding in the fields. I must save them."

Ananias stood on tiptoe and looked over the wall. "The sheep are fine. They're just bleating, like they always do. 'Baa, Baa.'"

"They're calling me!"

And Ba'al fled to begin the first of his many pastoral

missions.

Although Ba'al tried briefly and halfheartedly to find another patron in Damascus, Judas had been grousing endlessly behind his back about the odor, the charcoal dust, the expense of feeding him. Ba'al needed a fresh start.

His first impulse was to return to Anatolia. Although he had spent the winters of countless centuries there, he had rarely ventured from the warmth of the temple where the sacrificial fires soothed his toes.

As soon as he passed through the main gate, word ran up and down the streets. "Winter has returned! The barley will be blighted!" Denouncing the inevitable blizzard, the mob took up stones and descended on his temple.

He fled and holed up in a cave until the second solstice had passed. As spring approached, he donned a disguise and rented a hovel in the shadow of his former temple. Ba'al supported himself as a storyteller. He plagiarized the plot of Ananias's tale and used the gist as grist for his story mill.

Ba'al believed the basic idea of the original Jess script was sound. He could make it work with a simple rewrite and a merciless antagonist, one who could insinuate himself into the very core of humanity. He patterned his villain on Lucifer, painted in monochromatic evil, portrayed as a demon dragging the unwary to their doom. The children were thrilled, the adults, terrified. The authorities, their time wasted between checking under beds and rounding up neighbors accused of demon-craft, reached exhaustion and insisted he relocate.

In the new town, the people found Ba'al to be inconsistent. Not even the Greeks, they complained, had so many versions of one story. He tried to keep them interested by inserting long discourses on his theory of sanctimonious sensibility, a topic he was only vaguely familiar with. People dozed. He tried to recover his audience by truncating the tale and trumpeting the terrifying doom as both inevitable and avoidable. Those who questioned were silenced when he declared it a new religion of a new god sent from an old god who had decided to forgive everyone who could say his name.

The confused among the audience concluded the fault lay with their own understanding and took his word on faith. Thus, despite his shortcomings, or perhaps because of them, he gained a position of authority in his new church. The legendary land of miracles was remote from the new religion's prophet, but it did not take long for word to reach The Apostles, who were trying to establish their own new church. They did not like that someone had plagiarized their drama. Ba'al was unaware that they had called upon Unpronounceable to set matters right.

CHAPTER 26

THE APOSTLES STRIKE BACK

The eleven remaining Apostles, both as a company and individually, were deeply disturbed by the extrapolations, inaccuracies, and misinterpretations that Ba'al was thrusting on those who hadn't heard or seen the original drama. They issued a cease-and-desist order that ordered him to cease from desisting from circumcisions. Their pleas went unheeded and unanswered which cut them to the quick.

The angels contended that Ba'al's popularity resulted solely from the low bar for admittance to the inner circle. One need only to believe in the magic of a name, cut out the circumcision and dress in drab garb. Very few converts cared to investigate the truth because the cut-rate reward for belief was a direct flight into heaven. The Apostles were worried, not only about fidelity to the original version, but also about lost royalties. Amateur productions would certainly cut into their ability to draw an unbiased crowd on the road. Almost all the remaining eleven set out individually or in pairs to establish theaters in untapped markets. They hit on the unsubstantiated claim that Jess had sent word to deliver the play to all who had the price of admission, no matter where they lived.

On my usual rounds, I passed through Jerusalem and dropped in unannounced on Simon Peter, semiretired from show business. At dinner, he told me he had realized that attracting, training and rehearsing a new cast would be an insuperable burden. He believed a speaking tour would help shake off the depression that swallowed him after Steven's death. He also hoped it would be a profitable substitute for a play. A fortune would be saved without the expenses of a full cast, sets, and special effects. He planned to hone his spiel on the road to Rome before wrapping up at the Forum.

I didn't want to douse his fantasy with negativity, but I had to ask, "Have you learned Latin? I thought you spoke only Aramaic."

"That's why I'm delaying the tour. I hired a tutor, a Roman named Saul, but he wasn't friendly at all once he found out I was part of the 'Gang of Twelve.' He said he was going to have to check with his lawyer and rethink the commitment. He didn't want to get into trouble with the authorities. I couldn't blame him for hesitating, so I let him have the time he needed."

"Well, I hope you waited to pay him until after the lessons."

Peter went on without answering. "Then I heard a rumor that he was among the crowd that stoned Steven, but he disappeared right after, so I wasn't able to get his side of the story. James said that the Fallen Angel Ba'al had assumed his identity, but that can't be because his body was found in a nearby street."

"His body?"

Peter continued without a pause. "Thomas said Saul headed to Damascus, but I doubt it because I also heard reports that his body was found near the site of the stoning. Andrew told me they found an unidentified naked body that they thought might be Saul, but the guard at the Damascus Gate reported that Saul had left town right after the stoning."

"How many bodies--?"

Peter was not to be detoured. "On the other hand, the guard said it might have been Ba'al because he smelled like smoke, but Saul had told him that Ba'al had been accidentally stoned to death. And the circle of rumors starts again. Personally, I wouldn't care a whit where Saul is, but I paid in advance for the Latin lessons. Cost me a couple of gems, way below the going rate. I thought it was a steal."

"I've said it a dozen times, Peter: get the goods first and pay after, the later the better. I doubt if you'll get the gems back."

"I can't afford another tutor unless I do. We're a poor group here, especially now that most of the cast has taken off. And our reputation makes it hard to find work. People seem to think I'll break out the whip and lay into them at the slightest provocation. I may have to start fishing for fish again."

"I always thought fishing for men sounded like a bad career move. Anyway, the gems are gone and the troop's disbanded. Your options are limited. You could join a traveling show and practice your Latin on the way. All roads to Rome are long and rife with Romans. Not to mention, it's easy to take a wrong turn. Safer to travel in a group."

"I hear you, Angel of the Lord."

"Please, call me Samuel. Our friendship has moved beyond titles."

"Sorry. Habit. I err on the side of formality now. Better safe than sorry with these Romans. You remember what happened to Archimedes, don't you? You can't even make a simple request of a centurion without risking your life."

"The cost of parchment was high that year due to an epidemic of ovine rabies." Archimedes had been a good friend of mine. I loved his conundrums, although I never understood any of the ones involving math. Pythagoras irritated me with his puzzles so often that I felt he acted purposefully.

"Anyway, there's a rumor that a Fallen Angel has taken our show on the road and is mangling the message. If it's true, it would certainly help if I really did have the power to cast out demons. He's rumored to be in Anatolia now, or maybe Greece. As usual, the rumors are all over the place."

"I'm headed to Anatolia, Peter. I can look into it, if you'd like, but I can't promise to cast out any demons. They're a stubborn bunch. Of course, I'd have to clear it at the top first."

"It wouldn't hurt if you did look into it." He frowned at me then looked away. I waited through his lengthy pause. "I never liked that name, the one that Jess gave me. It sounds like an insult every time I hear it."

"I think he was trying to commend your dependable spirit."

"Well, it sounds like a cheap shot at my so-called stupidity." As he spoke, he became increasing agitated. "I come from a poor town and a poorer family. I never had the chances he had. You know already about his connections. It rankled me the way John used to schmooze with him, talking about the days in Egypt and the childhood trips to the Temple. They didn't travel together either time, but you'd think it if you heard them talk. Amazing how they managed to see the same sights, like they were on a 'Wonders of Egypt Tour' together. And when Jess was still a kid, hardly older than a lamb ready for the slaughter, he supposedly wowed the rabbis with his wisdom. It's a wonder they didn't slap the upstart down."

Jess was hardly a kid. At twelve years old, he was awakening to adolescence. Many--almost all--of his questions concerned the daughters of Lot and the charms of Delilah. The Rabbis (blessed be their hearts!) humored his pubescent interests.

Peter was growing more irritated. "I'd never been farther than the neighboring town until Jess came along and tempted me with this fisher-of-men hook. Always get the offer in writing. I know that now. Yeah, I know--you don't need to tell me--I can't read, so it wouldn't have done me any good at all."

He paused and I waited, watching while his breathing returned closer to normal. "Well, maybe I am dumber than a smarty-pants, but I know this much: Living in a big city doesn't make you more sophisticated than a fisherman." Peter spit before he continued. "I've lived in Jerusalem for years now, ever since Jess quit the cast, but I still don't even know which gate leads where. Put me as the guard, and I'll send half the people in the wrong direction. Big city living hasn't made me any smarter. And one more thing, Jess was wrong. My greatest strength isn't being steady on my feet, it's I'm a good listener."

"What should I call you, then?"

"Huh? Oh. Please, call me exactly what my mother called me." I'd never met his mother, so his answer didn't help. "There's no danger anyone will be confused about who you mean now that the other Simon has gone off east." That was a better clue. "I wish him and Jude the luck of the lord. Those Persians are a feisty bunch." A light flickered in his eyes. "Well, maybe better luck than the lord had."

"I'll be off, Simon, and I'll see about getting the go ahead on tracking down the imposters."

Eventually, Simon Peter arrived at heaven's gate. He spent centuries sitting outside looking for his key. He is still called by his nickname.

Jess had once promised that, should he ever miss an entrance, it would be Simon Peter who would assume his role. At least, that is what Peter claimed and John confirmed. There are many who wonder if it really happened. Simon Peter failed to realize that this promise, even if verified, was unenforceable. And if it came about, it was hardly a guarantee that he would be the Star of the Show. He underestimated the cunning cupidity of Ba'al who quickly and easily relegated Peter to the role of figurehead.

CHAPTER 27

TRACKING THE TRUANT

O btaining permission to investigate on behalf of Simon was as easy as praying. But there was no need to take my request to the top of the line. As soon as I mentioned to Gabriel that it looked like the start of a new religion, loosely based on Jess's life, he reclassified the project from curious to urgent. The higher classification allows a certain latitude with physical laws, if required. I have been an aficionado of magic ever since Raphael stoppered the spring in Eden. Rather than use logic to determine necessity, I am by choice a "loose constructionist" when I consider what is "required."

Conforming to the regulations that had been instituted following the embarrassment of angels' being mistaken for divinities, I turned my Emanation Filter to maximum and covered my robe with a more casual garment, the standard issue civilian merchant cloak, to wear around town.

I cut into line at the Travel Department Station. The

Messenger Angel who would have been next on the Tram objected, but when I flashed my travel authorization, she remarked under her breath, "Urgent? You should've taken the stairs."

The Guardian set the coordinates for Jerusalem. I sighed when I arrived in Alexandria instead. I walked casually to the lighthouse, swam out of sight of land, and then flew to the outskirts of Jerusalem.

My first stop was with the Supervisor of Stoners. It was a short walk to a gate in the inner wall. I turned left and followed the base of the bulwark, bathed in the dust cloud raised by a pack of unwashed mules.

The Supervisor was slouching on a mound of dirt in front of his home, a hut that enjoyed an unobstructed view of the two lowest tiers of the wall.

I strolled over to him, travel scroll in hand, and tried to look as if I were doublechecking directions. With a perplexed look, I asked him, "Is this Wall Street?"

He pointed at the ground. "I wouldn't call it a street. More like a path, except when it rains."

"I'm looking for a man named Gideon."

He sucked from his pipe, wiped his lower lip on his forearm, and squinted at me from my toes to my hair before he exhaled. "Gideon? That's me. Call me Giddy."

"I can hear fine. You don't have to shout."

"Was I?" He still was.

"Well, I never would have guessed a Supervisor could afford such a splendid neighborhood." I leaned back to see the top of the wall. "Do you ever climb up there and admire the view?"

"The stairs are rickety, so I wouldn't risk it. Besides, I got a bum knee."

"How'd that happen?"

"I falled on over a pile of rocks and twistered it."

"Ouch! That was a bad trip."

"On top of them reasons, I got a great view right here." He dragged air through his pipe. A minute later, after exhaling, he continued, "I'm planning on doing the adorning thing on that wall. Right there. I got me in mind a green scene depic'-defying morn a hon-nerd different and separate type of shrubs." Wide eyed, he held his hands up, palms opened out as if he were miming an invisible frame. "I seen it in a vision." Then he picked up his pipe from the dirt and gazed at his nose tip for a half minute. "Scald a mural, see?"

"I can picture it already."

"Wanda help?"

"I wouldn't know which end of the brush to hold."

He looked puzzled.

Instead of explaining, I said, "I think you might be able to help me find a friend."

He had little else to tell me. As far as he knew, there had been absolutely no bystander injuries during the fourteen years he'd been the supervisor. He thought it might have happened under his predecessor.

My next stop was at the Damascus Gate. Luckily, my traversal of the city coincided with the midday meal, so foot traffic was sparse. But when I reached the wall, a line had already formed.

I waited for my turn patiently. A few people fell in behind me. I used a simple confusion spell on the man behind me. He said to his wife, "There's four people ahead of us. It'll take forever to get out of here. This one," he whispered pointing at me with his right ear while looking over his shoulder at his wife, as if I could not hear or see him, "looks like trouble. The guards will probably spend a half day asking him about his ancestry. Let's try Herod's Gate. Somehow, I know it will be quicker."

His wife dutifully praised his perspicacity and followed him with the children.

Each traveler in turn removed themselves from the line, some with discourses to their companions, others simply grabbing their asses and leading them away silently by the reins.

The three in front of me were quickly passed on their way.

"And you, my friend, what--." As the guard raised his gaze from his scroll to my face, he lost track of his question and looked puzzled over what to say or do.

I said, "Good afternoon, my good man." I could see in his eyes that he was indeed a good man who loved and respected his wife and children, ate and drank wisely, accepted only the honest bribes he was offered, and prided himself on helping the people of Jerusalem remain on the peaceable side of the divine disposition. "My name is Samuel, and my occupation today is Special Envoy. What is your name?" I knew the answer, of course, but humans become suspicious if you know too much too soon.

"David." He still looked puzzled, as if unsure why he was answering instead of asking.

"I have some questions I would like to ask." While David worked out the problem of his preconceived role conflicting with his newly discovered desire to help, I turned to the man who had just joined us. "Herod's Gate is in that direction. There are only fifteen groups waiting to pass through it, so it will probably be much faster over there."

The man thanked me and left, wide-eyed and eager to

get in the longer line.

Shaking his head as if to clear it, David said, "I'm almost certain that I'm the one who asks the questions. I hope I'm right about that."

"Absolutely right in a restricted way, David. You see, my status as Special Envoy bends the usual rules."

"I don't think I've ever heard of a Special Envoy. Why should I, why should I--"

David seemed to be losing his focus again. I helped him to understand quickly. "Look. Here are my credentials." I stepped back, looked around to make sure no one else could see, and opened the front of my standard issue merchant cloak. The sharp pure white light, stilled muffled by seventeen filters, dazzled, amazed, and hypnotized him in the single half second that he saw it.

While he recovered, I sent another four travelers to Herod's Gate and two completely lost souls to the Dung Gate.

At last, David spoke. "Samuel--was that your name, the name you revealed to me?"

I nodded.

"Samuel, how can I help you?"

"I'm searching for someone who may have passed this way."

"Samuel, there are so many who pass this way. How could I possibly remember the one you seek?"

I wished that I could unveil and share the image of Ba'al as I knew him, but during that brief time, he was in his full radiance as an Angel of the Lord. I was sure that David would not recognize him if I showed that memory. And the image of Ba'al in that flaming trillionth of a second before he fell through the clouds I did not want to share, especially with a fragile human whose "strong" faith might be shattered, whose black-and-white morality might be appalled, whose devotion might be turned against the righteous perpetrator. I remembered how Unpronounceable had fretted, "We'll never hear the end of it. Constant criticism and second guessing! We'll never hear the end of it." At that time, I had briefly thought that these creatures might prefer the fullness of empathy and forgiveness, of compassion and understanding, over the emptiness of righteousness and retribution, of arrogance and power. I eventually rejected the notion.

I said to David, who waited patiently for my answer, "He may have used the name Saul. He may have had an aroma of smoke or charcoal or--" and the thought hit me unexpectedly "--sacrifice."

"Ah!" said David, reaching into the memories he had chucked into the unimportant file. "That would narrow the search. What with the Roman wind blowing so strongly these days, few take the time to honor the old, true ways."

I went on, "It would have been years ago."

"That would broaden the search." David looked dismayed and knit his brows as he continued to scratch in the dust of his memories.

Remembering that Ba'al had been sentenced to community service as a stoner, I added, "And he may have had some blood on him from a stoning."

David perked up, the light in his eyes returning from the interior search. "Yes!" he shouted. "Saul! I had thought it was strange that he smelled like smoke, but even more that he had the blood of that Fallen Angel Ba'al on his cloak. He told me Ba'al had been struck by a wayward stone. We talked about the need for professional stoners, and, and--." David looked like an artist searching for that one brush stroke that will change a painting into a masterpiece. "I couldn't believe that a Fallen Angel had died. That's it! He told me Ba'al had been killed by a stone. I told him I didn't think it possible. He said it seemed it could happen because it did. I still wonder."

David looked down, like an artist who had failed to find the key, until I said, "That is what I needed to know."

His smile was small but serene, his breath full and calm. "I'm pleased I could help."

"I have one more question, David. Can you swear and promise that you will never tell anyone about this meeting, including seeing me in my muffled magnificence?"

"I wish I could, but I know the temptation to tell will be too strong."

"Then--"

"I understand."

I swirled a finger on my left hand while I thought a single syllable.

David shook his head, looked at me with uncertainty, his eyes questioning. Then he motioned toward the gate with his right hand. "Pass. You may pass."

I started toward the gate but stopped and turned when David called to me.

"I forget why I called you back. Something tugs, seems to need--. Oh! Have we met before?"

"No. But I often give people that impression. I guess my face is generic."

As I walked into the desert, I experienced a new phenomenon that astonished me. It reminded me faintly of Unpronounceable looking in all directions at once and vividly of the beauteous longing of Adam on his deathbed wishing he could embrace Cain once more. I saw simultaneously the gate behind me and the road before me. David seemed perplexed as he worked with the next travelers. Then all at once, I saw a splendor with him, a light flowing and shining as through a prism and radiating like stars in the night.

I walked far enough away to be out of sight. I stopped. I felt something between regret and disappointment but didn't understand why. Then, I brought my attention back to my mission.

I flew nonstop along and above the road to Damascus examining every stain, stone, and rut, seeking a clue to the whereabouts of Ba'al. Of course, travelers, weather, and time had obliterated the traces. However, I sensed the aura of Lucifer several times along the road. I feared he too was looking for Ba'al.

In Damascus, I asked random people if they knew anything about a stranger from Jerusalem named Saul who may have arrived a few years ago. My description was too broad to stir anyone's memory. Including the blood-stained cloak proved to be a red herring. Saying that he may have been a Roman amplified the fear and feigned forgetfulness. But when I added that he may have preached about another man, a Hebrew named Jess, eyes brightened with recognition. Most differed with my use of "preached;" his claims, they said, were more like exaggerations of a tall tale.

I learned the details of the earliest versions of Ba'al's

story from Judas. We pretended not to recognize each other. He referred me to Ananias, who told me Psaul had wandered the town claiming a prophetic mission. But his reputation was already established; no one believed; he set out north. Not a soul mentioned Lucifer, but I caught his scent. I hoped that the convergence of our paths was a coincidence.

CHAPTER 28

BASKING ON THE BEACH WITH BA'AL

When I finally found Ba'al, he was sitting on a beach outside Corinth, on a wooden chair with a small table to the side. He was reviewing and revising correspondence. There were a few clouds on the horizon, but the sun was bright, the sea was calm, and the sandflies were keeping a safe distance. I conjured a chair for myself and settled in beside him. An intermittent breeze soothed my face, and the humidity and warmth encouraged indolence. I waited patiently while he finished reading a letter from a Thessalonian.

"I could smell you coming for the last half hour," Ba'al said, looking away from the papyrus but not at me. "You were exuding that same scent the last time we met. Celestial Crocus, isn't it? It's a bit dated."

"I prefer it to your perfume. Charcoal Chips, if I'm not mistaken?"

He smiled and turned his face toward me. "I've grown to appreciate its full-bodied aroma."

"I detect a hint of Lucifer."

"His odor does linger, but he left four days ago, more or less."

"If it's not confidential, perhaps you could tell me: what did he want?"

"To encourage me."

"Did he succeed?"

"It wasn't necessary at all. I'm on a buttered roll in a plush job. He asked for a percentage, but I told him he'd have to do something to earn it. He threatened to knock me back to the Fiery Pit; I don't care where I go, as long as it's warm. He bared his claws and told me I was putting my hands into fate. I smiled right back and asked him if he'd like a job. The offer won't last forever, I said, so he ought to cease the day while it's striking hot. He didn't seem interested in shouldering a wheel."

"He's not one to follow, even with an argument like that."

Ba'al smirked. "I can smooth talk as fast as he can fly."

"Pardon me if I jump to the reason for my visit."

Ba'al scowled at me. "Are you here on Sanhedrin

business?"

"No."

"But the Sanhedrin's still tracking me, isn't it? Well, you can tell them I won't be dragged back to finish their common nitty service. I don't care who they send. This time I'll put up a fight. I learned a lot about power after my escape." He scanned the beach and lowered his voice. "I know the magic word."

I skipped over the threat. "As far as I know, there's no plan to chase you beyond Jerusalem's walls. The Romans don't seem to care either."

"I wrote them a letter, but they don't seem interested. At least, I haven't heard any backtalk. They're caught in emperor worship, an easy mistake to make; like a mitten in a tree, easier in than out."

"I've heard about your progress. You borrowed a story, confabulated the parts you didn't hear about, added what you thought would be convenient, then revised it in every new town."

"I have to keep them guessing which version is right. It keeps them talking about me. And about the story, too. Lying is the cheapest way to get publicity. The wannabelievers have constant distortions about who's got the better memorial. They wrangle over and wag the tails as if truth lives in their petty parsing. Then, just before the smolder breaks into a flame, I send a letter telling them that they're in need of fresh instruction. It's the perfect time to raise the stakes. Both sides try to scratch their names off my list of hairy ticks by dashing to double down on their devotion."

I could not help but smile. His insight was unassailable.

As I sat in the light, swishing sandflies away with one wing and fanning my brow with the other, I watched the gentle lapping of the gulf waves. It felt good to see Ba'al again. I had always thought our first meeting had been too brief and less than satisfactory because of the confusion over my name, yet I felt a deep affection for this near-deaf angel who was nanoseconds older than I. In my heart, I knew that if I had been less enthralled by the incomprehensible vision of the void or better versed in basic arithmetic, I would probably, most certainly, have laughed along with the other half of the heavenly host. It was only by the grace of ignorance, or perhaps the injustice of a poor education, or maybe the luck of missing out in the random distribution of talents, that I remained on the A-list.

"What are your plans now, Ba'al? Where do you go from here?"

Ba'al smiled. "I readily admit to you that I was named Ba'al and that I stood beside you until I heard Lucifer's clever joke. But, please, keep my name a secret. I've got a new identity that confuses my enemies, a cushy job that lets me travel and meet new people, and the devotion of the young and beautiful who are all too willing to believe that my body is a direct conduit to heaven. It's just inconvenient to have to move on to another town when my indiscretions are uncovered. Then I talk about imposters and those who would overthrow righteousness through deception. Have you heard about Satan and his works?"

I felt compelled to confront him. "Unpronounceable has a perfect memory, and so far, he's been impossible to confuse or mislead."

"That's your biased opinion. You've got a lot of snake in this, and all your legs are in his basket. Let me tell you about my ministry." According to his account, his personal, expert knowledge of someone he had never met was based on a few days of unstructured instruction in hearsay, no mean feat for someone almost deaf. If he had claimed to be a mathematician with equivalent training, he would have been laughed off the planet. Ba'al claimed with confidence, "I can extinguish reality from fiction. But most people can't. Begin by demanding suspension of disbelief, then make belief mandatory."

"I can see where this will lead," I said. "Very soon, it'll no longer be necessary to ask. People will swear their belief is true because they were told it's true. It's a short hop to burning those who disagree."

"Don't mock it until you try it."

"Have you thought about starting a snake oil business?"

"I've got something even better: Holy Water! Low overhead, plentiful supply, insatiable demand. It's a miracle no one's thought of it before."

I sat for quite a while in silent wonder that such gullibility existed in the world.

Ba'al pointed at a darkening cloud on the horizon. "There's another delivery coming my way." We watched the cloud draw closer. It passed over us before it dissipated in the direction of Athens. "I guess it was for someone else. I wonder if someone stole my idea."

"Cute trick." Reminding myself why I came to see him, I said, "You've been a prolific letter writer, Ba'al, for someone trying to stay out of sight," I said.

"Not really. And please call me Psaul in case the Sanhedrin has spies close by. I'm writing under a false name twice removed, so it's hard to connect me to the Fallen Angel, especially because I write about how to be holy. I've only penned a half dozen letters so far; one of them came back as undeliverable because I used the city's Aramaic name instead of the Greek. The rest of the letters attributed to me are from people pretending to be someone they're not. I can hardly condemn them for that. I've been delighted to receive letters from myself that I don't remember writing."

"You don't find that unnerving? What if you wrote them

and senility prevents you from remembering?"

"Then I won't apologize for what I can't remember I said."

I asked, "Psaul, can you please explain to me exactly what happened that made it possible for you to become the leader of a small, insignificant troop of gullible simpletons on the road to disillusionment?"

"You sound biased."

"Just realistic," I said.

"Poisoning the well, Aristotle would have said. Never mind if it's true."

I felt like we were running another lap around the pigpen. "Let's begin with reality so we can have a common starting point."

"Pooh, pooh," he said. "The only good starting point is prejudice. Begin with what people already believe or we'll spend the rest of eternity debating misunderstood misperceptions, getting nowhere in the long or short run. You say they're gullible because they believe in events like rising from the dead and virgin births simply because they were told it happened. Can you say for sure such things didn't happen?"

"Yes."

He ignored me. "You think they're simpletons because

they refuse to use their ability to observe and reason. Logic's all a matter of personal taste. If it fits together in your head, it's true simply because it makes sense to you. And if it fits with your prejudices, then life feels comfortable and sane. You say the premises are unrealistic. Well, there's no guarantee that anyone knows reality, so we may as well play to the gallery and get a free meal and bed for the night.

"My followers won't end up disillusioned because they won't know they were wrong until after they're dead. Limbo and Purgatory, I hear, are quite cushy and satisfying if you haven't been to the real heaven."

"But nothing you write about is based on reality--"

"The Truth" he said, "is more compelling, more important, and a lot more believable than reality. Humans would rather think that God would prefer to kill them than to love them, or better yet, to get them to kill each other for him. I think they're in the right of it there. Some of my followers think that he regrets this creation; in his eyes, it's turned out to be an unholy mess. They say he's looking for an excuse to annihilate it in order to save his self-esteem. And there's a rumor that he's designing a second attempt at perfection."

I could only mutter, "I'm sure he's better than that." I had completely forgotten to deliver Peter's message. I mean, Simon's. However, as I dematerialized my chair, I said, "What was it that Lucifer said to tell you? Was it that he'd be by soon to collect his percentage?"

I heard Ba'al's startled inhalation. We both knew he had lied about his confrontation with Lucifer; we both knew he would be outmatched when Lucifer came to collect. As soon as I was behind a cloud, Ba'al gathered his belongings and left the beach. He surrendered his entire operation to his second-in-command. The word spread that Psaul had been cornered, imprisoned, and slated for execution. As a Roman citizen, Psaul appealed to the Emperor. The local centurion booked him a passage on a cargo ship bound for Italy. His second was seen waving to a parting ship from Sidon.

The sailors however quickly grew irritated with Ba'al. He criticized their personal hygiene, ridiculed their names, refused to help with the chores, and promised to do his "real work" by praying for them. They threw him overboard seven times, and seven times he skipped across the waters in a circle and landed back in the ship. They finally rid themselves of him in Malta by sailing away while he preached in a brothel. Accounts of his adventures after that are sketchy at best.

Ba'al was not aware that the real Saul had conveniently misrepresented his Roman status in what he thought was a no-where town without access to official records. I feel I can freely speculate about what would have happened if he had arrived in Rome. He would have been forced to pretend to die there. He would have disappeared from his grave. I'm sure he would have been tempted to impersonate a dead man risen from the grave, but he had used that patter before. Instead, he would have assumed a low-profile job, like carting equipment for a traveling theatrical troop.

Among angels, both leftover and fallen, the consensus is that Ba'al relocated to Bengal where he founded a music school. I haven't been able to confirm the story, but I did see him once cavorting on a tropical island with three Polynesians whom he taught to dance.

CHAPTER 29

THE RETURN OF THE KING

A traffic jam delayed my entrance into heaven. The excruciatingly long wait for the Guardian Angels to examine and verify each permission slip was worsened by being stuck between two Messenger Angels who were swapping insider information about the Athenian stock exchange.

Said the one in front, "It seems that cattle are trading for sheep at one to three, but an ovine plague is about to upset the ratio and turn fleece into gold."

From behind me, the other Messenger said, "Don't be fooled by it, Angela. I heard the plague is a hoax orchestrated by the Ministry of Oligarchs. They plan to buy up the cow herds and then apply a cure derived from pigeon gizzards."

Angela asked, "Then the real money's in pigeons?"

"The price will soar. If you throw in some seed money, it'll make an impressive nest egg in no time."

"And to think I almost planted a dream that legumes were a hedge against inflation. There's one seer in Delphi who would've been stuck with a hill of beans. Thank you, Angelica."

Each time another Messenger Angel joined the line, the advice was repeated.

Finally, my turn at the gate arrived. I handed over the papers Gabriel had given me.

The Guardian frowned sternly. "This form was superseded last week. How long have you been drifting around the universe?"

"Less than a week."

"Hmm. I wonder if these are forgeries. The date-time stamp is smudged." He held the papers in front of a candle. "Where's the watermark? Who gave you this?"

I didn't want to impugn Gabriel's reputation. "I have to take responsibility. I was in a hurry to deal with an emergency and I might have thought I didn't have the time to procure the proper paperwork."

"So, you're telling me that no one else knows about this emergency?"

I didn't want to tell an outright lie. "You could say that."

"How long did you plan to wait before reporting your alleged emergency?"

"It seems like eight, but it's only been four celestial days."

"Then you could have waited a few more days."

"I thought it was an emergency."

"When did this 'emergency' take place?"

"It's been unfolding over at least a decade."

"Then it could have waited another decade while you waited for the proper forms. Sit over there until I have time to send for the proper form for excusing missing forms and requisition a form for replacing them."

"But I'm on my way to Gabriel to ask his advice about a new religion that's taking root around the Mediterranean Sea. I'd hoped to stop it, but I, well, I--. I seem to have failed."

"Again?"

A bad reputation is a beastly burden to bear. "Yes. Again."

After offering up a hearty and somewhat lengthy prayer for my success in begging forgiveness for another failure, he waved me through.

The squabble between Gabriel and Michael during the production of the morality play had repercussions throughout heaven. Unpronounceable decided that the hierarchy of angels was an unnecessary source of disharmony. He proclaimed that he loved us all equally, like children love their toys. To prevent further animosity, he dismantled heaven's matrix in favor of a flexible plan of cloud-sharing among equals. We had all agreed in principle; however, aware of the sensitivity of archangelic egos, we lesser orders of angels still adhered to traditional protocols and followed the chains of command.

I was therefore dismayed that Gabriel wasn't at his mansion in heaven. His housekeeper (rumored to have been smuggled into heaven without the proper qualifications) informed me that he was jamming with his trio at Andromeda's Androgynous Asteroid, an exclusive jazz club deep within Jupiter's red spot. I knew I would not be admitted. Either I had to wait for his return or go to the next higher level. I decided to risk hitting a sour note with Gabriel by bypassing him.

Michael had been cranky with me ever since his stint as director. Whenever I found it necessary to approach him, he would brandish his sword, swing it in a wide circle, examine its edge--all the while pretending to ignore me. He had staked out his personal domain on a cloud abutting the Portal to the Presence. His plush mansion gleamed as white as an igloo in deepest winter. As soon as I came to the door of his house, he unsheathed his sword and cut off a slice of cloud. He asked me, while nibbling the cloud as if it were a piece of angel food cake, "What brings you here?"

"There seems to be a problem on Earth, and--"

He inhaled the rest of the cloud slice. "Isn't that your responsibility? Why bother me with mundane matters?"

"I felt you might be interested because it involves Jess."

Michael twirled his sword, balanced on the tip of his middle finger, then puffed a soft breath toward the blade. It burst into flames. He caught it a nanometer above the cloud. "Not my problem but go on."

I abridged and paraphrased my conversation with Ba'al. When I reached the part about holy water, Michael extinguished the sword. He tested the point delicately, but when I explained the difference between Truth and reality, he pricked his finger.

"Well," said Michael, "you just need to drag him around to all his correspondents and insist he recant. Tell him we're going to throw him into the Fiery Pit and set a Guardian to make sure he doesn't escape again."

"That would be easier if he hadn't disappeared."

Michael looked down the spine of the blade at me, like a gladiator in an arena. I gulped as he asked, "You let him get away? You haven't got a clue where he might be?"

"Yes. No. Respectively and respectfully."

Michael said, "Let me think." I saw his eyes narrow as if focusing on an imaginary point. Twice his brow knit subtly while his eyes widened a tad. Each time the brow loosened, and the eyes refocused on a distant point. Finally, he said, "Let's take the question up another level."

Gabriel, having learned on his return home that I had gone to consult Michael in his absence, caught up to us as we approached the Portal to the Presence. I told him, "It's about the mission of Jess and how it's being distorted."

Certain that we could handle the problem without his help, he bowed out and sauntered away whistling.

At the Portal, I raised my hand. Before I could knock, Unpronounceable called for us to come in.

Michael entered first and went straight to the point. He carefully and succinctly relayed the information I had given him, while detouring frequently to point out where and how I had failed to see and take the obvious, appropriate action. As a result, he explained, the situation had now reached a veritable point of no return.

When he fell silent, he looked down his nose toward my naval. I saw the reflection of a coiled, golden cord twinkle in his left eye for a moment. It disappeared at the same instant that a look of puzzlement flitted across his face.

"Never mind, Samuel. You all make mistakes. I will send Michael to rectify this one."

Jess materialized between Michael and me. He was sipping a cup of broth which he let drop in his surprise. Predictably, the cup fell faster than the broth and managed to catch every drop before any could reach the floor. Cleanliness is a must next to Unpronounceable. The cup returned between Jess's hands and hovered there until he was composed enough to take hold of it.

"Again?" Jess asked squeakily.

"A little different this time," said Unpronounceable.

"Not another crucifixion?"

"Let's hope not." I heard Unpronounceable's muffled chuckle. "It wasn't in the plan last time either. Free will can get out of hand. This time, all I need is for you to take a little trip, just a day or two, maybe a week at most. It's a speaking engagement."

"I was never good at memorization."

"This is extemporaneous. It's as easy as issuing a denial."

"Rhetoric's not my forte either." Jess looked guilty and puzzled. "What didn't I do? What am I denying?"

"That you ever pretended to be me or my close relative,

or the king of the Jews, or . . ." Unpronounceable held his palm up in Jess's direction. "I know. You never said any of that, but somehow the rumor is spreading all the way from the Tigris to the Atlantic. Just say it isn't so."

"Can it really be as easy as that?"

"Of course! Takes no skill at all except talking. That's why I'm sending Michael to help you."

Michael winced.

"Where do I start?" asked Jess.

"Jerusalem."

Jess opened his eyes wide and started to speak, but before he could say one word, Unpronounceable blinked. Jess and Michael flew backwards out the Portal, their bodies curved like sails in a gale. Unpronounceable said, "Stay close, Samuel. I have a feeling they'll be wanting your help." He chuckled and grinned with tightly shut lips.

I genuflected and backed through the Portal. The instructions I had just received seemed clear at that moment. I was to stay nearby so that I could be called upon if needed. The misinterpretation proved calamitous.

I wandered down to the gate and watched the queue lengthen. Often Guardian Angels would either cut in line or walk through the open gate without waiting or checking in. As they say, "C.H.I.P.: Class has its privileges." (About five centuries later, I suggested an express lane for humanity, an idea that still has not been approved. Under the current conditions, most people prefer to reincarnate, hoping to come back at a less congested time.)

I had just finished humming the second strophe of a dainty ditty I learned from a Cretan when Michael returned alone. He whispered urgently, "He's between a rock and a hard place down there. I don't understand these, what are they called? People? Better hurry."

I zipped as fast as I could, following the trace of Michael's passage through time and space so as to arrive soon after he left. I appeared before an astonished Centurion. I called out, "Jess! Where are you?" I heard a crowing and commotion at the center of the square and went to investigate, fearing the worst.

When I found Jess, he was sprawled face up near the Serpent's Pool, surrounded by a crowd of irate but satisfied people. His cloak was torn, disheveled and soaked in blood, his eyes wide open, an almost toothless mouth gaping at the sky, a look of disbelief on his face, his forehead concave on the right side.

Lucifer crossed the square, the crowd parting before him, and sat on the low wall where the Centurion still stood. Lucifer looked smug as he said, "You missed the action. Maybe you ought to go stick him in the side with that sword of yours just to make sure he's dead." The Centurion followed the suggestion with alacrity. Three more Roman soldiers arrived looking more curious than purposeful.

I sat down beside Lucifer. He said, "A bit late, aren't you?"

"What happened? Why didn't Michael protect Jess?"

"Michael, ha! All I had to do was tell that Centurion, the blond one with the aquiline nose, that Michael was a friend of mine who had a remarkable sword. Romans love their weapons, especially penetrating ones, so he went right up to him and insisted they compare swords. He was amazed, enthralled by the length and weight of Michael's and demanded to know how he managed to keep it up in action."

Lucifer was happy to divulge the story without prompting from me. Once more, he was enchanted by his own success and eager to share his victory.

While Michael was distracted by the Centurion's sword envy, Lucifer slipped over to the Supervisor of Stoners. Lucifer whispered in his ear, "Isn't that guy with the confused look one of the Temple Twelve? Looks exactly like the ringleader, doesn't he?"

"That he does. I better look into this." He went up to Jess and demanded, "Aren't you the one who claimed to be divine?"

"Not me. I would never say something like that."

A man nearby said, "I seem to remember that you did. You look just like him."

"It wasn't me. Why would I say such a thing? I'm too much a devout--"

Yet another man, standing behind the Supervisor, insisted, "But you are him! I know your face. You were the one who flogged me in the temple courtyard."

The Supervisor said, "I've read about you. I got a letter saying you were the Would-Be-King."

"Yeah," said the second man. "I got one, too, but it said you were divine, the messiah, son of the High One."

The third man added, "Yeah. He said you undeaded yourself."

The crowd in the square had drawn close together around Jess. Sweat dripped from the tip of his nose and the lobes of his ears.

"I never said any of that."

"But I read it in a letter. He said you told him in a vision. Why would someone waste a clean piece of good parchment on a lie?"

The three nodded together. "It must be the truth." People began to select stones from the piles scattered around the square.

Jess insisted, "That's what they say, but--"

The Centurion said to Michael, "Oh, look. Another stoning."

"Got to go," Michael said. He indiscreetly vanished before the Centurion's astonished eyes.

An instant later, I appeared in the identical place. I took a single step toward the crowd. I called out, "Jess! Where are you?"

I heard someone cry, "That's him! I knew he was Jess!"

And Lucifer crowed like a cock at dawn as the stones began to fly.

Part IV
Sin and
Punishment

CHAPTER 30

ROMAN FEVER

I seemed to be overachieving in discovering new ways to fail miserably. Before returning to heaven, to minimize the damage, I sent out a press release to all the gossips in Jerusalem, but the self-styled "eye-witness reporters" ignored my outline and imagined apocryphal fables. Thomas, Mary Magdalene, Herod: each skewed the story to make themselves look important. Pontius Pilate joined in and jotted some junk, although he'd missed the trial. While it was going on, he was out washing his greasy fingers between courses of a late-night dinner. According to these testifiers, Jess was married, single, head of a revolutionary gang, family man, loner, mystic, rabbi, comet-drover, shepherd, martyr.

Before long, three hacks were accusing each other of plagiarism and three apostles were claiming identity theft. Some self-proclaimed doctor from Greece claimed to know all the facts despite never meeting Jess. Then one of the thieves who had stolen the identity of one of the apostles complained that someone had stolen his stolen identity to promote a story about seven seals and seven cities. Apparently, an entrepreneur had arranged a forty-day, all-inclusive tour, The Cities of the Apocalypse, with an optional side trip to Salem-in-the-Sky.

On my return to heaven, the queue at the gate crawled slower than a dead millipede. In line, my bungled efforts to accomplish another simple assignment was the leading topic. The angelic ridicule heaped on me deepened the erosion of my self-esteem.

The second most popular topic among those in line was the paternity of Jess. No two angels could agree about the father's identity, but each had a theory. A committee had already tried to bury the controversy by declaring that his mother was still a virgin at his birth. Gabriel, who had a cameo in the first act, had been called as a witness, but he demurred when asked to verify her condition and denied first-hand knowledge. He merely pointed out that she would have been the first and only woman to lose her hymen from the inside out. The whole muddle had become as simultaneously complex and simplistic as a conspiracy theory. I half expected the speculators to swear Jess had been born in Kenya to a lioness.

I intended to spend this time in heaven reviewing my faults with Gabriel. Together we would examine my missteps and second guess my stupidity. If I could learn, I told myself, to inch my actions away from disastrous and closer to mediocre, then I might redeem myself in the eyes of Unpronounceable, who I knew in my heart must be disappointed. But when I checked in at the heavenly gate, the Guardian Angel instructed me to report immediately to Raphael. I choked on a chunk of pride. My assistant in Eden was now my boss.

I found him on the outskirts of Limbo, where he was assembling a team for a factfinding mission through China and Mongolia. The mission was to investigate the healing arts. I congratulated him on his appointment to the new position, Archangel of Sophomoric Science. "Will there be any use in this new field for those incantations you've mastered?"

"Yes, but only until we get some better equipment and work out the details of this theory the Greeks have recently promulgated, something called empirical thiggamadoodle. Unpronounceable tells me the hexes are being phased out due to their side effects on the space-time continuum. I'm still getting a handle on my new job. I heard the Far East is the place to be."

"Are you sure it's not the Mideast?"

"The Athenians told me to head east and said it was far. They even gave me a farewell gift: a map and a starter kit with all four elements. All I need now is a potter's wheel." He showed me the transparent glass vessels displayed on an attractive polished oak tray decorated with hand carved nude men. When I remarked that Air and Fire looked the same, he took the lid off one of them. Flames leaped out, singing his fingertips. "You have to be wary of Greek gifts," he said.

"Don't you mean Achaean gifts?"

"I've always had trouble telling humans apart. I could barely distinguish between Adam and Eve."

"I knew them longer than you did. There were some features that were noticeable if you examined them closely. Seeing such subtleties can be quite exhilarating. By the way, I want to go over what happened in Eden when you have the time. I'm looking for some suggestions for improvement."

"Is there going to be a second attempt? No? Then why dwell on it? We've got new assignments from Unpronounceable, and I need you to help my assistants on a couple of them."

"I don't know anything about science."

"You're going to be an observer, right in the thick of the experiments. Ignorance will be an asset."

"But I need help analyzing the debacle with Jess and Ba'al."

"Samuel, forget it. That was there then, and you are here now. Blame Michael and move on."

He sent me to Edesiel and Bibesiel who were

conducting cutting-edge research into the effects of decadence on career longevity and interoffice loyalty. Rome had experienced a dizzying turnover in emperors, generals, and senators. Evidently, attempting to achieve a position in senior management was proving to be a poor career choice. Success often led to the state confiscating retirement savings that were no longer needed. The astonishing number of premature deaths had led Edesiel and Bibesiel to hypothesize that dietary factors, such as overindulging in carbohydrate-rich foods and beverages, would lead to befuddled thinking by the military and sluggish response time from the officials--an unfortunate combination often ending in assassination. An alternative hypothesis suggested that repeated visits to the vomitorium resulted in malnutrition, leading to the same results. My instructions were to attend the feasts and orgies at the imperial palaces, quantitatively tabulate the intake of food and beverages, cross-referenced by type, and note any other behavioral factors that might be relevant.

I suggested the need for an assistant, but they vetoed the idea, citing budgetary concerns. I hesitated to take on another underfunded project. "Michael," I said, "is better qualified—"

Edesiel interrupted. "I see; you think you have a choice. This isn't the Fiery Pit. Options around here are limited by divine decree. When can you start? Now would be good for us. Here's your pass."

It was early autumn when I arrived. I can only guess that somewhere between two and three hundred years had passed since I sat on the beach with Ba'al. Conflicting calendars had sprung up after the exile from Eden. The Hebrews and Egyptians had untold local variations, often changing from one town to the next. The Greeks couldn't agree when the year started. The Romans enforced a supposedly universal system which was nothing more than a confusion of opinions. They were unable to agree how many days were in a year, how many months it had, how those months were named. (A reformer named Julius arbitrarily slapped in an extra month, without aiming at or achieving exactitude. I was not surprised by his arrogance. The one time I met him, he told me that he had been chosen by god. I said, "You don't look Jewish.") Beyond the lands bordering the Mediterranean Sea, the number of calendars leaped into the tens of thousands.

The conflicting array would prove to have a disastrous effect on a future mission.

I can't say who was Emperor when I descended. The Travel Department dropped me on the north bank of the Rubicon. In the time it took me to reach the outskirts of Rome, four contenders for the position had risen and fallen. I had hardly learned one name before he was buried. Some who aspired never made it as far as the Forum.

I found a cheap, cramped, furnished room above a

stable stall behind a butcher shop near the Forum. I wasn't bothered by the scent rising from the livestock, having grown accustomed to the odor while living in Nazareth. To earn my room rent, I applied the skills I acquired in Palestine. I replaced rotting wood around the pens, leveled the tops of the stone walls, plastered the interior of the shop, and served as barker on Wednesdays.

The landlords were an excellent match of chubby and portly, friendly but not intrusive. They worked quietly and efficiently. The husband bought cattle, lambs, and goats from farmers for slaughter. He would sink an axe into the animal's brain, rope together the hind legs, and hoist the body into the air. Suspended head down in the stable yard, the creature would twitch. The wife would swiftly slit the throat. The blood, collected in vats, was sold either fresh to chefs for soup base or dried to physicians for cure-alls. The meaty parts were sold in slabs or as sausages, the powdered bones as fertilizer.

Evenings, I attended as many palace events as I could. At first, I lived the dream of many people by becoming a fly on the wall. I convinced myself the disguise would make me an unobserved, unobtrusive tabulator. I was not entirely successful. On the one occasion when someone swatted me, I pretended death and spent half the evening wallowing in the grease of a slow roasted pig. While couples engaged in activities I hadn't seen since Eden (and hadn't understood), some of the participants would scream, "Oh god!" I was afraid they had spotted and mistaken me for a divinity. Why else would they close their eyes so tightly if not from fear of being blinded by divine resplendence? Dismayed that I might be accused of masquerading as Unpronounceable or of being a confidant of Beelzebub, I sought a better way to gain entrance.

While her husband was shopping at farms, the wife had an independent source of income, a side business that proved to be an opportunity for me. I had recognized one of her special clients as a frequent assistant at imperial palace events where he poured wine and dragged the incapacitated to safe havens against the walls. If he came to the shop while her husband was away, he would often spend time with her examining the private reserve in the back room. I dropped hints to my landlady to introduce us, and she ignored them. Respecting his professional privacy, I didn't share with her that I knew he was a certain Senator's Steward.

Finally, I asked her directly, discreetly, and politely if she could connect me with him. "Perhaps, the next time he comes to inspect the premium meat, you might suggest that I be introduced?"

I could tell from her smile that she was only too happy to oblige. "Would you like some of what he gets?"

At the time, I never ate physical food, only pretending when necessary to hide my identity. I told her, "I don't care for goat meat." She looked offended. Knowing that humans have thin skin, I tried to soothe her. "I would prefer a little lamb."

"Then you're on your own, my good man."

I took it upon myself to make his acquaintance.

Within a month, the Steward and I had formed a strong bond. He confided that he could get me, for a small fee, an invitation to one of the Senator's exclusive private parties, a Dionysian rite at the palatial estate on the road to Capri. I gladly paid the fee as well as an additional charge for a sky-blue toga which would allow me to mix inconspicuously among the other participants. I agreed without hesitation to use the name Casius Claudius Commodious. He reassured me I would not have to make any sacrifices to local deities. He would sneak me in through the servants' entrance. Once inside, I would be on my own.

The night of the rite promised to be warm. The moon was nearing the first quarter. I wore a simple cloak over my toga. The Steward came to the butcher shop in the late afternoon and, after striking a deal in the back room, bought a slab of fresh goat. We loaded it on the cart, and I joined him on the seat. We arrived at the estate at dusk. I helped him carry the half carcass into the kitchen.

The Cook complained as we heaved it on the table, "I don't know why you had to bring it all the way from Rome when we have perfectly good goats right here ready to slaughter. Seems like a waste of time and money, not to mention risking that half of it get carried off by ravens and rats and the other half spit on by every fly from here to the Tiber. I can only hope it'll be thoroughly cooked by the time it's served."

The Steward didn't argue. Neither of us pointed out to the Cook that he was the only one concerned about the skill of the Cook. We uncovered the side of goat, still almost intact except for a small slice the Steward had fed to the villa's resident cat when we reached the delivery entrance. We left it to the Cook to perform whatever miracles he could and would.

I kept quietly busy helping the Steward with the last-minute preparations for the event. I kept my back to the other servants and my forehead bound with a sweat rag.

When the Senator arrived, the Steward suggested that I change into my party togs. I slipped into a room off the pantry and out of my disguise, leaving on my inner sky-blue toga. I double checked my radiance filter and muted my aura to a murmur.

By this time, more than two dozen guests had arrived. I felt confident that I would go unnoticed. As soon as I entered, I spotted the Senator a couple yards to my left. He wore a finely woven, single layer, sunflower-yellow toga with a blue vertical stripe on each side. The fabric looked so smooth I felt what might have been envy. It was a fleeting feeling.

He turned his aquiline nose tip toward me and sighted my chin along its length. "Do I know you?" He separated each word carefully, making the simple question into a snobbish sneer.

Before I could react, a tall figure, clad in an ornate silk garb from chin to shin, standing beside and towering a foot over the Senator, looked over his shoulder at me. Both of us broke into vibrant smiles and greeted each other simultaneously.

"Samuel!"

"Lucifer!"

"Have you come to join us in our little ritual?" asked Lucifer.

The Senator looked from one to the other of us. He seemed irritated and flummoxed to be the one out.

"Just getting acquainted this evening," I answered.

Lucifer took the Senator by his elbow. "Let me introduce you. This is Samuel. We've known each other forever, it seems. He's practically my brother. Of course, Samuel, you know Gaius Petronius, esteemed of the Senate, a leader of the clan of Caesar, as well as the celebrated grandson of the inimitable author."

"As a friend of Lucifer, you are always welcome in my

house, Samuel."

I thanked him for his hospitality, saluting him with my straight arm parallel to the floor, fingers extended and palm down. He nodded.

Lucifer said to him, "Would you excuse us a moment? We have much to catch up on. We haven't seen each other in eons. Our paths often cross, but not at the same moment. The talk would probably bore you stiff-- family and insider religious stuff."

"Of course. Ah! There's Decius coming in just now." And off he went to entertain the guests he probably preferred over me.

Lucifer explained, "Officially, he's the one throwing this party, but it's really my affair. You see over there my signature dish, goat cheese and grapes? It's been a monthly tradition for me ever since I lived in Greece. It's still observed there, and in some quarters it's a weekly rite. Don't you love extremists?" Lucifer grabbed two glasses of wine from a passing tray and handed one to me. "Come," he said. "Let's sit beside the fountain in the courtyard and share a tale or two. There's still time to catch the full moon rising over the Apennines."

We slipped around a pile of people in front of the doorway to the garden. We had settled onto the benches on the far side of the fountain.

"I heard a rumor: you've been masquerading as a fly on

the wall."

I nodded.

"That's part of Beelzebub's act. I know he doesn't have a patent on it, anyone can use it, but you don't want to sully your reputation by borrowing without permission."

"The last time I saw him, he looked like he had retired his old act."

"Well, when you see him again, remind him that he still owes me for his unauthorized expenses."

I listened to the blended sounds of the gurgling fountain and the faint moans from indoors. The splash of the cascading water and the soft light of the setting moon lulled me.

"Just between you and me," said Lucifer, "I wish I hadn't been so hard on Beelzebub. Ejecting him from the Fiery Pit was acting just like the enemy."

"Regret's a start, but without atonement it's meaningless."

He sipped his wine. The last fragment of the moon dropped beneath the horizon. We sat silent, looking at the dark dome of the night and listening to the splash of the fountain.

Lucifer sighed. "Look at that sky, all those stars! It still amazes me. I wonder how many there are."

I told him the exact number.

"How do you know that? You were never good at math."

"Michael told me."

"Michael? You trust him? Haven't you noticed how he creeps his little feet closer and closer to Beelzebub's spot? He'd be in it by now if the enemy hadn't rezoned heaven."

"Michael does seem to have righteous ambitions."

"Honestly, you are far too trusting. Did he tell you that the count changes all the time? None of those stars are permanent. Some are born and others die every day."

"That makes more sense. I wondered if they felt burdened by an eternity doing nothing but radiating."

Lucifer sipped from his glass. "This is a lovely red wine from Greece. I imported it especially for this party. Try it."

I had never tasted wine before. Even drinking water was a rarity for me. I didn't require physical sustenance, and on the few occasions when I indulged, to fit in with the people I was with, the fare was simple and sober. The only fermented food I had ever eaten was a vinegar sauce over chicken and pearl onions. To be a gracious guest at his party, I imitated Lucifer and raised the glass to my lips.

My nose caught the blended aroma of plum, fig, and pear. The scent coaxed the wine into my mouth. My tongue was delighted by the texture, liquid yet subtly different from water, leaving a complex flavor that evolved over time. A soothing coolness flowed down my throat, pooled in my abdomen, then transformed to a radiance that spread, as if in rivulets, throughout my body. My mind was simultaneously hard clarity and soft cloudiness, frozen and sparkling. I hadn't felt good inside like this for ages.

I took a second sip.

Lucifer pointed to a spot above the eastern horizon. "Look, there's another star! Beautiful, isn't it?"

"And over there! A star just twinkled out."

"That's what I love about this universe. Everything ends eventually."

And I took a third sip.

CHAPTER 31

CLOTHES MAKE THE ANGEL

I overstayed my time in Italy. When Raphael called me back to heaven, I pretended I hadn't gotten the summons. My report not yet ready. I needed to copy my scrawls into something legible, delete what I couldn't decipher, and organize my notes into a comprehensible order. And I needed to sober up. I sequestered myself in a monastery in the south of Gaul, where no one could recognize an angel. I appreciated the silence and solitude; they made it easier to stay for several decades without suffering through serial interrogation. Once the data I had gathered on the rites and rituals of ancient Rome had been cleaned and properly sorted, I examined myself in the only mirror in the monastery, hidden in the muck room behind the refectory and used only by the Abbot and a few other high-ranking monks when they needed to visit the village across the river. I shook my head despondently. The garment was still too tight. It had indelible wine stains that I knew would be impossible to justify on my return to Heaven. The origins of some other stains were unknown, but I suspected they resulted from unauthorized interactions. I was ashamed that I had more secrets than I could remember.

A nomadic mendicant spent a week as a penitent hermit in our refectory. Although he had bad eyesight and poor taste, I asked him to recommend a tailor and suggested the more distant the land the better for me. The farthest one he knew about was starving in a small remote village in the Saracen desert, barely able to stitch together a living. The tailor's only real skill was cloud weaving, but that was a trade rarely asked for. According to the mendicant, Manny loved to chat while working. Some said his hawing while hemming hurt the quality of his products and made his customers suffer. Manny sounded like a perfect fit.

The mendicant connected me with a cargo ship sailing from Massilia for the Levant. He persuaded the Captain to take me on as seaman apprentice and arranged for one of the sailors, Ben-Jazmin, to take charge of my training. Between bouts of learning to sail and finding my sea legs, I reviewed my data from Rome.

On the voyage, Ben-Jazmin was slow to share anything with me, other than the ribald tales that are rife among sailors. After a few weeks, seeing that I was a quick study on board and a discreet companion in port, he grew to trust me.

We were sitting in a tavern in Corinth, close to the

beach where Ba'al and I basked long ago, when to my surprise, Ben-Jazmin told me about his experience with the very same tailor I was seeking.

"I thought I was taking a short cut from the Persian Sea to the Nile after I was abandoned in Maka. I came across a village so small and unsophisticated, I would've called it a backwoods town if the nearest tree had been closer than Lebanon and the population quadrupled.

"Down a path off an alley off a side street--there didn't seem to be a main street--I came across a tailor shop. I needed something to calm the storm I knew was waiting for me back home. I'd gotten overly talkative, you see, before I left to chase after a golden fleece, and she, the wife, was madder than Medea about something I said about every port." He clucked his tongue and slapped his forehead. "Never talk with your wife about your adventures, especially when you're soused."

He sipped his wine and looked at the table, shaking his head an inch and a half. "Manny was the worst tailor who ever stitched fabric. But," he said with a wink, "he can work wonders with cloud." He looked around the room as if to be sure no one could hear. We were alone; the barkeep was at the far end of the counter checking the quality of his mead. "That beggar-monk hinted you might be more than you are, same as him--that's why the Captain took you on, you know, as an amulet--and he dropped a word that you might be searching for

241

some special stuff. I'll give you a caution, so you don't stumble. Manny is proud. When I met him, he would not admit, even to himself when by himself, that his sewing skills were equal to a cat's claws. Everyone else knew, and they freely shared the word with me, just too late to stop me from signing the contract. He's a slow worker, so I had way more time than I needed to learn why his business was a failure.

"Most of his clients were obese, so his one-size-fits-all stock resembled small tents. Many men thought they were mockups and asked where the entrance was and if it could comfortably accommodate three men on a long journey." The sailor laughed and signaled the barkeep for another round. "Manny would blush and wouldn't answer or explain. I couldn't count the number of clients lost, dissatisfied before the goods were even ordered. The loss grew steadily, day by day, while I waited for him to finish the gown I'd ordered as an apology." He rolled his eyes toward heaven. "Never give your wife clothes that look like tents. Anyway, he lost more deals than he closed; I saw it myself every day. Funny thing is, there was a sign over his tent flap with clumsy lettering. 'ALL SALES ARE FINAL!' That was optimistic at best."

Ben-Jazmin signaled once more for that second round, but the barkeep found the mead more compelling.

I asked under my breath, "Did you actually see him weaving cloud?"

"Nah. No one asked for it."

I was convinced that no other angel would consider engaging Manny. His reputation assured me that my failings would not be accidentally un-Earthed. I desperately hoped Manny would be discreet once the transaction was consummated. Ruinous remarks race across space while compliments die in place.

I landed shakily on the outskirts of town and asked almost two dozen people where I could find the dressmaker. Finally, an embarrassed man admitted he knew him. He quickly added that he could recommend others, many others, who would do a better job at more reasonable rates and who lived closer to boot. I thanked him for his concern but declined the offer. Reluctantly, he told me the way. I noted that he steered me in a zigzag; I passed several other tailors along the way.

Manny was sitting on a lopsided wooden stool outside his dress shop. He was short and thin, with light brown skin and eyes and a full head of black hair under a loose plain square cotton cloth soaked in water. He sat beneath a sagging shade woven of hemp; a pitcher rested on the ground at his side; a scroll lay in his lap, and he held a stylus in his left hand. When I stopped in front of him, he looked up from his writings, scrutinized me from hem to collar, and said, "The cleaner lives two tents closer to the setting sun."

"Laundering won't help. Some of these stains appear to

be permanent." I explained, "What I need is a replacement, a simple garment of opaque cloud, loosely draped, without belt or sash, suitable for angelic chores."

"That is one of my specialties," he replied.

I swallowed my doubt.

When Manny quoted his price, I pointed out that even an angel with access to astronomical bodies did not necessarily have access to astronomical sums. "You mustn't confuse angelic powers with those of a genie. I'm in Human Relations, assigned to Earth from before it began, and I can swear to you there has never been a profit in caretaking shepherds and farmers. The genies in Finance have access to the treasury, but they don't share unless you can either free them from a lamp or promise them a better return on investment than divine law permits. Can't you give me a heavenly discount?"

"Anyone could walk in here and claim to be an angel. Those stains don't look angelic to me."

"I was on special assignment, and it got unclean."

"Can you prove it?"

"The stains are proof in themselves."

"I mean, can you prove you're an angel?"

"I have wings."

"Yeah, yeah. So does a gnat. And you're getting to be just as annoying."

"Would you be convinced if I turned you into a gnat?"

"Then who would make your robe? Cloud weaving is a rare skill. I'm probably the only tailor around here who can do it. And no one else would take you seriously as an angel. I can't be expected to take a loss just because you claim to be one. The price will barely cover my cost. Do you know how hard it is to get cloud strong enough to hold a hem?"

"Have you ever used cloud before?"

"I don't talk about my clients, especially those who need a cumulus covering. It would be unseemly."

I was happy to hear that, but I still needed a lower price. "I'm sure I'm smaller than most of your clients, and I don't need a blousy robe." I was trying to hold in my gut.

"No! You're suggesting I ditch my trademark; size has made me famous."

"I don't need a form-fitting robe either. It's considered in bad taste to show off your physique, especially when it's as far from the original specs as mine is. That should make it easier for you."

He jabbed in my direction with his stylus. "I don't do sloppy work, even on sloppy bodies."

Rather than reveal to him his reputation, I said, "I could promise not to tell anyone who tailored it. And the price would be our little secret." This was not a concession because I had already planned to keep the necessity of replacing my robe a tight secret. Manny called my bluff and sat firm.

I offered him a domesticated dromedary, but he said he was prone to motion sickness; a ride on a magic carpet, but he was a home body; three bags full of wool, but he claimed to have enough to pull over the eyes of everyone on Earth.

"What do you want then? Name your price!"

"I already have, but if you don't have cash, then you can get me a thousand loaves of bread, a hundred jugs of wine, and a cow."

"If I could conjure that, I'd be able to pay the original price and take a vacation on the moon with the excess."

Manny lowered his eyes and returned his attention to his manuscript. He ostentatiously placed his right hand on his chin and smirked.

Finally, in desperation, I said, "I see you're trying to write a book. I could help you with it, anonymously of course. I know a few pithy sayings. Some of them come straight from the mouth of Unpronounceable and are unspeakably clever. I'm sure the book would catch on and you'd make tons of money from it."

"I don't know. It sounds like a white elephant to me."

"How's this? 'Never bring a camel with a cold inside your tent.'"

Manny looked unimpressed.

"Or, 'Peace is for our enemies; war works for us.'"

Manny said, "That sounds reasonable. But it's too obvious. No one would pay good money for it."

"How about, 'Make them pay, more!'"

"No, no, no. These are stupid, bland--"

I pointed at the scroll in his lap. "If I'm reading it rightly from this side of the text, you seem to think that everyone will fall in love with 'There is no one but one and only one is alone the one and only one.'"

"It's a rough draft."

"For starters, the one's a little touchy about counting. I'd avoid numbers if I were you."

"I said I would revise it."

"Just junk it. You're capable of much better _if_ you work with me."

"I don't know if that's possible. You look unreliable. And how do I know you can write?"

"Are you telling me that you, the one and only dressmaker trusted by this angel, that you don't believe a good book can be dictated by an angel?"

"Is that an example of your prose?"

I ignored his snipe. "What about the ones the prophets wrote down up north? I had a hand in each and every one of them, if only a second hand with an eraser. But they are still sold and resold as authentic scripture. Such a book would be predestined to succeed."

"Are your edited versions the ones that sell?"

I skipped over his question. "You'll take so long to count the money you make, you'll be so rich, that everyone will talk about your day of reckoning even after it fails to pass!"

Manny hesitated.

"Manny, all you have to do is tell me the idea for each section. I'll dress it up in fancy talk and dictate the improved text to you. You'll write it down. It'll be as easy as stirring water with a fork!"

"Can we toss in a half a gross of virgins as a signing incentive?"

"I've sworn them off. I'm trying to get through rehab without a slip." I wondered how he knew my weakness. One of my weaknesses.

"I meant for me."

"Oh. I'm not authorized to go that far, but I can supply the ink and sheepskin."

He pressed for the virgins, but I stood firm until he was convinced that they were not negotiable.

As a last-ditch effort, he suggested we offer a sales incentive. "Each of our associates who sell seventy-two books will earn a commission of one virgin, with a certificate of authenticity signed by an angel, you."

I insisted, "Buying or selling or offering humans for any reason will never be acceptable." I hoped my tone of voice made it clear that this was not negotiable.

"But selling the book should get them some reward. Maybe entrance into heaven? We can call it Jannah."

"Doesn't that mean 'garden'? I absolutely refuse to have anything to do with another garden."

Eventually, he admitted losing the tug of war and accepted the exchange of one book for one robe.

Take my advice: When you sign a deal, be sure to include what was excluded and what was never promised. My reasonable contract devolved into the worst deal I ever made.

Manny was slow at taking dictation. I had to repeatedly return for the better part of three decades to fulfill my part of the bargain. An inconsistent speller with a poor memory, he often stopped to doublecheck the previous occurrence of a word and almost as often couldn't find it. He sometimes transliterated angel names into gibberish. He modified my grammar on every page and argued about word choice, insisting on changes that distorted my intention.

After two years, I asked if he could hire a scribe.

He insisted that was never in the agreement. That was true. "If you want a secretary," he said, "you'll need to cough up the cash, like a camel does his cud."

At the rate he wrote, I was afraid he would be dead before we completed the book. He made me nervous every time he got into a scuffle.

Five years into the project, I hired a cut-rate scribe, but Manny insisted that he could never work with a female. After a long discussion of whether qualifications were more important than gender, I relented and hired a male. Manny constantly read and reread every line over the poor scribe's shoulder. He offered improvements in spelling and penmanship during every session. He insisted on revisions, without me present, that ran up labor costs. To pay a fair wage, I had to take a job as a date harvester. I was in high demand because of how swiftly I climbed the palms. In the off season, I raised money by washing camels and shoveling sand.

Toward the middle of the third decade, I was pleased to

see that Manny had begun to collect strands of clouds. A few years passed before he accumulated enough to weave into whole cloth. From this filigree, he snipped and stitched together a robe. The garment pieces were held together with hair harvested from the foremost legs of camel spiders. (None were harmed in the making of the robe.) That the seams were clearly visible worried me. But Manny used a fine-toothed thimble to manipulate each one with incredible attention and patience until the garment appeared seamless.

It fit very well if a little loose around the middle; I had lost some flab after leaving Rome. I was pleased until I rolled up the scroll and found my name in the byline.

Immediately, I confronted him. "There is no justification for attributing any of this to me. I said in the beginning that you could not. And you've changed too much of what I dictated. I refuse to allow my name to be used."

"The gist is there. It's almost what you said."

"Even if it's verbatim, I forbade you to use my name."

"Really? Can you prove that?"

"Is your memory that bad?"

He sat on his crooked three-legged stool and folded his arms atop the hump of his belly. "You failed to specify in writing that I could not list you as coauthor." Suddenly he was talking like a lawyer.

"And here, a tenth of a cubit in, you act like you're speaking for Unpronounceable."

"You promised a few pithy sayings straight from his mouth."

"But none to be credited to him."

"You spoke for him."

"No one speaks for him but he. You can't claim Unpronounceable spoke through me. I haven't even seen him in centuries! I insist that Unpronounceable be unmentionable. And where in the world did you pick up this name? It's too close to the Greek for cow. One slip of the lip and we'll have another fall!"

Manny examined the nail on his longest finger. "Do you want the robe, or not?"

Caught in my own web, I acquiesced. But before I left, I dragged my finger across the width of the scroll. The spell erased the objectionable passages.

Without my knowledge, but at my expense, the scribe had been ordered by Manny to make a copy. When I reviewed this copy centuries later, I saw the unmistakable hand of Manny smudging the clarity of my phrases.

CHAPTER 32

THE TRIALS OF MY TRIBULATIONS

I didn't know until I reentered heaven that I could have returned immediately from the assignment in Rome.

When I arrived at the gate of heaven, carrying my soiled robe in a banana leaf sack, the Guardian Angel suggested, "Why don't you try to find a more suitable robe?"

I dissembled that the one I was wearing was an original.

He shook his head. "Clever crafting, but the seams look like they were sewn together by a spider."

"It's from authentic cloud. I had it made to my specs."

"Looks more like you made it out of whole cloth. In fact, I'd say it resembles cotton more than cloud. Did it shrink when you washed it?"

I promised to replace it at the first opportunity.

As I started past him, he said, "By the way, Samuel, you need to report directly to the SAC."

"Wonderful!" I ejaculated in as thrilled a voice as I could muster, but mentally I growled a grating moan.

The Supreme Archangelic Council was in session when I entered. I couldn't understand what was being said, but it sounded like someone whining. Not long after I arrived, the complaining voice stopped, and the Chief Archangelic Decider (the CAD) signaled me forward.

"Word has come that you, Samuel, have spoken to Earthers about divine adages without being authorized to discuss the matter. At first, he laid claim against 'angel or angels unknown' due to an inability to spell the name properly. We have, however, concluded that you are the source of these sage sayings." She then rattled off a half dozen phrases most of which I had repeated to Manny.

"Some of them, your Archangelicallousness, I did indeed say in the presence of this tailor. But I expressly forbade him to attribute them to anyone but himself."

The CAD looked at the parchment in her hand. I took the opportunity to ask the bailiff, "How did Manny get here before me? I left first and came straight here."

"Complainers are given a faster pass, right to the head of the line, so they can be disposed of quickly before they incite the rest of the line to riot."

The CAD cleared her throat, not because she needed to, but as a way of calling my attention. "This Manny, a simple tailor who, judging by your robe, does a passable job when working with cloud-like material, also claims that you gave him exclusive rights to all sequels in the prophecy genre."

My mouth dropped open. I insisted, "I acted as a free agent on a single project and never promised anything that would bind others, especially Unpronounceable, his heirs (just in case the rumors are true) or his assignees, be they prophets or astrologers."

The Archangel to the right of the CAD pointed out, "Even if he made the deal, he did not have authorization to consummate such a transaction. It would be, therefore, invalid."

His counterpart on the left asked, "Manny the Tailor, did you prequalify for the SAG?"

Manny asked, "SAG? What's that?"

"Ah! Evidently not. The Sacred Authors Guild has been tasked with vetting and training those who would like to pen spiritual guidebooks. Once candidates pass all the exams, they undergo trials by fire and--"

The CAD interrupted. "He can't have prequalified because the SAG has yet to accept any students. All the applicants have been rejected based on their desire to speak for the divine instead of listening to him."

The left-hand Archangel said, "My point exactly."

The right-hand Archangel, said, "Terrifying presumption!"

The CAD instructed the bailiff to blast three times on his trumpet. "I hereby throw this case into the jaws of the nearest possessed pig."

Manny objected. "I appeal to--I think you call him Unpronounceable."

The unmistakable voice of Unpronounceable sounded as if through a tube. "No need to listen to any arguments. I've heard the trial. I hereby invoke the principle of arbitrary flexibility and squash any further discussion."

"But--" cried Manny.

"And I declare Manny persona-non-gratis and order him never to show his face again." His public relations team managed to convert that condemnation into an approbation.

At that moment, Manny disintegrated in heaven and reassimilated in parts unknown.

Unfortunately, the book that I helped Manny write became a best seller, and, before anyone in heaven realized what was happening, a new religion had started. When I informed Unpronounceable, he groaned, "Haven't we got enough confusion down there already? Did they start another calendar? The Travel Department is having enough trouble as it is."

Waiting for me a half step outside the court was another Guardian Angel. "The ASS is waiting for you, Samuel. I've been asked to escort you to them."

I said, "I thought they'd disbanded the Anti-Sodomy Society."

"They did. This summons is from the Agency for Science and Sorcery."

"Is that Raphael's organization?"

"Yep. It used to be the Agency for Scientific Study. They changed the name a few decades ago, and Raphael quit in protest. But his resignation was returned, unread it's said. Still Michael seized the opportunity and tried to usurp the leadership spot. He renamed it the Panel Loathing Observable Truth and plied anyone who would listen with alternative and anecdotal explanations that supported his favorite causes. It didn't take long for Raphael to realize his mistake and take control again."

"I bet it was a struggle to dislodge Michael."

"We don't wager in heaven, but you're right. It had to be resolved at the top. Now the Agency's swung the other way. A clique of statisticians dominates it and won't let anyone publish without sufficient data to justify belief, even in obvious cases."

He was about to open a doorway in a bulbous cloud so that I could enter the Society's chamber when he paused and looked me over carefully for the first time. "Is that the best robe you have? It's hardly fitting for formal proceedings."

"It's better than the one I was created with. That one's stained badly."

"So! The rumors <u>are</u> true." His broad smile had a tinge of satisfaction. "I know a shaman in Amazonia that does wonders with stubborn stains. The process involves passing the garment through an anaconda then rinsing it in the mist from Angel Falls. He comes highly recommended by the Amazons."

I shuddered at the name that many considered an idealized vision of the Earth's future. "The tribe without men?"

"That's right. Great warriors. Lousy housekeepers."

"Thanks, I appreciate the offer, but I'll take care of it myself."

Once inside, I was surprised to see that Raphael was not presiding. The Archangel in charge asked me to present my notes and figures on the rites and rituals of Ancient Rome. I wondered why a city that was still inhabited would be called ancient, but I offered my cleaned and recopied data without comment.

"Where are your original notes?"

Reluctantly, I brought the crumpled papers from the inside pocket of my robe. The Archangel studied them, passed them to the angel on his left and waited until that extremely slow reader finished perusing them. I was impressed at how many times per paragraph she could clear her throat.

The notes were then passed to the angel on the opposite side. She pored over them while sniffing with a sneering twist to her upper lip, as if she could smell my sins.

I was accused by these holier-than-thou angels of attending orgies.

I reminded them that my original instructions were to do exactly that.

The Angel on the right asserted that I was not told to participate.

I pointed out that the Agency had sent me there with no training and had not listed prohibitions.

The left-hand angel labeled my account "unspeakable smut."

The Archangel said, "The council will adjourn to consider the evidence. We will reassemble in forty-seven minutes."

I did not like that he called my data "evidence." While they withdrew, I rushed to the cleaners across the cloud and dropped off my stained robe. Hiding it was no longer useful.

By the time I came out of the laundry, the details of my deeds were known through all the heavenly choirs. Later Raphael intervened and forbade recounting my adventures in the presence of Cherubs.

When I reentered the chamber, I saw the original commissioners of the study had joined us. Although Raphael was present, he didn't take an active role in the proceedings.

Bibesiel and Edesiel declared that no certifiable conclusions could be reached due to dirty data. They accused me of squandering my time and their efforts.

A statistician was called to testify. "This data set is skewed by the high number of unverified observations that can only be classified as subjective and/or biased."

"I admit it was hard to remain a neutral observer while attending an orgy, but I stand firmly behind my data."

"How can you vouch for observations made after you passed out?"

"Every dubious memory was verified the following day with an independent source who had managed to stay sober the entire night or who had passed out after me."

Edesiel suggested, "It's possible your sources suffered from confabulation."

Bibesiel asked, "Perhaps you led the witnesses? Some of these 'observations' appear to be outside of the norm."

I suggested politely, "Perhaps your system can't handle outliers, even when they're the truth." I still had hopes of clearing my name. "If you doubt the facts, then we can rerun the experiment. I volunteer to return to Rome and--." I stopped in midsentence, realizing that I was about to offer to be placed in the path of a temptation I couldn't resist the first time.

The Archangel said, "The failure of the Western Empire to maintain a viable and verifiable hedonism has made replication impossible."

The angel to his right tore up my original notes. "Lest these fall into the hands of Cherubs, I will dispatch the tatters to the Fiery Pit."

All my work flew out of her hands and through the cloud floor. In the pit, a tumultuous clamor arose, the sound of the fallen attempting to preserve salacious fragments from the conflagration.

A Guardian Angel approached, took me in custody and led me to my second appearance that day before the

SAC. On the way, he said helpfully, "If you buy a size too large, the cotton will shrink to fit you."

The Divine Accuser, famous for his expertise in the laws of clean living, proceeded to prosecute me before the almost full SAC of seven archangels. Normally there are nine, but Michael and Raphael had recused themselves.

The DA was known to push for the maximum sentence with the harshest punishment. He liked to downplay his preference for severity by saying that he was just doing his job as best he knew how. He went so far as to claim that all sinners are masochists yearning to be chained and beaten. As soon as I saw him, I could feel my feet warming up.

The court appointed an Excuse Attorney. He smiled beatifically at the judges and said, "Your honors, I don't like to complain, but I haven't consulted with my client."

The CAD responded, "There's really nothing new to know. The rumor is that the rumors are all true. I'm sure you've heard them all."

"I'm not one to object, I rarely even hint at disagreement, but I've got to say, I ought to at least hear his voice once."

"I agree," I said.

"There," said the CAD. "You've heard it."

"Thank you." My Excuse Attorney smiled. "Let's get going."

The witnesses were interrogated under a bright lamp. One tall angel singed his halo. From time to time, the Excuse Attorney would object. "Your honors, I'm not feeling the love here." No one was cross examined. No closing argument was presented. My attorney just cleared his throat and mumbled, "Well. There you have it."

I was found guilty on 36,547 counts of professional negligence, 73,094 counts of double entendre, and 1,584,017 counts of impure thoughts of which 956,011 were fulfilled.

I was sentenced by the SAC to seven hundred seventy-seven years in India where I was forced to sit in a bare, cold cave and answer random questions from lost, wandering souls who insisted on calling me Baba. Although the penalty seemed severe, I knew that I had escaped a prolonged punishment in the Fiery Pit for committing what I knew to be unspeakable offenses. I shared the cave with a Yeti who ceaselessly shed, continually burped through chattering teeth, and frequently mentioned how delicious my rump roast would taste in a stew with a few carrots, onions, potatoes, and a dash of ground coriander.

CHAPTER 33

HIGH TEA IN THE HIMALAYAS

Well, well, now isn't this cozy?"

Lucifer stood outside the entrance to the cave. He stooped to peer at me sitting in the darkness at the back of the cave. "Looks like they put you on ice with a Yeti to watch over you."

This morning marked the halfway point in my time served. I had expected before now at least a pity visit from Raphael or a mockery of my failed righteousness from Michael, but Lucifer was the first angel to drop by. My only other visitors so far were lost souls seeking a way home.

"How did you know I was here?"

"I didn't. I heard some rumors about a holy man in a cave, but I didn't connect it to you. I knew you'd been imprisoned, but I didn't know where, and I couldn't imagine anyone calling you 'holy' after that business in

Rome."

"I have a feeling it will take an eternity to live that down." I stepped forward into the dim light that shone over and around his shoulders.

"A spotty reputation can be an asset, especially if you act like a reformed sinner. But, anyway, I'm here to see my other friend, your cave-mate."

"What could be so important to bring you this far from civilization?"

"I was in the neighborhood. Where's the Yeti?"

"It's out throwing snowballs at tigers. Didn't say when it'd be back. Please have a seat. No need to run off. Shouldn't be long now before it's home. Come in, come in!"

My heart felt as if it were bound up in burlap. Fear that he would turn away gripped me as strongly as suspicion of his motive for the visit.

He stepped over the threshold and gave me a warm embrace with his wing tips.

I had spent fifty years trying to decipher the Yeti's grunts and groans. The effort was far greater than the benefit. Now, at least, I had the prospect of intelligent conversation.

I moved the ice block I'd sculpted into a rude table to

the center of the room and asked if I could get him anything.

"Just a fire for now."

I piled some wood in the pit near the entrance and set it on ember. "Wood's hard to find in the winter. It's rare at this altitude, and the harsh weather keeps the shrubs short. I can make you some tea, but it'll take some time."

Lucifer wiggled his pinkie at the fire, which responded to the tickle by flaring up. Consternation flooded my eyes. "Don't worry," he said. "The wood won't actually burn. It's a little trick I learned back home."

"I heard tell about eternal flames, but I found it hard to believe." I put a kettle on to boil some snow for tea.

"Some optimists say it's just perpetual. I've grown accustomed to it. Nothing says 'home' like a warm hearth in a cold world."

"Can you show me how to do that?"

"It's an easy bit of magic." He swore me to secrecy then revealed how to work the trick. It was as easy as watching ice melt in the tropics.

I went to the shelves that I had carved into the wall. "You say you were in the neighborhood? Surely you're not sightseeing?" I held up two bottles of tea leaves. "Lavender or Jasmine? I've got a few sprigs of mint. It's not high quality."

"Have you got belladonna?"

I reached into the back of the cabinet and pulled out a half-full jar. Today it looked half-empty.

"I was visiting with Shiva over on Mount Kailash," Lucifer said.

"Ha! I've been his neighbor for more than three centuries-- I can even see his house from here--and he still hasn't dropped by to say hello. I gave up on getting a welcome basket two centuries ago."

"It's the ganja. He used to be quite the entertainer, wild parties with the finest riffraff you could hope to meet. The crowd loved to watch him spitting up roaches and blowing centipedes out of his nostrils. And that little woman gushing a river out of his tangled hair was a hoot! He put those Romans to shame, made their orgies look like shams."

He looked out of the corner of his eye at me. I got up to fetch the teapot.

Lucifer shook his head mournfully. "But now, he just sits in the corner and puffs on his pipe and babbles incessantly about not knowing how loud he's talking. Not even Shakti can get him off the stuff. Kali shook her necklace at him, and all he did was smile stupidly."

"He's lucky it's not addicting." I stood with my back to

my visitor, waiting for the melted snow to boil. "At any rate, that's what some tokers say."

"That's the only positive thing I could see. He blows smoke about it being better than tobacco."

"Didn't you used to promote both? Come to think of it, I seem to remember you were a big retailer of opium, too."

"That was before I knew how addictive it is. They can't shake it. Even in the Fiery Pit, they crave it. <u>And</u> they expect to get a fix for free, as if I owed it to them. It's annoying, and it burns a hole in the profit margin fiercely."

I poured the boiling water into a cup, added a couple leaves of belladonna, placed it on the table before him, and prepared a lavender tea for myself. "It's hard for me to be sympathetic. You did your best from the beginning to lead humans onto the path to perdition. That's how I recall it."

"You're referring to the help I gave Eve with her relationship?"

"That's right. My reputation has yet to recover. The other angels can't stop taunting me. 'If it'd been a snake, it would've bit you.' And all I can answer is, 'Ha, ha, ha.'" I almost tipped my cup over. "At least, they didn't accuse me that time of being in league with you." I couldn't stop myself. "But after that business in Rome!

Would you like to talk about it? I'm sitting here waiting out another three hundred plus years because of it."

"Do you really blame me for that?"

I took a sip of the lavender brew and turned the memory of Rome over and around. Then I sipped the tea again and looked out the doorway. Did I really want to insult the only guest I'd had in centuries? "No," I said. My third sip of tea washed the blemish off my attitude. "It was my decision. I could have stopped, but I--wanted to immerse myself in the experience." I looked away and down. "In retrospect, in spite of the consequences--." A slow nasal exhalation followed a deep breath. "I learned."

Lucifer asked for a second cup. As I poured the hot water for him and refreshed the leaves, he said, "You've taken a step in the right direction. From the unforgiving, uncompromising heights of the heavens to the discomfiting world where the rest of us wallow. You can learn to love it down here in the mud."

I smiled. "Some of my best friends are possessed pigs."

He laughed. "All of mine act like they are."

"But aren't you the one who brought all this suffering about?"

"Since you brought it up, I'll tell you the truth as I see it. I would love to take responsibility for snaring Eve and tricking her into seducing Adam. It would give my arrogance a shot of fertilizer. The fact is, I can't take all the credit. I realized long ago that disobedience is built into the system. I've learned a lot more about these inquisitive, impulsive, and reckless creatures since that day. Eventually, they would've let their curiosity take over. Not only would they have eaten all the apples, but they would've dug up the roots, cut up the wood, and set fire to the whole garden. I just sped them along the path. The animals should thank me for saving them from being burned to death." He looked toward the entrance. "Here comes the Yeti."

As soon as it stepped in, the Yeti grunted a greeting.

"Yes, my friend, it's good to see you, too."

The Yeti grunted about fifty noises.

"You're right," answered Lucifer. "I've been reduced to visiting my furry friends for entertainment. What's up with you?"

It roared and growled for several minutes.

Lucifer said, "I'm worried, too. I'm just hoping it's nothing stronger than ganja."

They talked--rather he talked and it grunted--far into the evening. I poured tea for them both. At nightfall, I chopped a chunk of lamb off a carcass and served it to them raw.

Throughout the evening, I grew calmer and lighter, as if confessing my Roman fever and dropping the weight of blaming Lucifer had loosened my shoulders.

At the entrance to the cave, as he was leaving, Lucifer pointed to a fresh speck of light in the sky. "Do you still delight in a new star's twinkle?"

I wondered if I was falling into another snare. "Drop by again, any time."

He cloaked himself in purple clouds, struck the mountain top opposite the cave with lightning, and thundered down the valley, leaving me alone with the Yeti. The moon renewed three times while I sat weeping at the threshold of the cave.

I felt more than ever that the Yeti was my warden, tracking me diligently, ensuring that I didn't wander from my cell before my parole date. On the one occasion that I went for a cold dip in the river below, it kept an eye on me. The better I understood its grunts, the more I realized how much it loved to insult me. It seemed to take special delight in inconveniencing me. At least twice a month, it would spill tea in my lap. It would then laugh as it watched me descend to the river to rinse my robe before it stained. If the creature had turned out to be a skillfully disguised Guardian Angel whose sole task was to make my imprisonment miserable, I would not have been surprised. I buckled under the weight of persecution, but I refused to label it paranoia.

I felt overwhelmed, depressed, empty. My sinfulness, it was clear, merited nearly complete isolation. Lucifer was the best companion I could hope for.

CHAPTER 34

BREAKFASTS WITH BEELZEBUB

After long decades of frustration, I had finally learned the rudiments of the grunted language. The more I could understand, the more inclined I was to consider the Yeti as an intelligent being.

Even after a good night's sleep, the Yeti cultivated its morning grumpiness as if it were a rare orchid. Its early yawns filled the cave with a scent reminiscent of the corpse flower of South Africa.

I asked the Yeti on the four hundredth anniversary of my arrival why it was invariably grouchy before noon.

It grunted at me. "I can't help it. I'm always irritable before my first cup of coffee."

The first chance I had, I asked a poor soul with sufficient money and abundant guilt to have delivered to me a half a peck of dry Ethiopian beans as a dharma task. The morning after the two quarts arrived, I offered the Yeti a freshly brewed cup as soon as he woke.

It declined. "Never touch the stuff. Makes me jumpy."

I donated the remaining beans to a farmer in Mysore.

Although from the beginning of my stay the Yeti had occasionally adventured away from the cave, often for as long as a week and twice for a month, I felt watched every moment. Perhaps my paranoid guilt amplified the occasional, slight signs of surveillance into continuous, overwhelming evidence.

In the final fifty years of my confinement, when we were alone in the cave and I adrift on a sea of silence, with steadily increasing intensity the Yeti would pace the length of the cave. Without warning, it would flail its arms and emit incomprehensible, harrowing howls and garbled grunts. It would then ignore me diligently, with pointed negligence, until another outburst would shatter the icicles. Then, without an explanation, it would take its mood outside and seek its favorite remedy for cavern fever: fresh air and a bare-claw hunt. I had to enlarge the pantry to store the carcasses.

Two weeks before my release date, I was feeling as irritable in the morning as the Yeti. The day before had been brimmed with people who wanted to know what and how many rewards they could amass in exchange for good deeds. For most, the goal seemed to be to identify the point of maximum gain for minimal effort. I was never good at math, so my answers were neither consistent nor reliable, but they were sympathetic.

Some seekers asked more challenging questions. A wife from Calcutta wanted to know if maiming her husband instead of killing him outright would mitigate her karma. My answer was, "If you can wait another week, your neighbor upstairs will resolve the problem without your having to accrue karma."

A Prince of Kashmir asked, "Can you tell me how many years I will need to be confined in a Tibetan prison in my next life to atone for usurping my older brother's throne this Thursday?"

"If you leave for Tibet today, you'll still have your head on Friday."

A worker from the British East India Company asked me if it was possible to gain riches in this world with the promise of performing good deeds in heaven. "The effect before the cause? Go for it. But be aware! The road to the Fiery Pit is paved with alternating bricks of good intentions and bad science."

That night, in my sleep, with no pauses between preaching vehemently against the snares of the flesh and snoring like angry elephants defending their calves, I kept the Yeti awake. In the morning, we had matching moods.

I was trying to shake off the clinging mental numbness from the day before, when the cave entrance darkened.

The Yeti growled menacingly.

My whole heart agreed with the Yeti. Welcoming the sun, much less a lost soul, was beyond my capacity, but when I saw who it was, my reluctance evaporated into eagerness. Without hesitation, I invited Beelzebub in.

He had successfully cleansed his robe of the last remnants of charcoal, its scent now replaced with hints of jasmine and geranium. He stood taller than I remembered him, and his jaw was set yet relaxed. What amazed me most was his pure white halo.

The Yeti, still growling, asked me if we were going to have to feed this one, too.

"It would be polite to offer," I said.

The Yeti showed its pointed yellow teeth to the visitor. "I hope you brought your begging bowl."

"I'll just have tea, thank you."

From the visitor's soft, manicured hand, the Yeti yanked the bowl-cup, scratching it with his claws.

I said to my visitor, "You understand Yetish! It took me centuries to figure out the simplest phrases."

Beelzebub said, "We go way back. We met shortly after I crossed the Indus the first time. We didn't hit it off."

"Then my theory about its being a Guardian Angel sent

to keep me in confinement is false."

Beelzebub heartily guffawed. "Believe me, that's no angel. The stories I could tell--But I don't want to risk getting my wings ripped off. If you get a chance, Lucifer and Shiva have all the dirt."

"Lucifer was here a long time ago, but he hasn't been back for a second visit."

"He was never good at social niceties."

This was my first opportunity to sit with Beelzebub since that day under the bodhi tree when he opened his eyes and found a multitude around him. I had wanted to step up and chat about his post-celestial adventures, but the people who had gathered around him, who believed they had so much at stake in his mediated wisdom, needed his time more urgently. I knew another chance would come for me eventually. Now, after the fiascos of the failed plays, I felt I should congratulate him on having drawn larger crowds than Jess, seemingly without trying.

"The crowd count amazed me, too. To think that all I had to do was sit there with my eyes closed."

"This peace permeating you wasn't the result of shutting your eyes. For the first couple centuries, in between trying to find homes for nomads, I dropped in and out of the crowd around you. At one point, I noticed a change in you, and right away I became enthralled, watching you relax one thought at a time until you were ready to see past yourself to the rest of us. Tell me, what brought you there?"

The water began to boil. The Yeti poured a bowlful, sprinkled some leaves in it, and handed it to Beelzebub. I started to sound a warning, but Beelzebub said, "Hemlock! my favorite! How did you know?" The Yeti snarled in disappointment as Beelzebub slurped it down all at once. Turning to me, the visitor said, "Samuel, you already know the important points."

"I want the details. I wanted to meet with you after seeing you in India, but I was kept busy putting out sacrificial fires deemed unacceptable by the SAC. Unpronounceable muttered something about a rebellion. He wasn't talking to me, and I thought it would be best if I could continue to claim ignorance. At any rate, it's not a good idea to ask him too many questions." I realized I was rambling. I took a slow sip of my tea and waited for Beelzebub to begin.

Telling the tale of his travels through southern Asia took most of the day. The achievements, the disappointments, the witticisms, the insights, the pithy parables delighted me endlessly. The Yeti became crankier each time we asked for more tea. Pacing at the entrance, it growled and howled like a hungry, wounded werewolf on a deserted island. There were no other visitors that day.

We must have had ten cups of tea each. When Beelzebub recounted a story about the reciprocity of karma and dharma, I remembered to pass on Lucifer's request for restitution.

"He'll have to wait until he gets over it. It was never his anyway."

We talked through the night, disturbing the Yeti's sleep yet again. The fifth time it complained, Beelzebub said, "Practice equanimity, my friend. If you can't sleep, then meditate. I can show you how if you'd like."

The Yeti snarled. "What's gotten into you, Mr. Meditator? Who made you master of the zafu?" It retreated to its corner where it mumbled gruffly. After two and a half hours of muttering what had begun to sound like a mantra, but felt like a curse, it growled at Beelzebub, "I thought you were supposed to be the avatar of compassion, but instead of letting me sleep, you drone on about how much you've suffered."

"Sometimes when you tell the truth, people accuse you of self-pity. If you show yourself compassion, they accuse you of self-indulgence. And then they take serious offense when you tell them that they're not being compassionate. Here is what I will do for you. I'm going to demonstrate compassion and willingly give you this opportunity to develop a smidgeon of empathy for my plight. It will serve as a door to compassion. The practice will help you gain composure when you're in the grip of your own irritation."

The Yeti snarled again.

Beelzebub turned to me. "Now it's your turn. Tell me everything."

I was surprised. This was the first time any of the host had asked me to talk about my own life, if you exclude demands for explanations and justifications. I started with Eden. He interrupted to tell me that he had met Adam and Eve twice. The first time was under the Bodhi tree. They had reincarnated as gardeners. The second was in Limbo when Beelzebub was on his first Empathy Tour. Eve was still working out her resentment over Abel's death. She refused to enter heaven. In her eyes, Unpronounceable had played her sons against each other. She had complained to Beelzebub, "He's got some problem with firstborn sons. Adam's lucky he didn't have a younger brother." Hearing that Adam refused to move on without her consoled me. And I was puzzled that I felt a taint of envy.

I recounted my visit with Ba'al on the beach. Beelzebub had seen him pretending to be a merchant on his way to sell silk in China. The real destination, Beelzebub confided, was Polynesia. Ba'al had heard good things about abundant fish, coconuts, and grass skirts. Although wary about learning to sail without a map, Ba'al reckoned floating so far out of the mainstream would make finding him unlikely. When Beelzebub pointed out that the Sanhedrin had no real power over him, he answered that he had heard they acted for Unpronounceable. Beelzebub and I both doubted that sincerely.

I skipped most of the details about my Roman adventures and parried his question about the nature of the infractions that resulted in my confinement. I suspected he was well informed before he arrived and was merely showing a polite interest in my story. I didn't want to risk reawakening the cravings for corporeal stimuli, and he seemed to understand and respect my decision.

However, before he left, he mentioned to me that someday I would need to find peace with my so-called mistakes and embrace the wisdom they had given me.

"If you mean the wisdom of avoiding temptation, then I have learned my lesson."

"Lessons are the way to learn, but they don't leave you wise."

I refused to budge. "I must be where I am, in school, with the abecedarium open before me."

"Avoiding the memories of pleasure prolongs its grip on you. Understanding pleasure's source is wisdom."

I suggested, "Why don't you open a booth in Kathmandu and sell aphorisms by the dozen?"

"I've got thousands of them on forgiveness. Would you like to hear a couple?"

I declined.

We sat through our second breakfast in contented silence, neither of us partaking of the gruel the Yeti offered us, but both of us enjoying the pungent aroma, a pleasant contrast to Beelzebub's floral scent, which had become cloying. The food had a granular texture that served well as a hand scrub.

When I accompanied Beelzebub to the entrance to bid him farewell, we found a crowd on the slopes below, looking up at us with expectant, hopeful faces, more numerous than the spectators at an execution. He offered, "If we divvy them up between us, we can make short shrift of this."

We finished the interviews at noon. He followed the last of the seekers down the icy slope without looking back. Twice the man slipped, and twice Beelzebub caught him before he knew he was falling.

The Yeti emerged yawning from the cave. It mumbled about needing to stretch its legs and kill something for dinner. It lumbered up the slope and vanished against the white background.

Alone, I sat at the lip of the cliff past sunset. My wings shivered in the cold air descending in a stiff gale from the snowfield above the cave. It reminded me of returning to heaven after a blistering day repairing Eden's wall, of slipping between cool sheets at the end of a heated night of observations in Rome, of skinny-dipping in the stream at the base of that very cliff when the Yeti decided to build a bonfire.

The sun rose; my eyes turned from the glare. My chest absorbed its faint warmth, and my mind cleared with its rising light. I opened my eyes and faced east. I remembered sitting on the beach outside Corinth, standing before the fire in a Roman villa on a particularly glacial day, the brief flash of heat when the angels disappeared. I sat, as still as an ice sculpture, deep into the night.

I gazed into the numinous depths of space. Far away, in the constellation Capricorn, I saw a flicker, a glimmer that transitioned into steady light.

"Ah! A new star."

Instead of inspiring joy or hope, it reminded me of my cold, unforgiven darkness.

Part V
Trying to Try
Again

CHAPTER 35

THE INVITATION

M y release papers arrived ten years late. No one apologized. The Guardian who was to escort me to the parole office noticed that the Yeti was holding back tears. The angel said, "She's going to miss you." I wondered how I could have been so obtuse.

I laid low in heaven for centuries. Although I had remained sober and chaste throughout confinement, I had not yet regained confidence in my ability to refrain from relapsing. In fact, I resisted redemption, longing to tiptoe to Earth. Whenever I thought an escapade might remain unnoticed, I recalled Unpronounceable's ability to see in all directions. What had been a wonderment was now an oppression. I could have filled a heavy book with my lamentations over pleasures no longer possible. I was torn between angelic devotion and demonic craving. At any rate, I lacked confidence in my ability to deceive or resist.

But Earth was my assignment. Someday, I would be

forced to return. To avoid or at least delay the inevitable summons to service, I tried to evade the Messengers. I didn't sleep on the same cloud twice. I bunked with lower orders of angels. I checked out with the Guardian at the gate and slipped slyly back over the wall. When cornered between a cloud and a fogbank, I scrawled my name illegibly on the receipts. The stress of evasion became too much to bear. I fled heaven altogether.

I used a pseudonym when I leased lodging in Limbo and later exercised squatters' rights for a house on the edge of Chaos, in the same neighborhood where Adam and Eve resided. I watched time drift like a twig in an eddy, a monotonous triviality making another round. I cowered in my closet, shuddered and refused to answer when I heard the doorbell. Although the rehab centers in Purgatory would probably have been better for me, I was afraid to enroll.

The inevitable day of reckoning arrived: Unpronounceable himself knocked on my closet door. I recognized his tap, as distinctive as his voice, as fear-inducing as his sidelong glance. I thought he would clip my wings for ducking my duties and then send me to be slow roasted. There was no escape, it was clear. On all fours, I crawled out of the closet and belly flopped at his feet, my tonsure near the hem of his robe, my palms turned up in submission.

"It is time," he announced in a voice simultaneously

stentorian and encouraging. "Time for you to return to active duty. Stand up, face me."

Once on my feet, I glanced into his eyes and immediately averted my gaze to his knees.

"For too long now you have eluded my messengers, or perhaps I should say, deluded them. I have had to come myself, as if I were the hound of heaven or the robin of radiance, to hunt you, as if you were a fox in flight or a slug in slime. Lay aside your doubts and cravings. I have a simple task designed to help you remember my kindness and regain your confidence." His voice softened. "By the way, it doesn't involve alcohol or sex, so you should be able to keep a steady keel. Are you ready to willingly accept the assignment?"

Dumbfounded, I wondered if he was asking me to volunteer? If this could be a test to see if I'm truly rehabilitated? I had never heard him request compliance. I reminded myself that a question from Unpronounceable wasn't really an offer of options. The consequence of refusal, I was certain, would be removal to the Fiery Pit. No matter how I examined the question, the answer involved simmering in sulfur soup. If only this cup could pass from me! At best, I could only sip timidly at its bitterness. Better to offer it to some other angel, someone willing to quaff the liquid and then beg for a second gulp.

But I realized that only divine intervention could save

me from the divine mandate. Whichever way I chose, I would be skewered. I decided to acquiesce. I could always deliver myself later to the Fiery Pit when it became clear that failure was inevitable. I would then stride courageously into the flames, wrapped in the satin of my dignity, though stripped of my last splinter of pride.

I was about to squeak my answer when Unpronounceable said, "This is not a trick question. You may accept or decline freely. Say yes and you will gain no reward; it's too easy a task. Say no and you'll suffer no punishment; other angels can do it. Someday, I will offer you another simple job when it arises. Like this one, it will be within your reach. Eventually, you will have to accept a new mission, so why not now?"

I wanted to banish the arguing voices in my head. "I beg your permission to seek clarity."

He nodded and shook his head simultaneously, as if granting permission while dismissing my hesitation. The motion resembled looking in all directions, but on a lesser scale.

"If it's so simple, why not entrust it to some idiot angel?"

"You mean some other idiot angel?"

"Can we upgrade me to moron?"

"The mission is too easily twisted to the messenger's benefit. You're the imbecilic angel most likely to deliver the correct message. I know you would never unknowingly manipulate it to benefit yourself. And it would be a miracle if you manipulated it knowingly."

I decided to think that through later to see if any part of it hid a compliment. "What if I fail?"

"When have you ever succeeded? Achieving my goal has always been just beyond your reach, so far. I'll move on from your failure (let's be kind and call it partial success) and try to find a way to rectify the damage, as always. I'm not called All Merciful for no reason."

"Who called you that?" I couldn't remember a single instance or reason.

"Don't get sassy."

"Sorry." I resolved to check the records later.

"This task is so easy! As easy as a child's maze, or baking biscuits, or picking ticks off a monkey's back. There is no way to fail."

"What's the goal?"

"To help a new religion get off on the right foot."

"Another?"

"The man is going to start one on his own, anyway. I think we should set him on the right path. He's praying for guidance, and I think it's a good idea to give him some. Otherwise, he's got some strange ideas that could take root as dogma. He's almost ready to give up on us."

I sighed noisily. "These humans start a religion based on someone's poor relationship to his father. They write a bunch of stuff, say it came from you, and twenty years later they split into fifty sects and declare war on each other. Why not just let them fight it out on their own?"

"That was then. Can we blame Manny for what happened after he died?"

"Yes. He started it."

"Should I blame you for helping him start it?"

"I never intended--"

"Exactly my point. This one needs guidance, too. I've written it down for you."

"Why not just give him the paper?"

"Never put anything in writing for humans. Haven't you learned that from the last time? Trust me. Are you game?"

The expression reminded me of slow roasting. However, recalling the principle of arbitrary flexibility and my history of catastrophes, I still hesitated. This unexpected generous donation of understanding and willingness to let me decide for myself seemed totally out of character for Unpronounceable.

I asked, "Will this be the one true religion that the sons of Adam are perpetually seeking to devise?"

"Actually, no. But it will be the only honest religion so far."

"Honest religion." Oxymoron? Impossible dream? Miracle?

Although tempted, I thought it best to ask him to delimit the task, hoping for an oral contract that might protect me from the canonic team that was sure to follow up by dragging me into the courts. "What exactly do you want me to do?"

"Tell the would-be prophet that the only true testament is that no one can possibly know the divine, the divine will, or the divine plan. Any description of me is not a description of me. Any proposed way that leads to me does not lead to me. Anyone who says that they have heard my voice is either lying or hallucinating. Anyone claiming to know my feelings, thoughts, or intentions is lying or simplistic. How can words tell you who I am? How can human minds comprehend anything about me? Even speaking to you, one of my angels, I must dummy it down to an unspeakably simplistic level while omitting the interesting parts. To understand my dilemma, imagine trying to explain geometry to an amoeba. I could do it, but to what end? As soon as I quit talking, it would forget all the subtleties; it would declare itself in possession of the righteous angle and proceed to condemn and execute all the paramecia."

"You're telling me that I'm to tell him, 'This is the word of God: There is no word of God.'"

"If he can spread the word that there is no word, then I can get on with my original plan."

"Would you like to tell me what that is?"

"It would take an eternity to explain."

I could put off my decision no longer. We both knew what I would say, but he waited for me to voice it. I acquiesced. He handed me a gold trumpet. I said, "This looks like Gabriel's."

"It is."

I was puzzled. Gabriel was Unpronounceable's usual choice for delivering important messages. I thought I saw a way out. "I don't want to encroach on Gabriel's territory. Shouldn't he be given the opportunity to handle this?"

"I'm giving you this opportunity to do something new."

"Why not him, if I may ask? He's got experience and talent."

"He's--occupied--for a while."

"What happened?"

"Never mind. I don't want to talk about it."

I gingerly took the trumpet and practiced blowing into it until I achieved a tolerable blat. I smiled, fondly remembering making music with Raphael on the day we awaited the two trees in Paradise.

CHAPTER 36

THE CASE OF THE VANISHING TABLETS

Unpronounceable assured me that arrangements were being made at that very moment. The newly reorganized and renamed Department of Humane Relations was coordinating with the Travel Department to ensure that I would arrive at the correct time and place to fulfill his mission. He handed me a scroll, a rolled slice of cloud with written instructions. As I read, each word vanished and the scroll vaporized line by line.

The first step was to alight in woods in upstate New York near the house of a man named Joe. Although no one had promised them a celestial visit, he and a neighbor, I was told, were anticipating my arrival at any moment, waiting on a hilltop near a village in New York.

I went immediately to the departure station nearest Purgatory. A rainbow bridge stretched across Chaos to the universe. Groups of humans wearing oversized, rose-colored glasses studded with rhinestones were toting bundles and singing about bringing in the sheaves. They sidled and stumbled toward heaven, but many of them tripped over the purple and fell into the grinding quarks.

I asked the angel at the transport, "Are there plans to install railings?"

"Worker safety isn't scheduled for another century."

Turning my attention back to my mission, I checked the settings on the transport. "Are you aware that New York is not the same as York?"

"Do you think I don't know my job?"

I stepped into the module. "Now that you ask me outright, I have my doubts. Not particularly about you, but the system in general."

"Doubt? You should talk." He punched a button with his wing tip while glaring into my eyes.

It was a fine spring day. Joe was walking across a sunny, verdant field speckled with paste-white lilies. As I descended, I realized the trajectory was too low and too fast. I would barely clear the treetops. I tried to slow down and pull up by spreading and angling my wings, but I reacted too late.

I crashed feet first seven feet in front of him. My arrival, a streak of brilliance cutting across the sky, was like a meteor plunging to Earth. And, like a meteor, my impact created a thunderclap, a flash of light, a shallow crater, and a gust of wind. It deafened him, blinded him, sprayed moist, hot dirt in his face, and knocked him on his back.

I knew it would take Joe a few minutes to get his wind and sight back, so I leisurely brushed the soil from my raiment and bent forward and to the side as I twisted to reach behind my knee to scratch a persistent itch that had been irking me since sharing the cave with the Yeti. When I twisted back to face Joe, I realized that Joe's eyes had opened. I immediately tensed, straightened my posture and squeaked nervously, "You have been chosen by God."

I smiled, feeling self-satisfied, and relaxed my shoulders. Joe's jaw hung ajar. Although I was at least a meter taller than he, my eyes were level with his because of the depth of the crater. I felt three soft taps on my left shoulder, as if to nudge my memory.

"I got the order wrong," I said. "We have to start over." I pulled my shoulders back and my spine erect once more as I brought the long gold trumpet that hung from the sash girding my loins to my lips and blew a long note. It sounded, to my ears, more like brass than gold. Nonetheless, I looked him squarely in the eyes and declaimed, "I bring you good tidings: You have been chosen by God." I smiled for a moment. Then my eyes clouded over, and my smile wilted. The setting didn't feel quite right. "Wait a moment." I climbed to the rim of the crater. From my new perch, I looked down at Joe and raised the trumpet to my lips.

Before I finished inhaling, Joe asked, "Are you an angel of the lord?"

I knit my brow. I was familiar with mankind's penchant for asking stupid questions. I answered patiently, "What other kind is there?" I didn't wait for his answer. I trumpeted and issued my call. "Good tidings I bring to you. You have been chosen by God." I brought the trumpet to my lips a third time, but before I could sound it, Joe interrupted.

"Hey! Cut it out! Are you trying to wake the dead?"

"Not yet. Wait! What year is this? Never mind, it can't be the end time judging by the way you're dressed."

"What's wrong with the way I'm dressed?"

"Never mind. It's a matter of personal taste. Apparently, you're not familiar with the concept of fashion."

"Could you at least point that thing away from my ears?"

I lowered the trumpet to my side. "Sorry, but I'm supposed to blow this thing three times. It's in the protocol, you know. I just got the order wrong. Sound the note, read the memo, repeat, repeat."

"Three times?" asked Joe. "Why blow it at all? You

already got my attention by falling from the heavens."

"It's not for you. It's for the official record. Without drama, there are no followers. And for the record, I left from Purgatory."

My face lit up and I raised my brows as I took a deep breath. The trumpet arrived at my lips a third time. The blast was so loud that it scared all the cows dry within two miles and terrified the pigs on a neighboring farm. In a panic, they fled into a lake. Their deaths set free a dozen demons who then sought new bodies to possess. The nearest available were bats. The only other damage happened after midnight; the local coven was forced to adjourn early due to an infestation of oinking bratty bats. The next morning, the witches had to discard twenty-seven quarts of undercooked dragon's blood. I am tempted to leave these facts out of this unofficial record because farmers and witches can become litigious over such details.

"You really ought to stand, you know, or maybe kneel. It won't look good in the paintings to have you sitting down with your legs pointed at me. Unpronounceable wouldn't like it. He thinks it shows disrespect, and he's got a reputation for being a stickler for trivial details. Maybe we should start over."

"No, no! Let's just say that I was knocked down by your arrival and as soon as I got to my feet, I knelt in your presence."

"Are you in the habit of lying?" I asked.

"Who is this Unspeakable?" he asked, evading the question.

He was finally on his feet. I aimed the trumpet at his nose, tried to blow some sense into his head, sounded off the memo, and repeated and repeated the ritual.

He was on his knees, clutching his ears and wincing as if in pain. "Are you done with that thing?"

I nodded and sheathed it in my sash.

"Who is this Unspeakable?"

"Unpronounceable," I corrected. "We call him that because no one but he can say his name correctly. We've tried to convince him to use a nickname that someone else can pronounce, but the idea seems to irritate him. The amazing thing is the staggering variety of names he's been saddled with on Earth."

"And what is it that he wants from me?"

"He has a message that he wants you to promulgate in that new religion you have set your heart on starting. Personally, I think that's a terrible place to set your heart, and don't get me started on how there are too many religions already. Every time a human thinks he knows what he wants, he treats it like a god. Anyway, the message he wants you to relay--"

"But I've already started my religion."

I was dumbfounded.

"Don't look at me like that. It wasn't my fault."

"How can you choose to act and then claim it wasn't your fault?"

"I was forced to begin without you. I'd told everyone I was expecting a visit and prayed for it every night back in New York. But nothing happened. I thought for sure that the father and the son would drop in together."

"Which father and son?"

"You know, the One and his Son."

"He doesn't take kindly to that name, and there's no proof he has a son."

"Anyway, as I was saying, the duo didn't appear on my schedule, so I had to tell everyone back in New York that the vision already happened, just to keep from being embarrassed. I said, me and you (meaning you, not them) were going to be hobnobbing next time. You don't mind being called Moron the First, do you? I was ticked when I picked the name, but my intuition told me it would fit."

"According to Unpronounceable, my title is Imbecile. I don't know the number. I was never good at math."

"It's too late to change it now. I wish you'd gotten here on schedule back in New York."

"Back in New York?" I gasped, finally understanding the third time he said it. "Where are we?"

"When no one showed up, I guessed I would get some instructions in writing. I especially wanted them on gold leaves because that would be most impressive, not to mention the resale value. I prayed and I made predictions, but no parcel arrived. Not one page, much less a whole book. I was forced to guess what the message would be. I did the best I could with only my own desires to guide me. So, I cranked out a few dozen plates, used paint as close to gold as I could find, and kept the lights down low. I convinced eleven family and friends to give sworn testimony they saw them in exchange for power and glory in my church."

"Where are these tablets now?"

"Uh--I don't know. They--vanished. In the night."

"Didn't that make the witnesses suspicious?"

"I told them you took them back."

"They bought it?"

"I was shooting from the hip, all alone in the spiritual wilderness. It turned out it didn't matter what I said. Not a one of them could find a bible in a gunny sack. When they started arguing about niceties like who gets first shot at marrying the girls--"

"Girls? Don't tell me—"

"Squabbling got so bad, I had to excommunicate all the witnesses, but they were in too deep by that time, so there's no need to worry about them turning honest on us."

"Excommunicated? But isn't that Cath--"

"Well, shoot me if I'm wrong, but they were getting unreasonable. I explained to those sons-o'-guns that I headed the church--"

"Where are we?"

"--and I wrote--I mean, translated and wrote down--the newest book of scripture, just like the pharisees in Babylon and--"

I shouted, "Where are we!"

"How can you not know? Are you sure you're an angel?"

Gritting my teeth, I growled, "Where are we?" I reached deep inside to find enough patience to let him live. I directed my frustration away from him. I knew he was too fragile to survive a single angry thought from me. I reminded myself that I was not the Angel of Death. In the back of my mind a mantra ran nonstop: "Not my job, not my job. Don't kill him, don't kill him." I couldn't control my wrath. It flared out and struck the ground to my left, accidentally setting ablaze a passing garter snake whose last thought was, "Why me?"

The puff of flame and smoke focused Joe's attention. Then he scratched his nose from the inside and flicked something into the grass. "Illinois, of course," he said offhandedly, as if no other possibility existed.

I couldn't fathom the depth of his placidity, undoubtedly from profound arrogance. I smacked my forehead with the heels of both hands, raised my wings heavenward, and shouted toward the sky, "The first line of the instructions, and they couldn't get it right!"

Joe asked, "Who are they? Who are you talking to?"

"Too late and in the wrong place. I've got to go. I need supplemental instructions. I wasn't told a plan B. I'll have to speak with Unpronounceable and see if we can get another shot at this."

"Don't fly off like that. Keep calm. There's still time to make some corrections, as long as they aren't too far off from my gold tablets."

"Gold. Tablets. Unpronounceable only writes on clouds." I couldn't help but sound scornful.

"What about those stone tablets?"

"That story! The guy couldn't find his way around a puddle. He spent years following clouds across a wilderness."

"When you get back, ask him to prepare the celestial orb. We're counting on it."

"Orb?"

"I promised the kids a planet all our own. Not that we're elitists. The beauty of this paradise is that you don't have to be good to get there. All you'll need is a descendent who'll be sorry for you and vouch for you. That's why I went with polygamy--to maximize the chances that one of your descendants will find you tolerable even though they never met you. There were other reasons, too. Of course, I never mentioned the others to my first wife."

"You expect--"

"I'm confident Unspeakable will have no problem conjuring up a planet for the saved. I call it Kaboob. I've got a real talent for making up names that sound silly and sacred all at once."

"Have you estimated the eventual population of this planet? I'm awful at math, but I can guess it's--more than I can count, maybe even astronomical."

"Unspeakable can do anything."

"What makes you think that?"

"I read it somewhere, and then I confirmed it by saying

so myself."

"Can doesn't mean will."

"I'm sure he can squeeze everyone in since we'll be spirits by then. Don't you know about the old question, how many angels can stand on the head of a pin?"

My patience exhausted again, I swept the trumpet out of my sash and shook it at him. "The answer's one, but only if he's a master of balancing." I bopped him on the right shoulder with the trumpet bell. "And you'd better start calling him by his preapproved name, Unpronounceable." I belted him on the left shoulder with the other end, wielding the trumpet the way Little John taught me to swing a staff. "Tell me there's no promise of virgins on this planet." I was growling like the Yeti.

Crossing his arms and rubbing both his shoulders, he said, "It's not official, nothing written down at least. I may have implied it when Brig and I were chatting behind the barn one day."

My wings drooped. "I wish this horn had a mute. I'd stuff it into your maw."

"Ma's got nothing to do with it. She's not a virgin, anyway, as far as I know." He smiled timidly. "If you could start a rumor? By the way, about that planet, I promised prime real estate, adjacent to the throne of Unsayable. When we get home, I'll give you a copy of the books so everyone's clear on what to deliver."

I heard clamoring in the distance. I rose above him and wrapped myself in a cloud. "Looks like the sheriff's coming. I'd better go."

Fearing the pain of punishment as well as bearing the shame of failure, I slunk back into my closet in the suburbs of Limbo. When I felt that I had truly resigned myself to my doom, I meekly crawled to and through the Portal to the Presence and sprawled before Unpronounceable, my face buried in the cloud.

He said without hesitation, looking up, or turning toward me, "It seems the space-time continuum is too complex for the Travel Department. I might send the lot of them on a long, slow trip to nowhere."

"There's the matter of the garter snake."

"I know all about it. I've made it up to him. He's reincarnated as a cobra. It would be wise if you avoided him for a while."

"I bent and dented Gabriel's horn."

"No problem. He'd been blowing a sour note lately anyway."

Matthew Stramoski

Part VI:
After Math

CHAPTER 37

LUNCH WITH LUCIFER

About a hundred years later, I received an invitation from Lucifer by way of a possessed carrier pigeon that seemed to choke on each word. Lucifer asked that I join him the next day for lunch at noon local time and suggested a small café in an out of the way town in the Gobi Desert. The pigeon then vomited and asked if I would like to send an answer. I thought the bird had already undergone enough stress, so I told it I would send a note by cloud mail, and it flew away, looking relieved.

Thinking it would be good to catch up on the latest in-depth news from the depths, I referred the invitation to the inner circles for approval. There was a time when I would have readily accepted on my own responsibility, but each failure to carry out Unpronounceable's wishes undermined my confidence. Subjected to the strains of ridicule sung sotto voce by entire choirs of angels, I constantly anticipated the inevitable summons to the SAC. The tinkling of whispered voices behind my back persisted, a ringing in my ears. Many angels voiced fears that I was endangering this universe. After all, another existed that was more amenable to divine will, or so said rumors said to be started by those who said they knew. How demoralizing to hear that my counterpart in the alternate universe was doing a joyfully better job. It was hard for me to ignore my own shame and jealousy, to find room in my heart to forgive them for saying what I knew must be true. No one could say for certain what would be the fate of the choirs of angels at the end-time.

When Angelina, the Messenger Angel, delivered the permission slip for lunch with Lucifer, I thought she was mocking me. She said, "I got the impression that Unpronounceable thought it would be a good idea for you to meet with Satan." She smirked as if she had inside information. "Will we be seeing you again?"

I condensed the wisp of cloud and dropped the sleet at her feet.

I forwent arranging passage through the Travel Department. It was unnecessary; I would probably never need to re-enter heaven. My home in Limbo was the best I could hope for. Facing expulsion into the Fiery Pit, I tried to make light of my doom by referring to it as my pending Limbotomy. Still, I knew I would miss the place. I had grown fond of my neighbors, although with most I had only a nodding acquaintance. When Judas moved in a few clouds down, I worried about the sanctity of my isolation, but we hadn't spoken yet.

Adam and Eve often entertained Jess, and Judas would frequently join them, but they had yet to send an invitation my way.

The day of the lunch, I left early, landed in a secluded canyon, and entered the village by way of an alley, and turned into the market.

The air was shimmering off the baked mud walls lining the dusty square. Tattered canvas awnings and faded cotton curtains shaded the windows and concealed the interiors. Several vendors sat languidly at tables in the shade of a long beige canopy. As I passed, one man bent forward and extended a wizened hand holding a misshapen copper figurine, as if to offer it for my money's consideration, but said nothing and instead leaned it against a sisal basket at the edge of his table, obviously too expensive for me.

Lucifer materialized with a puff of dark red smoke in the middle of the square. No one seemed to find this magician's entrance remarkable. He was probably a frequent visitor. We arrived at the café simultaneously.

"Good to see you again," I said.

"Good? I haven't heard that word in a long while."

We walked single file between the two tables of patrons who sat in front of the café in the shade of a ramada. As we passed, all eyes remained carefully trained on the tabletops. At the doorway he swept aside the barrier of vertical strands of multicolored beads. Lucifer led the way to the table nearest the bar. I sat opposite him. On the far side of the room, the café's climate control, one open bare window, waited for the next breeze to cough.

The server was a petite young woman with black hair, brown eyes, and a pleasant shape that aroused my memories of research in Rome. She asked Lucifer what he would like to drink. Her left hand caressed her earlobe; she bent her head forward and to the side. She couldn't take her eyes off him.

Lucifer ordered a hot toddy.

I asked for a glass of water, and she jumped as if startled. Apparently, she hadn't noticed me. I was tempted to turn my radiance filter off, just to see if the brilliance would attract her attention.

When she returned with the drinks, Lucifer, without looking at the menu, asked her, "Can you charbroil a steak for me?"

She wasn't sure what that meant.

"Cook it until it's charcoal."

"I'd be out of a job for suggesting he could burn anything."

"Yeah, I know. I was just trying to make trouble. You know me, I like to sow a little discord wherever I can."

She giggled. "You're so cute."

"Seriously now, can you bring me a tri-tip of yak, rare. When I say rare what I really mean is raw. Believe me, you can't undercook it."

The server started toward the kitchen without asking me what I would like. Lucifer called her back and suggested that she take my order. She seemed surprised to find me still sitting there.

"I'll have the same, but medium rare," I said. When she left, I asked Lucifer, "It hasn't changed, has it? Whenever you're around, humans don't even see me."

"I have that effect on people. You shouldn't take it personally. They know intuitively that I have the keys to their happiness. When did you become carnivorous?"

"While doing research in Rome."

"Research? Is that what it's called in heaven?"

I ignored the jab. "I acquired a taste for goat while I lived above the butcher. It's juicier than you'd expect if you prepare it well. Your friend, the Senator, served a scrumptious filet mignon with a wine sauce that I've never found the equal of. Then the Yeti taught me that red meat, literally red, has its own charm."

Lucifer laughed lightly. "Aren't you the little learner!"

Waiting for the food, we caught up on the weather in

heaven (white clouds underfoot) and hell (dark clouds overhead), the whereabouts of a few Fallen Angels, the newest drama from Michael, and the latest world to blow itself up. Lucifer kept in touch with Ba'al by letter. I was vague about where I'd seen Beelzebub.

Lucifer said, "I haven't seen Gabriel in quite a while."

"That's good news."

"Where's he hanging these days?"

"Not a clue," I said. "I heard his trio disbanded. Don't know why. Some say he was turning the Red Spot blue."

"I heard his trumpet was damaged."

"I'm sure that happened after he disappeared."

Lucifer stirred his toddy with a fingernail. "You're looking glum."

"Really? Glum?"

"A vacant or pensive mood, perhaps."

"You could say that. I've been wandering, lonely, on my cloud, while those on high have spewed a crowd of golden mockeries."

"It's that Joe incident, isn't it? When I suggested he make his own tablets and sold him some yellow paint, I didn't know I was setting you up for trouble."

I wasn't surprised Lucifer was involved. "Would that have stopped you? Would you have told him to wait for me?"

"No. And no. It might have made it more satisfying for me, knowing I was betraying a friend."

"You think of me as a friend? I find that--a curious pleasure."

The server brought a plate of raw yak. Lucifer asked her to bring my food as well.

While we ate lunch, Lucifer did most of the talking. "On a lighter note! Yet another human offered to sell me his soul. I didn't point out that I had it as soon as he'd wished for me to buy it. But I humored him and asked what price he had in mind."

Lucifer sighed. "It's been eons since I enjoyed buying souls. Nowadays, it's already a done deal before puberty. Once upon a time--oh my, but it does seem like long ago and far away in a fairytale time and land when there was enough good to corrupt without the risk of exhausting the supply. In those days, I had to work to win a soul. But too soon, it got to be too easy to return much satisfaction. People would ask for wealth or the violation of some woman or power over enemies. I finally outsourced that business; it's boredom incarnate."

He took a long sip from his toddy and stared at his

bloody meat with a thoughtful expression. "I mean, really, if you can't figure out the basics of life, then what makes you think you can handle your most cherished wish? I take your soul, I give you money, you squander it at the roulette table. Next! I take your soul, I give you the woman or the man of your dreams, she turns out to be a shrew or he's a beater. Next! I take your soul, I make you king, you live in fear of assassination for the rest of your life. Next! On sale, cheap: Come and get your wish fulfilled and live in your own private hell before you die." He sucked blood from his fingertips. "It's all too predictable."

I asked, "But you were tempted this time? What was it that caught your interest?"

"He hooked me with his arrogance. This man thought he could outsmart me. It was a small challenge, smaller than I hoped for, but I've always been a sucker for a chance to puncture hubris. He asked me for eternal life with guaranteed wealth, youth, good looks and excellent health. He insisted that no injury be able to harm or maim him, that nothing could diminish his vitality. I was in a mood that day, a little more irascible than usual, so I demanded to know if he was aware of what his request meant.

"He assured me that he did and proudly told me he'd thought it through from every angle. Just to be clear, I asked him what he meant by wealth. He wanted more than he could ever use up. I told him to initial there and sign here and the deal was done."

Lucifer smiled. His lip curled. "As soon as I countersigned, he laughed, taunted me triumphantly. 'You will never see me in hell because my life is now eternal. I would have to die to go to hell!' The man thought he had duped the devil."

I asked, "Surely you'd thought of that?"

"Of course. I let him relish his victory for a few days. Then, he was lured by a vengeful acquaintance (I think his name was Edgar or maybe Allen) into a neglected basement. The bait was the promise of a cask of Amontillado. (I never cared for the stuff myself, but this man fancied himself a connoisseur. All he really knew was his personal preferences.) He was so eager to get the first sip of Amontillado that he didn't notice the cuff until it was on his wrist. He had managed to get himself sealed up behind a brick wall, chained to the opposite wall so he couldn't reach the sherry that he craved. There was his wealth! More wine than he could ever drink! Thirst, hunger, loneliness!"

Lucifer tore off a chunk of raw meat; blood dripped into his lap. He swallowed the mouthful without chewing and continued speaking with an ecstatic gleam in his eyes. "The best is yet to come! When the seas rise, he'll be submerged, gasping saltwater into his lungs, mercilessly tickled by minnows and shrimp, anemones rooted to his eyeballs. He'll beg every passing angel for deliverance, but he'll find out his life is out of their control. I've got the contract to prove it.

"Eventually, when the land is subducted, he'll be compacted under millions of tons of rock, roasted by magma, then finally thrust back into the atmosphere. And what will he find? The sun turning into a red giant! He'll be blasted into space by the explosion. And again, he lives hunger without hope of food, thirst without hope of drink, suffocation without hope of air, loneliness without hope of death! All the while, he watches as matter expands farther and farther away, out of reach for eternity, just like the Amontillado he couldn't resist and never tasted.

"Yep. He's well on his way to learning what it really means to have eternal life."

I said, without conviction, "Maybe Unpronounceable will have mercy on him."

"That would be out of character, now, wouldn't it? Have you ever heard him forgive anyone? Has he forgiven you?"

I didn't argue. I hadn't forgiven myself. Why would I expect another to do it for me? What good would that do me?

It was obvious that Lucifer still resented his exile. He was not yet ready to find enough space in his heart to forgive. I had seen this phenomenon too often in men.

Some were unable to forgive themselves for resenting their own fathers for being human, for being imperfect, and therefore unable to grow fully into their own masculinity, much less their own humanity. A cycle of resentment, domination, abuse passed through generations like a precious heirloom. I shuddered to think of humans molding spiritual relationships on human families, with the absurd assurance that everyone would be wonderful once they were dead. Somehow, a grave was going to magic Uncle Joe into Mr. Nice.

Lucifer wasn't ready to hear my opinions on his personal development, and I was not at all certain that I had anything important or efficacious to share. My beliefs sounded, even to me, too much like loathing. They were disturbing enough echoing in my own head. I couldn't see a reason to spread the discomfort. At any rate, I was doubtful about the wisdom of likening Unpronounceable to a human father, even as a contrast.

Lucifer sucked down the last of the toddy and ordered another. "A little hotter this time, if you could."

He looked me in the eye. I felt again his ability to mesmerize. "Samuel, I asked you here for a reason."

I broke away from his gaze. "I'm not going to join you. Arabia was way too hot for me, so I know there's no way I could be comfortable in the Fiery Pit."

"Oh, Samuel! I'm not extending an invitation; I'm asking a favor. Besides, you don't have the sense of humor needed to survive and thrive in Hell. When was the last time you laughed? Look. Picture this: the antics of the mouse with cosmic consciousness. The little bugger dances on his two back legs, blows up his cheeks until they're as big as an elephant's head and pulls his nose long, all the while singing out, 'Look at me! I'm Pinocchio!'" Lucifer laughed heartily.

"I don't get it."

"Exactly my point. You'd just stand there thinking the rest of us are stupid. When <u>was</u> the last time you laughed, Samuel?"

"Oh, I remember it well. It was while doing research in ancient Rome. I've got to tell you, I--Uh, never mind about that. I was taking time off, walking across the Sahara, searching for a lost sheep, when I suddenly understood about the zero. I sat down on the hot rocks and laughed, so hard and long the lost sheep had already died of old age when I found it. Luckily, Unpronounceable didn't hear me. Pity the lamb was too rotten to eat."

Lucifer ignored the answer to his question. With a soft, nostalgic glow in his unfocused eyes, he murmured, "Ancient Rome. What fun that was. For the rich. How I love a wealthy empire built on the misery of the poor! It's the best of both worlds!" Lucifer clasped his mug between his hands and squeezed until the toddy steamed.

"Samuel, you've got something I want: Space."

"Space? I think you're talking to the wrong angel. Isn't Galgaliel in charge of that?"

"Him and his constant music of the spheres? I can't endure his harmony. It's so predictable even the clams know what's happening next. And the tune--the same silly ditty over and over. Besides, what I want is space, room, emptiness."

"Don't you have enough of that in your heart?"

Lucifer said sarcastically, "Ha, ha. Is that a beam in your eye?"

"Touché. Why do you need more space?"

"The martyrs are arriving in droves and cluttering up the pit."

"But they've been redirected to you by orders of the Almost Most High. When they first started arriving, the gatekeepers didn't know who they were or why they thought they deserved heaven, so they put them in a holding tank just outside the gate. Sometimes, the names of some arrivals don't get on the list--it's often out of date--but there's always the chance they're nothing more than gate-crashers."

"Why not park them in Purgatory?"

"Admittance to Purgatory implies eventual acceptance into heaven. We think of it as a way station on a one-way street, a Vichy shower before a massage, an hors-d'oeuvre as it were. Granted, some angels go there on vacation when they want to rub elbows with the not yet cleansed. You understand. Sometimes you need to let your hair down. I've got a cottage there, although I--." I stopped short rather than share any more secrets with someone who already knew too much about me, someone who was already grinning as if he understood all too well what I didn't want to share.

I willed myself back on topic. "Investigations on Earth revealed that some self-named prophets promised self-proclaimed warriors a free pass to heaven if they die in holy battle. The warriors started claiming that any little slight, even disagreement over a name, was grounds for a holy war and any minor scuffle counted as a chance to die in sacred battle. They took the idea to absurdity and claimed it was martyrdom even if you killed yourself as long as you took someone else with you! Innocent people were said to qualify. The next thing we knew, we had martyrs piling up on top of each other. The bystanders they killed claimed to be martyrs, too. They started banging on the gates, causing the heavenly peace to go south. So, we stuck the innocents with the other martyrs while we tried to sort out the truth. Talk about a ruckus!"

"Well, I didn't promise them free room and board--"

I interrupted. "Their sins are enough to merit Hell. You'd expect the holier-than-thou to have at least <u>minimal</u> respect for life. I heard one of them sneer, 'You call that a pilgrimage?' Crawling on your belly from Prague to Compostela isn't good enough. For goodness sakes, the martyrs on the same side can't agree who they're fighting for or how to spell the name. They go on and on arguing if it's three in one or one in three or one in all or all in one. There's even a Frenchman who keeps screaming, 'All for one!' A woman from India keeps yelling, 'I must be dreaming! Somebody, pinch me!'"

"I sympathize, but--"

I barreled ahead, too agitated to be polite, too irritated to be reasonable. "Finally, Michael took responsibility and personally cast out all the martyrs, every last one of them."

Lucifer frowned at me. "Are you done?"

"For now."

He sipped his toddy then said, "Heaven's still underpopulated and Hell's already overcrowded. The martyrs are pushing out the original settlers and complaining about everything and the kitchen sink being filthy. They claim I'm taking up too much space and have too much authority. Apparently being The Satan is not justification enough to have a ring to myself. And each and every one of them demands I personally escort them to heaven to tell the gate guards there's been a mistake. As if they'd listen to me!" Lucifer had worked himself into a lather. "On top of all that--on top of all that! They keep demanding virgins. Seems those alleged prophets promised six dozen a pop. How's anyone going to find even one virgin in Hell? Yes, sometimes one will show up, but the chauvinist pigs grouse and insult them to their face. 'You're so ugly, it's no wonder you're still a virgin.' Now we have women scorned in Hell. I never thought such fury was possible. Lately, the martyrs have been screaming that they are going to agree to disagree, which just prolongs the conflict because they can't agree on what to disagree on. They all need to pull their heads out of their asses and shake the shit out of their own ears."

He was pounding the table with his left fist and shouting.

I signaled him with both palms pushing air toward the tabletop. "Calm down. Take a breath."

Through clenched teeth, Lucifer said, "One of the virgins organized the others, all three of them, into a brothel. When a martyr skulks in and enjoys his reward, the others mock and condemn him. Then they take their turn, always pretending that none of the others know what they're up to, and then they endure their turn at being mocked and condemned."

He frowned and gnashed his teeth. My water glass shattered.

I looked across the café to the window and waited for him to cool down. "I hear you, Lucifer. The martyrs told us the same thing when they arrived. I pointed out that six dozen won't last an eternity. Virgins aren't durable, the least little thing and they're done for, and there's no repair shop. The martyrs were duped."

"Rats are more rational."

"They claim the prophets wrote down the words of some god and that guarantees it! Can you believe it?"

"A spider's web is crafted more credibly than their books."

Lucifer drained the last of his toddy. The server returned to the table and asked him if he'd like desert. He said he'd come back later for her. She smiled and returned to her station near the kitchen. Of course, I may as well have been lost in a Saharan sandstorm for all the attention she gave me.

Lucifer asked me, "Who designed these creatures, anyway?"

I thought it safer not to answer. "I can do this for you: I can ask Unpronounceable about bringing the martyrs back to heaven, but I doubt if he's going to agree. You know, Lucifer, he places a high value on the serenity of heaven. He thinks it's a big draw that'll bring in the masses. I think a bar with a good dance floor would work better."

"You're in the right of it there." He inhaled. "Don't bother asking him." His sigh singed the tabletop. "I just had to get it off my chest."

"What's the matter, Lucifer? You seem more out of sorts than usual."

"No one in Hell listens to me anymore. I guess people don't believe me when I tell them they've been lied to by their holy men. I tell them egregious lies, and they think I'm telling the truth. I tell them the simple truth, and they think I'm lying. They put more credence in the self-serving scribbles of dead men than in the obvious. There's no winning. I wish I could damn them all, but that would be redundant. Where would that Hell be? Would that solve the problem or just give me another ring to mind, a subbasement as it were?" He rubbed his temples gently. "I've got a hell of a headache."

CHAPTER 38

THE EPISTLE TO THE RECORDERS

My annual report on Earthly progress was several months overdue. My official excuse was my move to a new home, forced on me by an influx of astonished ancestors of members of Joe's new religion. They were unexpectedly yanked from the Fiery Pit. Most had grown fond of the stimulating activities there and were having trouble adjusting to loitering in Limbo.

The new cottage assigned to me was thirteen clouds up from Adam and Eve's place. Our relationship had improved somewhat. Whenever we saw each other, we waved and smiled and quietly went our separate ways. They had grown more reclusive the longer they stayed in Limbo. I noticed Judas seemed to avoid them. Their only regular visitor was Jess. On occasion, they would ask him to track down lost sheep. He was relentless.

Judas had the most palatial home on his level, seven clouds lower than mine and six up from theirs. His balcony had a superb view of Chaos. (My view was blocked by a thunderhead that hung constantly over Stephen's lot.) Judas, although friendly toward other residents, avoided me. His role in closing the show was hardly the topic he'd want to discuss over a cup of cocoa. And I wasn't eager to review about what happened the night Jess was arrested. When most needed, I was up a tree humming a happy tune, watching the stars go round. Judas and I kept a comfortable distance. Raphael, on a rare visit occasioned by accidentally bumping into me while returning from Andromeda, suggested that being completely open about the past with an accomplice might have therapeutic value. I never followed up on the idea. The unbridled joy of heaven doesn't necessarily survive the review of guilty secrets.

I unpacked the spare robe, the one Manny made for me, and hung it in the closet next to my desk. Having no other delay handy, I unrolled a blank scroll and sharpened a new stylus. Reluctant to put any precise statement on paper, I examined the length of the scroll for imperfections, studied the taper of the stylus, and checked to see if I had left any notes in the pocket of the spare robe.

The Sacred Council of Angelic Recorders (SCAR) invariably slashed my accounts with the enthusiasm of editors deleting adverbs. After my untimely intervention with Joe and then the failure of the locust plague I organized to force the new religion to disband, the SCAR reflexively dragged every word I wrote down a salted winter road.

I thought I would begin my report with a summary of my lunch with Lucifer. But, how to relay his request to allow the Fiery Pit to disgorge the martyrs? My priority, I decided, should be an account of Earthers striving toward--what? I had less of a clue about what they wanted to achieve than they had.

I had asked decades ago that I be allowed to transfer my assignment to Sandalphon. After my fifteenth request, he agreed to take over my position. Unfortunately, my application to either retire or take an assignment on an asteroid was denied without explanation. To my surprise, I was merely demoted. The SCAR noted smugly in brown ink that I was given a special, additional assignment in Australia, due to my familiarity with "down under."

These wandering thoughts were merely my way to avoid starting the report. Still hoping for an urgent interruption or any other distraction, I began to write. Luckily, the bureaucratic language loved by courts and theologians required little mental effort.

 "I, Samuel, Angel of the Lord, Deputy Custodian of Earth, and Special Envoy to Koalas, do hereby submit to the Above the testament below of my latest brief but humbling bumbling of the will of Almighty. While attempting to fulfill his impeccable desires, I had the opportunity to notice a few human traits and trends. In the interest of kindness, I will skip over them and go directly to the recommendations for further contact.

"First, due to the proliferation and increasingly antagonistic attitudes of Earther religionists, it is recommended that all would-be prophets of existing or new sects be summarily execu--"

Before I could write more, I heard an unmistakable knock on my closet door. It was soft and severe, stern and sympathetic, authoritative and permissive. Only Unpronounceable could convey so many contradictions in a single tap. He didn't wait for me to invite him in. The wall vanished.

Before I could stand up, he started talking without greeting me. "I'm sure you remember that I promised the Travel Department a trip to nowhere, but I haven't quite decided how to uncreate," he said.

I felt a certain relief but wondered if this foreboded a reassignment for me to warmer quarters.

"Besides," he continued, "I've grown rather fond of all the alleged imperfections in my flawless creation, and uncreating even a small particle would undoubtedly leave an astronomical vacuum in my heart. While I was observing everything all at once, I noticed the demons and devils can arrive anywhere they want whenever they want. So last month, I sent the Travel Department on temporary assignment to receive corrective instruction in the Fiery Pit under their Chief Demon of

Assigned Duties, Crusolini. When I summoned him to discuss the training, he contended that the heavenly Department's incompetence and corruption were the causes. He's rather hard on the Leftovers, as he calls them." He chuckled. "Leftovers. Isn't that clever?"

I said, "Our Department members seem to manage their own vacations without going astray, but I doubt if they're corrupt. There might be another explanation."

"Incompetence is a judgment call, and I'm the only one qualified to make judgments. Crusolini suggested alternative explanations. Too many calendars for starters."

"I agree! It's better now than it was while I was in Rome, but it's still confusing." I hadn't meant to bring up Rome.

Unpronounceable went on as if I hadn't. "Lately, groups of wannabe ancients have resurrected defunct calendars from all over ancient Earth, without bothering to verify the math."

"I heard about people scheduling the end of the world because their calendar ran out of days. It didn't occur to them to start over until the next day. I was surprised that no one celebrated the cosmic renewal."

"If people celebrated every day that started someone's new year, Earth would be one constant party town." Unpronounceable seemed to think that idea over for a moment. Then he said, "Ok. Let's stay on topic. Crusolini thought there might be a problem with the interface between sidereal and universal time. It has to do with a phenomenon called the precession of the equinox, a result of humans neglecting to take my infinite subtlety into account. He calculated they were out of sync by as much as thirty degrees when Jess started his career. It's hard to be exact because the Romans couldn't figure out how to divide 365 by any numbers other than five and seventy-three, but they wanted a timeframe that was easier to track."

He shook his head quickly, like a dog drying its ears. "I'm wandering off topic here. The Travel Department suspected that the clocks were uncoordinated, so they tried to compensate when you were sent to guide Joe, but apparently, they hadn't realized that the calendar changes were ongoing. Crusolini promised to synchronize temporal and heavenly time so the Heaven to Earth shuttle can leave and arrive predictably. It's a big job."

"I'm glad someone else has to do it." I was hoping I wasn't going to be assigned to it. I was prepared to point out my ineptitude with math.

"Of course, odds are they'll invent another religion and start a new calendar as soon as we have everything running like clockwork."

Unpronounceable materialized a chair and sat down.

"These Earthers are most illogical for rational beings. Whenever they're at a loss to explain some simple phenomenon, such as water evaporating, they invent a supernatural power who makes it happen instead of thinking it through, conducting experiments, finding the mechanism. At one time in Rome, it took eighty deities to open a door and ninety to close it quietly, plus another forty if a child was involved. It was a wonder anyone could enter or leave a building. At least, it kept the demons busy. I ask myself sometimes why I bothered to make it all so seamless. Some Earthers think that they can make a few sacrifices and bow a half dozen times to an idea of divinity, and that these idea-deities will be forced to accommodate their every whim. When nothing happens, Earthers blame the inscrutable will of me. On the few occasions when the wish comes true, Fallen Angels rush in and take advantage of happenstance and claim after the fact that they're the ones responsible. Then they demand more tribute and expect to be treated like divine beings. As a result, there's a god on every corner, in every bedroom, anywhere two people can agree on a name. It's no wonder the masses are confused."

I started to speak, but he would not be interrupted. "I know what you mean, but organized religions don't help. First, they're only organized to promote the interests of their own clergy and long after that their own members if it helps the clergy. Second, almost every one of them claims the power to make everyone on Earth the most powerful, the richest, the happiest, the most revered person on the entire planet. And third but not the last one, they all claim the deity they worship is the most powerful of all the deities. Of course, all these omnipotent gods eventually become vanquished by a neighboring omnipotent god. The clergy explain this contradiction so simply that no one doubts it: Our one god loves us, and when we please him, he shows that love by allowing us to be ever victorious, but if we displease him, then he shows his tough love by allowing our enemies to defeat and enslave us. Some of the vanquished admit they displeased their god, even if no one among them or the conquerors can tell with certitude what the offense was. To ice the cake, it only takes one displeasure to end the deal."

I said, "I can't believe they think so little of you."

"They don't think of me at all. They only think of theories. Humanity is being crushed by theories. Gods with unreliable skills sometimes get it right and sometimes wrong. Or gods who get very hormonal when things don't go right. Priests insist on total devotion to dark designs. Disagree and die, heathen infidel! The survivors define heresy. Then they claim all heretics are suffering eternal punishment in the Fiery Pit. If they really understood how long eternity is, they wouldn't wish damnation on anyone. And it would get very crowded down there if they were right. They're not.

"Everyone's invited to come to heaven. Even the Fallen Angels if they do the right penance the right number of times."

I opened my mouth, but he continued. "I know! Beelzebub thinks he can sneak away if he hides in a crowd. Ba'al thinks he'll someday be forced to atone for masquerading as an apostle. His first three apologies won't be sincere. He's always been on the slow side, but he'll come around eventually. Adam and Eve are already comfortably settled into a cottage near a pasture on the outskirts of Limbo with their flock of sheep and several German shepherds who tickle Eve's fancy. You could see their house if this hut didn't have walls. They think they're close enough to heaven."

"It's best to let them live in their personal paradise, don't you think?"

He went on as if I hadn't spoken. "Lucifer! Now there's a conundrum! Only to himself! His place is beside me, and someday he'll come back. He may be the last to return, but he can, and he will. I'll welcome him no matter how long it takes. Of course, ultimately, it's up to him, but it will be very lonely in the Fiery Pit all by himself."

I said, "I hope he does return. I miss him. That voice, those eyes. . ."

"I miss him, too, so much that at times I am tempted to descend into the Fiery Pit and--. I've kept his halo in cold storage. I already have his replacement robe picked out."

"You're saying all I needed to do was ask for a new robe? Now don't get me wrong. The cleaner did an amazing job, but I think I'm still having a bad reaction to the cleaning fluid."

"Oh, Samuel. Are you suggesting you're on the same level as Lucifer?"

I wasn't sure which level that was at that moment. I stayed silent and nursed my feeling of chastisement.

Unpronounceable seemed to sense my hurt heart. "Tuck in that lower lip, Samuel. Lucifer loved me first and strongest among all I created, which is why he hates me so fervently. Someday, I might share what really happened, before the rest of you appeared."

Unpronounceable stood up; the chair vanished. "You really need to get out of this hut."

"I've been—"

"I heard a rumor once that fear of the lord is the beginning of wisdom. Not true. Curiosity about the creation is the beginning of wisdom. Understanding the universe is on the road to wisdom. If you know how, you can eventually know why. Forget fear! Fear is the first step on the road to the Fiery Pit. Fear makes you doubt your own worth."

"But I—"

There was no stopping Unpronounceable. "Consider this. Creation requires an enormous commitment of power, resources, time, and love. If you could create a real, corporeal human being, would you discard that person in a snit? Never! Your craving would be so compelling that your creation would brand you a stalker."

Although I hadn't decided to follow his advice to leave the safety of my cottage, I felt a need to breathe freely in open air. The walls of my closet and cottage became transparent. I could see the outskirts of heaven in one direction and Eve's pasture in the other. Through the thunderhead I could see Chaos. In the opposite direction, a Void promised unimaginable wonders. It was all sweeter than a Roman orgy. Before I could chastise myself for the thought, I was grateful for knowing better.

Unpronounceable spoke softly. "I have another mission for you. This time tell my new chosen one that the primary commandment is this: Do no harm. Accepting this message will synchronize the world with my will. I'm sending you because you have the most experience at starting new religions."

I was incredulous. "Do no harm? I'm supposed to tell him that you, the god of vengeance, the god of retribution, the god of judgement--that you who have sent your own angels to the Fiery Pit, apparently without a thought or regret, who have never hesitated, by all accounts, to squash enemies and friends alike for the least reason, even when your devoted followers have mistakenly thought that they were doing your will--that you now want the rest of us to do no harm? Who would take me seriously? Is it even possible to live without doing harm?"

"Do you remember who I am?"

"Sorry, I got carried away by my bafflement over your mysterious ways. But could you admit I've got a point?"

"They could give it a try."

"I suppose so. This time--" I braced myself before I went on. "This time, it might be better if you deliver the message yourself. I haven't been able to get it right. You wouldn't come back to me if another angel could do better."

"Myself? The risk is too great. I need someone to blame in case the message gets garbled or adulterated. I'd have to admit that I was the one who spoke to him; it would be embarrassing to reveal that my choice turned into a poor one. What have we had so far? A bad actor, a liar, a self-serving pedophile? It's the free will paradox."

I was mulling this over when Unpronounceable interrupted my thoughts. "By the way, this time you won't be delivering the message to a man. Time to shake it up a bit. You'll need to lay aside your Roman nostalgia and keep focused. I can arrange for a few practice sessions so that the announcement can flow more smoothly. 'Sound it, read it; repeat; repeat.' That could have been ironed out in rehearsal, but I didn't think it was difficult."

"I still think you should take this job on yourself. Personal responsibility is the new watchword on Earth."

Unpronounceable looked simultaneously in all directions in that unsettling way he has that always leaves me dizzy. "Now creation is telling the Creator what it wants. I would have smacked down democracy back in Athens, but it's even harder dealing with dictators. They can't follow the simplest instructions." He shook his head deprecatingly. "Do you recall that two-pfennig dictator from Austria? My Struggle, he called it. His struggle was learning which end of the paint brush to hold. Couldn't figure it out, so he decided he was destined to rule the world. Like all the other dictators, all he did was ruin lives and make an ass out of himself. He thought he was hot stuff until they burned his body. When he woke up in the Pit--. Well, Lucifer can tell you all about it."

I hadn't thought about it in a long time, but I suddenly felt compelled to ask, "How's that parallel universe coming along?"

"Ah! Don't ask. It would take an eternity to explain. The problem with parallel universes is that they run in the same direction. And right now, it's time for you to go. You're going to arrive a little early just in case the Travel Department has erred again."

As I turned to leave for Earth, I was struck by the similarity between the moods of Unpronounceable and Lucifer. The level of frustration, the yearning for success squashed against the intractable determination of people to do what they want. The main difference I could discern was Unpronounceable's absolute certainty that, at the end of time, all would turn out well. And why, I wondered, do I think there will be an end to time?

In my heart and mind and soul, even in the infinitely fine matter of my body, in my totality and with an overwhelming singularity, a gratitude arose in me for his eternal effort, his boundless patience, his seemingly unrealistic yet unwavering faith in me, the most incompetent among the host of angels. Yet, against all the evidence, his faith in me was steadfast. Who was I to doubt what he believed? He had put his whole self into this universe and gotten back little more than criticism, fear, lip service, empty rituals, doubt. Compassion poured through me. I turned to thank him.

I intended to address him as Unpronounceable, but instead, from the depth of my heart and with the fullness of my being, I spoke The Name that I had heard only twice before. At that moment, I glimpsed for a nanosecond a trace, a suggestion of an outline, saturated and overflowing with a brilliance that seemed to sweep from and through him from somewhere and sometime, everywhere and always, unlike here and now yet ever present.

When I awoke, the familiar form, bending over me and smiling, said, "Run along now. We've work to do."

CHAPTER 39

DINING WITH THE DEVILS

I landed on Clouds Rest above Yosemite Valley. This time the Travel Department was closer to being accurate. I arrived ten minutes late instead of a day early and landed lopsided. Because I bent my knee at the last moment, I stubbed my right toe instead of embedding my foot up to the ankle in granite.

"Ow!"

The two hikers already sitting there were startled by my sudden appearance. They lost their balance and rolled fifteen yards down the slope. I caught them in an angelic net before they were seriously injured. While they applied antibiotic cream to their scrapes, I planted the idea that I had appeared from the opposite side of the ridge while they were looking away. They accepted my apology for frightening them.

Returning their attention to the view, the objective of their hike, I pointed to the vast expanse before us. "Have you ever seen such a spectacular panorama?"

They were too enraptured by the view to think carefully about inconsequential events like the sudden, poorly explained appearance of a man from behind a ridge they had just crossed a few minutes before.

"Never!" said the woman.

"I've been here several times," said the man, "but it blows my monkey every time."

"I beg your pardon?"

The woman smiled at me and poked him on the shoulder with a soft fist. "He means 'monkey mind.' It's a meditation term." She whispered something to him that sounded like, "Behave yourself."

The three of us sat quietly for quite some time, absorbing and absorbed by the spectacular expanse before us.

Then the woman, looking at me with curious concern, offered me a sandwich in a plastic bag. "Would you like something to eat? We brought extra."

"Thank you, but I'm not hungry."

The woman said, "Still, you shouldn't wait for hunger to tell you that you're running out of fuel."

The man asked, "Do you have enough water? I don't see any. You'll never make it back to the trailhead without water."

I realized that my human appearance had caused them to be concerned for my human needs. To have come this far on a strenuous trail without provisions must have seemed to them like unmitigated idiocy which could only end in death. Touched by their kindness, I twisted halfway around where I was seated and pretended to reach behind a bush. Magically (and without prior authorization) I produced a navy-blue backpack. "Let me see. I've got two quarts in the side pockets and another half-gallon inside. Here's something you might like." From the top pocket, I materialized a trio of baggies, each containing a generous square of fudge with walnuts.

Her eyes widened. "They look divine."

"And they taste devilishly delicious. I made them myself. There's enough for everybody." She still hesitated. I assured them, "No ingredients your saintly great-grandmother wouldn't have known and used." I took a bite of one square.

As she savored the first nibble, her eyes rolled back in her head, and she made an appreciative guttural sound. "Adrian, you have to try this."

"Don't tempt me, Evelyn. You know I can't stop once I get going on sweets."

I piped up, "There's just one square for you, so you won't stray very far off your diet. Two hundred fifty calories, tops."

"I do love walnuts."

As he and I bit into our fudge squares, I thought of Lucifer offering me a glass of wine. I started to regret tempting Adrian off his diet, but it proved impossible to repent while simultaneously relishing the exquisite flavor. I suddenly understood that I was no longer unhappy I had accepted the wine.

Adrian murmured, "This is to die for!"

Evelyn asked, "You made this yourself?"

"I outdid myself," I confessed.

"This is inspired." Adrian took another bite, smiling at Evelyn as if she had handed him the fudge.

Another couple arrived, admired the view, and left a few minutes later.

Evelyn and Adrian packed their empty plastic bags into their backpacks, thanked me for the fudge, and ambled down the trail. I watched her go. I hadn't delivered the message.

All alone, I sat silent. A pale light radiated all around. The rocks glowed faintly; the dirt nestled in the cracks of the exfoliating granite shone steadily. The fallen leaves and twigs emitted a slightly stronger light. The grass, bushes, trees--even the lichens--iridesced. The auras of the squirrels and birds, lizards and gnats were more brilliant with a broader spectrum of colors. In the distance, I could see the radiance of human beings; some brilliant and clear; others faint, as if seen through a fog or a soiled and scratched windowpane; but all stronger than any other light. I breathed in the light, held it as it filled me afresh, then exhaled it permeated with love.

A dark storm formed swiftly over the far end of the valley and swept toward me from the west. Lightning bursts, thunder crashes, shrieking gales: I recognized my old friend's typically melodramatic entrance. I held onto my halo and waited to hail his arrival. The dark purple clouds engulfed me. The winds buffeted me. The center of the storm opened, and there in the eye of the hurricane was Lucifer.

At first, his back was to me. But as he suavely rotated, still in flight, to face me, a table and two chairs swept into view. He, the table, and the chairs settled lightly on the uneven crag. At the very moment I took the seat opposite him, a third chair materialized to my left. The storm calmed. Thunder stopped, lightning ceased, clouds became a dense fog.

"Good to see you again, my friend. I see you're expecting another guest."

"That would be Beelzebub. There might be another. RSVPs don't get delivered reliably now that Crusolini has defected."

I couldn't contain my excitement. "You mean, he's

come over from the enemy?"

"That would be <u>gone</u> over to the enemy. But no; he's just on temporary assignment."

Not wishing to argue the direction of travel, I changed the topic. "That was quite a dramatic entrance, even for you."

"I've done better."

"When?"

"Take your pick: typhoons, revolutions, earthquakes. Histrionics are fun, but my most effective and subtle entrances have been through religions. Most of them don't even know I've gotten my foot in their head."

"Religions? Tell me more!" I reminded myself that Lucifer was an unreliable source and prone to unsubstantiated bragging, but I wanted to learn which religions and where they were practiced.

He said, "For example, I instructed the Satanic Travel Department to warp the interface between celestial and earthly time so that you would arrive too late to deliver Unpronounceable's message to Joe. In the meantime, I convinced him he wasn't going to get a divine meeting. He needed to start now or forever lose his chance. I planted the idea in Manny's head that he could make sense of the cosmos. And I was the one who drove Beelzebub out of his comfortable temple so he could start his sit-in. Would you like a complete account?"

"I get the idea."

"As do I," said Beelzebub as he simultaneously arrived, pulled out and sat in the vacant seat. "Although I don't concur."

"Smoothly done," I said.

"Nor do I," said Ba'al as he materialized to my right. He provided his own chair, which listed a little to his right.

"Ah, ye of little faith," said Lucifer.

"Ah, ye of little proof," said I.

"Can I give you a better chair, Ba'al?" asked Lucifer.

"Why?" said Ba'al. "This one seems fine to me." He moved his left hand, palm down, over the tabletop. A bowl of steaming liquid appeared before him. "I don't recall you hanging around when I was slipping out of Damascus, writing letters, heading off to Rome. I take great pride in starting it all by myself. I did appreciate your encouragement that one and only time you bothered to notice my efforts." Ba'al drew the bowl close in front of him and solidified a spoon from the fog. "Do you mind if I start without you? A little vinegar and jalapeño soup to warm the heart. I'm ravenous today. Must be the altitude."

I reminded him, "Do you remember our discussion back

on the beach? I still say that stuff you wrote was--not factual."

"No one cared then, and few question it now. Ideas are what matter. Creating facts to support a theory is easier than finding a theory to explain the facts. Throwing in a quotation from a dead expert ices the cake, especially if you misquote and mangle the message. Nowadays, they call it politics."

"Someone's coming," said Beelzebub. I could hear him, too.

Lucifer muttered, as if speaking to himself, "You do your best to keep people away, but some idiot thinks he'll be safe in a storm." A roll of thunder accompanied a sheet of lightning. We heard an unpleasant shriek, a disconcerting counterpoint to Ba'al's slurping. Lucifer said at a normal volume, "He'll be okay in a few minutes."

"Well," I said, "you did want to radiate light. I thought you meant in a different way."

"I was young. I had a lot to learn about what life was really like. We all evolve." Lucifer glared at Ba'al. "Did you bring enough for everybody?" he asked in a full voice.

Ba'al looked embarrassed. He didn't answer, but three more bowls appeared on the table. I pulled one close, materialized a spoon, and surreptitiously changed the soup into gazpacho.

Lucifer said, "I remember the beginning time. I wanted to hear from every one of the angels what mission they each thought they had, what each of us would choose to do. I was under the impression that we had tons of time. Beelzebub had only said a few words when the plan went south."

I noticed Beelzebub was having minestrone. He smiled at Lucifer. "What I remember best is watching all those animals fly into storage. I thought it would be grand to find them all and bring them back, so we could all live together in heavenly peace."

Ba'al broke in. "I didn't hear you right, Lucifer. I thought you were asking about shoes. I was perfectly content with my sandals." Ba'al shook his head. "I'm still searching for a hearing aid. So far, none have done anything but amplify the noise inside my head. I even tried hiring a boy soprano to shout in my ear, but the musicians' guild cut him off. He made a good living as a castrato."

I heard the intruder stand up. Lucifer stared in his direction. Instead of moving away, the man began to stumble toward us. Lucifer growled. A bolt of lightning flashed, and the man shrieked. Lucifer smiled. "He'll be okay; he'll need to learn to walk again, but he'll be fine. Someday. Samuel, have you discovered what you want to be, or not to be?"

"Hail to thee, blight spirit. Bard thou never wert."

"You found a sense of humor? That is an outrageous fortune."

Ba'al said, "I never understood what that had to do with swings and barrows."

"Not to mention that creep in the putty face, all round and furry," I said.

Beelzebub chimed in, "It's a pail sold by a kitty-cut."

The four of us nodded in unison.

Lucifer said, "You realize that there's a special place in the Pit for those who make bad puns? Originally it was the eighth ring, but I moved them to the second. The eighth was too close to my digs, and the first would scare off the new arrivals."

We all looked at him with wide open eyes. The puzzlement was clear on all our faces. At the end of a protracted pause, I whispered, "Mercy? From you?"

"It happens. I--" Lucifer appeared to be thinking over what to say next. "I get tired, exhausted really, by my campaign. The whole mission to spread evil throughout the world is too easy. In fact, it's self-perpetuating, built into the system."

Beelzebub leaned forward and stared at Lucifer's face. I leaned back and folded my arms. Ba'al pinched his earlobes and raised his eyebrows.

Lucifer sounded dejected and demoralized. "Evil used to be a challenge to create, but now it's a spectator sport. Boring! Predictable! And the whole effort's inane, it doesn't give any satisfaction. In fact, it makes me feel empty, like I'm wasting my talents."

We all sat silent. Lucifer suddenly shook his head like a wet puppy and changed his soup to split pea. He looked around the table as he lifted the bowl to his lips. "Oh, never mind. I get into these moods." Golden fried chicken and salty fries appeared heaped in the center of the table. "Help yourself. My special recipe."

Beelzebub nibbled a smidgeon off a drumstick. "Ha-ha! Too funny, Lucifer!" He handed me a breast. "Try it. It's tofu!"

"I call it toficken."

Ba'al exclaimed, "It's toficken delicious!"

During the repast, we spoke only of trifling matters, like how many humans can die for a principle.

After the apple pie, I stood up. "I've got to fly along now. I hope you'll forgive me."

"Another divine mission?" Lucifer sneered.

"Unpronounceable gave me a message to deliver, but I decided against it."

The others fell off their chairs. Being angels, they landed on their feet.

I could feel Lucifer lusting for my soul. I said, "Thanks. I've never felt so wanted before. I'm flattered. If you wanted me to join you because of who I am instead of how it would hurt another, I just might investigate the darkness seriously. But my plan is to spread a little light in the world. There is a great longing for more light in the world. I remember the moment you pledged yourself to spreading it."

"If it's wanted, I should have said. Have you ever noticed," asked Lucifer, "what happens when you turn on the light in a filthy kitchen at night? The roaches and rats flee faster than frost from fire. Black widow spiders react more slowly, but they still climb the wire into the haven of darkness. There are those that do not love the light. I didn't create them. I didn't seduce them."

"And yet, there they are, right alongside us," said Ba'al, "falling in step with our drummer and using our shadows to hide from heaven. I wonder what made them afraid?"

Lucifer laughed. "I'm sure Unpronounceable knows about the unspeakable. I don't blame the vermin for running." He turned to me. "If you're not delivering the message, what's your plan?"

I took a deep breath and fluttered my wing tips. "What I remember about day one is that you, Lucifer, said that

Unpronounceable had 'let light be,' as if he had given permission to something that was hanging around waiting for the chance to make a grand entrance into the universe. I didn't think about it at the time, but now I wonder if you were trying, perhaps at some subtle level, to minimize his accomplishment."

Beelzebub looked at me with surprise. "Now that you mention it--. What Unpronounceable really said was, 'Let there be light.' At the time, I didn't think about the nuance."

Lucifer said, with a hint of exasperation, "You're trying to find the devil in the details."

I said, "I'm going to give you the benefit of the doubt, the same as I've done for Unpronounceable."

Lucifer asked me again, "What's the plan if you're not delivering the message?"

"I've decided to begin my own mission, one that means something to me, one that will challenge me while giving me a sense of purpose."

"Big words for a fetch-and-retriever," said my friend.

"The more I know about people, the more I love them, and the more love I have, the more I want to help. I've learned what it's like to be absorbed by the pleasures of the world. And I've learned what it takes to get control of yourself. It's enough to make you want to help others find out what they are capable of."

Ba'al said, "I don't think I heard right." The rest of us ignored him.

"But first, I want to visit Hells Canyon. I mean the one in Idaho. I've heard so much about it. I'll just drop by for a quick look on my way to The Congo. A doctor and his wife are working there to help people recover from atrocities. I hear they could use some help. I can handle the laundry or maybe some kitchen duties. I know which end of the mop to lean on."

Lucifer looked me up and down. The sparkle in his eyes reminded me of our first moments, when his glance swept over me. My heart went out to him. "My brother, I long for you to come home."

"I'd rather harp on a grudge than strum on a harp."

I turned to leave, wondering why I had bothered to reach out to him. Then he startled me. "Someday perhaps," he said, "There's so much to do. I don't understand the plan. I asked him, way back in the beginning, and now I ask myself--. Well, it would take an eternity to explain."

I said, "If you care to join us, Lucifer, you're welcome. Maybe you could shed a little light on the path."

"Not yet." He stood staring to the north in silence.

Through the cloud that surrounded us, I heard the

stricken man groan and stand up. The faint sound of his feeble footsteps retreated. Lucifer concentrated his storm around himself and flew west. Ba'al headed south humming a single, wavering note. I watched as the specks of light within them melted into the background glow.

Beelzebub smiled. "Would you like some company, Samuel?"

"Come along," I said, "I'm walking. I'm sure we'll find a lot to keep us busy along the way. I've had a habit of arriving too late, anyway, so I may as well turn the tardiness into a talent and see what I can do along the way."

As I turned to the north, I saw a glimmer transform to a steady glow; a new star was born at the edge of the galaxy. "Welcome," I thought.

Beelzebub pointed in its direction. "Look!" he whispered. "Someone has found the light."

I resolved to visit it once my work on Earth is done.

ABOUT THE AUTHOR

A native Texan, Matthew has spent his adult life in diverse careers. He defended democracy as a member of the United States Air Force, spending a considerably time overseas. He then passed three years in various temporary jobs, from shovel operator to file clerk and receptionist. He has since worked as a bookkeeper, massage therapist, and spa manager. He earned undergraduate degrees in Music Composition and Psychology from universities in California.

His most persistent interests are music, ancient and medieval history, literature, poetry, comparative religions, and languages. His favorite genres to read are mystery, fantasy, and science fiction. However, his eclectic tastes frequently lead him into other realms.

He is now retired, living peacefully with his long-time companion, Barbara, in suburban Idaho.

www.ingramcontent.com/pod-product-compliance
Lightning Source LLC
Chambersburg PA
CBHW070841260626
47170CB00007B/2453